The Professor of Poetry

Grace McCleen

SCEPTRE

First published in Great Britain in 2013 by Secptre
An imprint of Hodder & Stoughton

An Hachette UK company

1

Extracts from 'The Love Song of J. Alfred Prufrock' and *Four Quartets*
taken

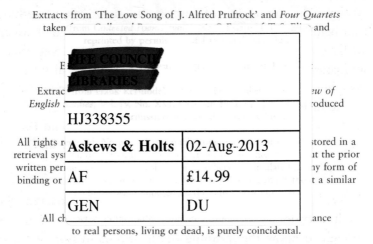

Extrac   *ew of*
English   roduced

HJ338355

Askews & Holts	02-Aug-2013
AF	£14.99
GEN	DU

A CIP catalogue record for this title is available from the British Library

Hardback ISBN 9781444769951
Trade Paperback ISBN 9781444769975
Ebook ISBN 9781444769968

Typeset in Sabon MT 12/14pt by Palimpsest Book Production Limited,
Falkirk, Stirlingshire

Printed and bound by CPI Group (UK) Ltd, Croydon CRO 4YY

Hodder & Stoughton Ltd
338 Euston Road
London NW1 3BH

www.sceptrebooks.com

'"Sometimes," Père de Grandmaison tells us, "during the contemplation of a work of art, or while listening to a melody, the effort to understand relaxes, and the soul simply delights itself in the beauty which it divines . . . or merely a memory, a word, a line of Dante or Racine shooting up from the obscure depths of our soul, seizes hold of us, 'recollects' and penetrates us. After this experience we know no more than we did, but we have the impression of understanding a little something that before we hardly knew, of tasting a fruit the rind of which we have scarcely nibbled." Such an experience is, among others, an instance of those "profane states of nature in which we can decipher the great lines, and discern the image and rough sketch of the mystical states of the soul . . ."'

Henri Brémond, *Prayer and Poetry:*
A Contribution to Poetical Theory

'It has been deduced from the belief in Pure Sound that the resultant meaning of the words need not be known, that it is enough to know the meaning of the words in isolation and enough of their syntax to read them aloud rightly. In a degree this is often true, but it is best to regard this state of limited knowledge as a complicated state of indecision which involves much estimating of probabilities, and is less ignorance than an ordered suspension of judgment . . . a musical chord is a direct sensation, but not therefore unanalyzable into its separate notes even at the moment of sensing. It can be either felt or thought; the two things are similar but different; and it requires practice to do both at once.'

William Empson, *Seven Types of Ambiguity*

BOOK I

'If all time is eternally present
All time is unredeemable.'

*

'Burnt Norton'
Four Quartets, 1936

The Dissident Corpus

It was not, to begin again, what she had expected. She had been waiting a month now for the results of a scan to reveal whether her renegade brain cells, caught late in the game of incestuous duplication, had been eradicated, and knew the outcome was unlikely to be favourable: Doctor Robertson, a greying, sprightly beanpole of a man, had told her so. The size of the tumour had been considerable, surgery had removed less of it than had been hoped. In such circumstances therapy could be counted upon to do only so much. And yet here was the doctor, looking even more sprightly than usual, handing her a sheet and informing her that not only had the rebel cells been disbanded but her white-blood-cell count was the best it had been for over a year, since the trouble first started.

She peered at the paper over the tops of her glasses as if at an impostor. A moment passed before she said: 'Are you sure these are mine?'

'That's your name, isn't it?' Robertson said. 'To all intents and purposes you're a well woman, Miss Stone. We couldn't have hoped for a better result.'

She sniffed and raised her eyebrows. The paper trembled a little as she replaced it on the desk.

'Of course,' he said, 'we'll keep monitoring you, but things look good. Have you had any more headaches?'

'No.'

'Nausea?'

'Sometimes, after eating.'

'That's normal enough. Your body will take a while to

feel like itself again.' He swivelled in the chair and smiled at her. 'So, what are you going to do with yourself, now you're up and about?'

She pursed her lips, flicking a speck from her skirt. She knew how she appeared: a spinster, bespectacled, sensible shoes, skin and lashes of a pallor that suggested dim rooms and silence; her eyes were the only thing that didn't fit the rest of the picture because they were dark, flashing, almost feral and most people didn't look at them for very long before turning away. She said, smiling a little: 'Oh, back to work, I should think. I'm behind with my book and the department can't do without me.'

'Take some time out. Get away for a while – have you got a friend you could visit?'

'Of course,' she said, glancing at him.

He regarded her quizzically for a moment, perhaps a little sadly, then stood, holding out his hand.

At the door he said: 'Remember, no work.'

And she indulged him with a smile and said: 'I promise.'

She stood in a long corridor with a shining floor. In front of her a column of dust eddied in sunlight. It was dust, but as Professor Stone looked the particles glinted, pirouetted, were alchemised into some grander matter, not dust but gold, and gold tinged with rainbows. To her left, beyond a glass wall, trees swayed, leaves whirled in blustery sunshine. They were trees, but as she looked the boughs became arms reaching towards the sun, fibres of some eternal matter imploring mediation.

A noise startled her and she turned to see a man pushing a trolley towards her, pursing his lips. The word that came to mind to describe the sound, however, was not 'whistling': that was not nearly strange enough for the music, neither human nor inanimate, she was hearing.

She blinked, the trolley passed, the dust scattered, the

leaves went on whirling. Something had happened: what was it? Words seemed to lag behind her perception of things this morning, sorry messengers of a secret too subtle for comprehension. She said, 'I am well,' but these too were inadequate to describe the disparate thing her body had become ever since Robertson had handed her the paper.

She was now standing in the column of sunlight, dust whirring madly about her: fabric, flesh, veins, nails and sunspots were all suddenly quite dazzling, touched into being by a luminescence she felt all around her. She said, 'Thank you,' cautiously, as if testing the words, and these alone seemed to retain some of their meaning this strangest of mornings – though she was not sure to whom she was speaking and did not like to think what talking to herself in the middle of the day suggested.

Professor Stone began to walk slowly, and then with more certainty, down the long, shining corridor.

Elizabeth Stone (professor of English poetry, celebrated author of *The Dissident Corpus: John Milton and the Poetics of Difference*, fellow of two bodies of higher learning, chair of two; contributor to ten journals, editor of one) was in her fifty-second year when life as she knew it came to an end. As it happened, she was standing in a lecture theatre about to demonstrate the swoon that 'by communion raised/from earth to heaven' the rapturous Wordsworth, when in striking counterpoint, and to the surprise of more than two hundred undergraduates, the earth raised itself to meet her, a light flashed across her brain, her left hand dropped the papers it was holding and the world went black. She woke to find Matthew Cullum, head of English, bending over her, saying: 'Elizabeth, can you hear me?'

She put the fall down to low blood sugar and resolved not to skip breakfast. A week later she got out of bed and the world went black again; the next morning while she was brushing her teeth her left arm went limp, her hand contracted to a claw and the vision dimmed in her left eye. After twenty minutes things were back to normal, though her arm remained weak for the rest of the day.

She told no one; it was tiredness, a trapped nerve, some sort of deficiency. She had had similar symptoms once with migraine. She would get it checked out next week when she had finished the Donne lectures, at the end of the month when she had sent off the paper on Dryden. The fact was Professor Stone was used to dealing with her body's revolts. Over the years it had supplied her with a baffling array of ills and she had become a skilled opponent of it, though it had never before behaved with quite such abandon. She drank tincture of opium when she was afflicted with diarrhoea and needed to give a lecture at Harvard, hobbled about on a stick when a bout of lumbago threatened to prevent her travelling to the John Ryland's Library to consult a manuscript, woke herself up at random intervals when writing her first book on Milton to play the insomnia at its own game; she prevented her hands trembling at conferences by gripping them so hard that half-moons appeared in her palms.

At the time of the fall she had just begun the long-awaited second instalment of her *magnum opus*, *The Dissident Corpus: John Milton and the Poetics of Difference*, the culmination of a love affair with the literary giant that had occupied her to the inclusion of little else for eight years, though perhaps 'obsession' should be substituted for 'love' and 'battle' for 'affair' because there were times when the combatants had come to mortal blows and it was doubtful that one of them would survive the encounter. Survive the professor must, however, because the grim truth was she had not written a book, despite eager anticipation from critical circles, since her first foray into Milton's Hell;

6

though she hadn't been wasting time – on the contrary she had been researching obsessively; indeed, towards the end the temptation was to continue researching because the thought of transforming the teetering piles into some sort of structure itself bordered on hellish.

When she was sure of her argument she began to write up the first draft. This took three times as long as she had expected, first because of the quantity of material, and second, because of her desire to include as much of it as possible. She was contending with the weakness of her left arm and an odd but fleeting darkness that would descend upon her left eye when the headaches appeared. They were unusual in their severity, began on the left side and, if she didn't catch them early, soon rendered her immobile. Nothing, though, was as debilitating as a growing fogginess, an ability to fall deeply and sometimes dangerously asleep at a moment's notice: she arrived in Epping instead of Holborn on the Underground and would have travelled back to West Ruislip if the guard hadn't woken her; called to a faculty meeting to discuss the necessity of enlivening the syllabus, she was nudged by the new historicist Felicity McGowan and woke to find herself attached by a chain of spit to her own cardigan; marking papers at home, reading in the British Library, sitting in Lincoln's Inn Fields working on her book, she had felt her grip on the world weaken.

She woke from the naps thick-headed and disoriented. Coffee made the sleepiness worse. Fresh air, brisk walks, early nights and fewer carbohydrates all failed to invoke industry. She skimmed the mellifluities of Milton's lines and the world darkened, anatomised Satan's soliloquies only for her eyes to begin to throb – was the problem the thesis itself? she wondered. Was it her argument? Had she researched too much?

She had started and restarted four times now but the

work refused to become a gestalt. Sometimes she felt she was seeing things clearly, but when she looked again, she had fallen short.

The truth was, there had been times even before the fall when Professor Stone had written no more than a sentence a day, when she had paced for hours before sitting down in front of the computer screen. It was as if her body was turning its back on an old lover, for so she had always thought of poetry, as one who gave or withheld favours. Now though it looked as though she might no longer have stamina for the pursuit, knowing through experience what many (especially those who contended that the pen was lighter than the sword) did not: that in order to write anything at all one had to be just as vital in spirit and body as in mind.

Years before, the professor had made a discovery: whenever her body sent her a new ailment all it needed was a shock of some sort, another assignment, a deadline brought forward, a bad review, the realisation that there was material for another whole book awaiting development in an appendix – in short more, much more, to do than it had imagined and less time to do it in – and, hey presto, it began functioning normally again; sometimes even better than before. The present events, she felt sure, were merely a case in point. Nevertheless, despite the annual Milton conference she was heading, extra faculty work and two journal articles to finish within the month, the symptoms not only failed to improve, they worsened. She told Professor Cullum she was experiencing some minor health problems. It was preferable to his thinking the reason was a more mysterious complaint – one lurking in the corridors of the mind, for instance, an affliction to which a worrying number of the English faculty had at some time fallen prey. He urged her to take a sabbatical and she declined.

Ironically it was mental rather than physical disturbance that finally prompted Professor Stone to seek help. It was early September, the evenings drawing in and London preparing itself for what looked set to be an unseasonably chilly autumn. She was not usually perturbed by the arrival of the darker months but walking home along the Strand she could not shake off a feeling of impending doom. The lights of passing traffic, white noise of the city, hurrying shapes of commuters, the sky seething pink and then orange and then blackish ochre, all seemed to presage some unspeakable disaster. In addition to anxiety, she began to experience startling fits of anger: jamming her key into the front door so hard that she bent the metal, trembling with rage as she rifled through the teetering pile of post in the hall, denting the plaster of the wall as she burst through the swing doors in the English Department, Dr Chakrabarti, head of Middle English, along with it. Worst of all, she found herself weeping often, profusely, and apparently for no reason: when opening an invitation to the annual Donne conference, when marking a quite astonishingly bad essay on Lovelace; midway through steak and kidney pie in the cafeteria; on the top of a double-decker bus.

Professor Stone had always made a point of engaging in outbursts as little as possible and found the latest development distressing in the extreme: how could she analyse Milton's Michael when it was all she could do not to screw up the page? What good were floods of tears when dissecting Satan's rhetoric? Things came to a head when, taking Witwoud's part in a tutorial, she was surprised to find she couldn't speak; she mastered the obstruction only for the letters to blur. Her students glanced at one another. The tutor they privately referred to as 'The Stone' appeared to be dissolving. She rose abruptly and went to the window; but now the roofs of Somerset House were moving, tears were falling. 'Excuse me,' she said, and strode to the door.

She spent the next twenty minutes locked into the small bathroom down the corridor, attempting to compose herself.

Fainting, neuropathy, headaches, narcolepsy, fits of anger could all be borne, but not weeping in a tutorial. Professor Stone made an appointment to see the doctor.

Past, Present, Future

That her GP thought it necessary to refer her to a neurologist Professor Stone found excessive, that she was fast-tracked laughable. That Doctor Robertson ordered an MRI and a CT scan was an irritant: she had to cancel a lecture and two tutorials. Not even as she travelled in slow motion into the belly of a giant space-age pupa and listened for the best part of an hour to the aural equivalent of Chinese water torture (for though it did no observable damage, she was convinced by the end that her skull was caving in) did she suspect there was any cause for alarm; serious illness simply wasn't an option; the gods had decreed a different fate for her. She was to be tormented by ailments that were interminable but essentially harmless. She was Sisyphus and his boulder, Prometheus chained to his crag.

Nevertheless, despite the inconvenience Professor Stone was glad the investigation had taken this route. What she had secretly been dreading was a referral to a psychotherapist. In fact, it was what she had expected Robertson to suggest when she returned to Praed Street (a suggestion she had decided she would agree to wholeheartedly, then do precisely nothing about). So she was not prepared in any way when, before she was even properly seated, he said: 'The tests revealed a brain tumour. That accounts for the neurological symptoms. It's pressing on the right frontal lobe. That accounts for the mood swings.'

He said other words too – 'aggressive', 'malignant', 'options', 'prompt', 'debulking', 'growth rate' – but they sounded strange, second-hand, and not immediately relevant to her. When he had finished speaking she sat in silence for a moment. Then she said: 'I've got a book to finish.'

He waited for her. Then he turned the screen so that she could see in irrefutable black and white a cross-section of her skull: humbler than she had imagined, more idiosyncratic. She could make out her crooked incisors, the flattish part of her head near the crown, and there, nestled like a downy bird in the whorls of her cerebellum, a dense white mass the size of a plum.

She blinked twice, then turned to the window. When she didn't speak for several minutes – indeed, to all intents and purposes, appeared to have left the room – he said softly: 'Have you got someone you can talk to? I can put you in touch with someone here, if you like.'

She appeared to wake then and turned back. 'I don't need to talk, I need treatment,' she said. 'When do we begin?'

The gods had a new agenda. Her body meant business after all. It would not consider rapprochement, diplomacy would be in vain. It had been waging an underground revolt, for goodness knew how long, stockpiling armaments, recruiting adherents – and now it would be all they could do to wrest the things from the rebels' bloody hands. But the insurgents, unbeknown to themselves, were attacking their own side; or there were no sides; or there was one, because what was cancer after all but a case of mistaken identity? A belief that the enemy was within when in fact there was no enemy at all? A purgation that infected the purgers in the very business of cleansing? An explosion of free-thinkers, mavericks, a frenzied division from the body politic under the assumption that such a policy could contain the threat and usher in a new order. But the threat was illusory, the new order fatally flawed. A dissident corpus indeed.

She said she was taking leave to finish her book. Professor Cullum was glad she had seen sense at last, and told her not to hurry back. The surgery went as well as could be expected. They should start therapy, Robertson said, as soon as possible.

She could afford taxis to and from the hospital; that was the good thing. The bad thing was everything else. Apart from the litany of nausea, dizziness and exhaustion, the weekly appointments with a plastic sac that delivered a moment-by-moment infusion of poison, the obvious mood dampener of being fixed to a table by a frame drilled into her already fragile skull while beams bored into its depths. She began losing her hair.

Professor Stone was not a vain woman but her hair was the one physical feature she liked: its mass offset her shallow forehead and lessened the abruptness of her nose; its weight suggested health and abundance in one who was slender to the point of thinness; its chestnut warmed an otherwise wan complexion, made excuses for the porcine fairness of her lashes, and added a note of colour to a person who would otherwise have appeared muted in the extreme. In fact, her attachment to her hair was even more complex than this, because its very abundance suggested things about the owner that were themselves redeeming: that here was a mind intent upon loftier things than appearance; that cardigans and pleats, sensible shoes and thick tights were beside the point, the point being merit, the point being Art. She had been privately elated when she learned her head would not have to be shaved in preparation for the surgery, and afterwards, while still in hospital, spent many minutes alone, gazing with infinite relief upon her reflection; a reflection that, unless she turned her head to the side and lifted her hair to reveal a jagged white scar three inches long, did not betray anything abnormal at all. Now it did, however; and if Professor Stone's hair was more than just hair, she was losing it. Each morning the brush came away wound so thickly you could hardly see the bristles. She gave up brushing and woke to find strands on her pillow; lost, infantile, adrift on the cotton like riverweed.

It wasn't easy to distract herself. On days at the hospital the wasting hours were brought home most unpleasantly by the drip of the liquid hourglass beside her; a trickling, once noticed, no less unwelcome than the ticking of clocks. There was one thing, though, that this strange new world of taxis, vomiting, daytime television and sunlight at bedtime did afford, and that was time. One afternoon when rain lacerated the bedroom windows and the lamp probed her eyes mercilessly, she read her thesis from the beginning and came to see it was not the masterpiece she had thought. She couldn't tell why it wasn't working but the more she read the more convinced she became that it could not be published; it was exhaustive, worthy, immense, but also plodding, circuitous, and in places, she was distressed to see, downright pedestrian.

For years now Professor Stone had imagined herself travelling down a long road. To begin with the distance between herself and her destination was invigorating; the lack of gratification, the hardships of the journey merely highlighted the fact that she had not yet arrived. But with each year the situation became more critical. Now, quite suddenly, the destination looked as if it might be imminent, and she was not ready. To the world she had made great advances – there was even talk of 'pre-' and 'post-Stonian' readings after her first book – but the germ she had been looking for, the divine spark, had never materialised. Her work was insightful, controversial, sometimes brilliant; but never original, not in the larger sense. Now, on this rain-riddled afternoon, Professor Stone was alarmed to discover, in what alcoholics term 'a moment of clarity', that her lifelong search for something to say had ended in speechlessness. A voice said: shall I say I have gone through half-deserted streets? Was that Eliot? Yes. How strange it was to remember the old poem and all of Prufrock's verbose pomposity; but the fear of death – the head brought in upon a platter – was the same.

The fact was, the professor's imagination had long been preoccupied – and why should she hide it? – with one reader in particular, a reader who presented himself whenever she sent a book into the world, delivered a lecture she was proud of, or a paper she was not. The reader had said he would be watching her. In a city filled with books he had sat in a room overlooking river meadows, with a view little changed since the days of Milton, and read aloud Wyatt and Herbert and Donne; he had locked her into a chamber filled with straw which it befell her to spin into gold – so she spun, at night mostly, and in the morning, when the sun lifted spider-legs over chilled quadrangles and others tumbled into lectures or Hall, crept into bed; so she learned to use words, to measure what was needed and trim the surplus, learned to arrange words pleasingly – and he was, on the whole, pleased, though the fabled gold had always eluded her.

In darkest London Professor Stone began to think of the reader and of the city and of the room; the bells, the mornings, the evenings and afternoons; the ruins and façades and long, empty views that hadn't changed for centuries and probably wouldn't for centuries to come. In her bed at nightfall, in the hospital when sunshine illuminated the steel tree's translucent fruit, in the back seat of rain-spattered taxis, the edges of things were lost in whiteness, the fabric of the present gave way and her hand passed through some gauzy membranous wall to a continuous, indivisible present. Returning was unbearable; she had not spun gold, he had not got to hear of it; she had turned out to be ordinary, her work too little – and now, it appeared, too late.

Of her period of sickness two days stayed with the professor, the first an afternoon in hospital, dark shortly after four, the outside world enveloped in freezing mist, the inner smothered in fluorescent light and the dusty fumes of central heating. She was connected to her drip and before that had waited hours, during which she had been forced to engage in an activity she found even more enervating than chemotherapy itself; an activity inappropriately called 'passing the time of day' but one that she found made time go infinitely more slowly. During the course of her life, the professor had cultivated the ability to detach herself at will from her immediate surroundings. Now it seemed she could not get away from them. She was forced not only to talk to her fellow patients but look at them, look at faces hollow and pale, at elbows and knees protruding through jumpers and jeans; at shaven heads, stitched heads; faces, bodies and heads that probably in some ways, she admitted, now resembled her own.

On that afternoon, when she was finally sitting in the treatment room, the nurse taking her blood pressure, other patients picking up magazines, talking to their companions or leaning back and closing their eyes, Professor Stone noticed something: the chair opposite her was empty. Each time she had visited the hospital before, the chair had been filled, though not very much, by a young woman with skin as grey as that of a cadaver. Professor Stone knew very little about her because, like herself, the woman apparently did not feel the need for chit-chat. She hadn't spoken more than a few words, in fact, in all the time she had been there.

This afternoon the room was unusually quiet. Professor Stone could hear her breath and the tinkling of the radiator and a fly at the windowpane. It was tired of battering the glass and resorted to the odd millisecond stab, its anger reduced to a caricature in the realms of the surreal and absurd. Professor Stone glanced again at the empty chair. It was green nylon, a recliner, with a large headrest and curved back, exactly the same as every other chair in the room, but the longer she gazed at it, the more certain she became that the quietness was emanating from there; she thought she could see it diffusing, like plumes of milk in water. As she listened, the muted snippets of conversation, the deranged fly at the windowpane, the turning of pages, the soft, shifting sounds made by the nylon skirts and stocking-ed legs of the nurses were muffled by the quiet. And then she saw that at some level everyone else was aware of it too. They gave themselves away by the angle of a head, the fidgeting of a foot, a page turned a little too quickly, the particular downward cast of their eyes. Professor Stone saw that the quiet had always been present and everyone had tried to ignore it. Before long, however, it would once more be incorporated into the stream of living moments, indistinguishable, a background hum. Today, owing to the empty chair, it was almost palpable. So, she thought. This is how it is. Death comes in ordinary clothes, is accepted by degrees, becomes another event.

The second moment Professor Stone remembered clearly was on an afternoon even gloomier than the first, a Sunday towards the end of December. She was at home, too weak to sit up, the apparatus of living gathered around her, attempting to read *Paradise Lost*, thinking perhaps even now she would see a way out of the morass that was meant to be her opus. More importantly, she was trying to read, an activity that had until recently been as integral to her life as food, though was now a statement of will. She had balanced the book on her stomach with the help of a pillow, resting the tips of her fingers at the bottom of the page, and had read for more than half an hour when the nausea became too great for her to continue. She let the book fall back, turned on her side and saw a clump on her pillow. The hair looked violated, lying there against the cotton. Foetal, untimely ripp'd, a sickly vestige of human or animal rendered mute and expressionless in death. She didn't know why shedding this last piece should move her, because what was one handful when the rest had gone? Indeed, being completely bald might be an improvement. But for a minute she could not get her breath. She glared at the ceiling, daring the tears to brim over.

Presently her breathing became regular again. She repositioned the book and went back to reading, but Milton was being difficult and refused to stay where he was propped. She gave up balancing the book and attempted to read it flat, but her eyes ached too much. A wave of heat passed over her and she hurled the book to the floor. She regretted it immediately, lay still for a moment, then turned on her side and tried to reach. She hung there, half on and half off the bed, grains floating before her eyes, then clawed herself back on to the mattress. Her heart beat so hard she thought she would suffocate. She tried again, leaning further, pressing her face into the mattress, to no avail.

This time she did not immediately turn over, and when she did her face was wet. She lay staring at the ceiling for a few minutes, not conscious of anything. What happened next was unclear: she was shuttling backwards and at the same time absolutely still. Afterwards she thought she must have fallen asleep because she heard voices and saw people but no time seemed to have passed. Then she thought she must have fainted, but that didn't explain how she could remember everything so clearly. Then she thought that for a moment she must have died. But there was no tunnel, no white light, no revelation, and the scene, far from heavenly, was very much of the earth. She was sitting at a kitchen table.

The table was long and rough-hewn and she was busy with some task there of great importance but one that could better have been done standing, for it required leverage. The room was dark, perhaps medieval, and the walls whitewashed. Light fell from high windows. There were also children and a dog, and she was trying, in addition to finishing her task, to watch a baby, who was crawling under everyone's feet. The noise was considerable and she felt her work would not be so onerous if only it could be done in silence. Then a figure appeared and drew up a chair beside her.

His face was dark and shrouded in something she could not pull back. He smelt of rain. He was wearing an old jumper. His voice was familiar. He asked her what was wrong, and she told him, about the baby and the dog and the work she must do, whatever it was that was laid out on the table, but he didn't seem to hear her because his face was blank. Then he put his arm around her neck and pulled her head on to his shoulder and everything became hazy.

The figure held her as though she was a child. She could hear his breath and feel his face in her hair and tell how much he was enjoying it, breathing deeply and savouring the moment. She could feel the thinness of his body and the hardness of his skull and her hands slipped from the table and lay in her lap. After a while she was too tired to hold herself away any longer and let her head rest on his shoulder and it seemed completely natural, as if she had always done this or was always going to and was perhaps even a little tired of it.

For a long time she was nowhere and everything was still. She couldn't hear the children, or the dog; could feel nothing, except an unearthly heat where he touched her, where his hand cradled her head – this charge – so that when he pulled away, her hair rose up and she was on fire and could hardly bear it.

In a little while he asked her if she felt any better and she nodded. In another he said, 'Up to walking?' and she nodded again, though the thought of moving grieved her. Then she remembered the work laid out on the table.

'Leave it,' he said.

'I can't,' she said. 'He needs me.' And now she saw that

she was holding the baby, who was crying. Then the dog jumped up, excited by the noise, and she sat down again.

He pushed the dog away, gave the baby to someone else, and led her through a door low down in the wall by the fireplace. He shut it behind them and they heard the dog's claws on the wood. He said: 'You're not going back. We'll never get out.'

They were standing in a passage. One wall was made of glass and looked on to a garden. On the other there were hooks and an assortment of coats. The coats didn't fit but he helped her into one, shrugging her arms into the sleeves and doing it up at the neck. He took an anorak that was too small at the shoulders and short in the sleeves, and she saw again his hands and studied the lines on his face, but his features eluded her.

They went through a pointed doorway, which resembled that of a church. Wind buffeted them and rain stung their faces. The sky was so low they seemed to walk into it.

They went along what appeared to be a cliff path and there were yew trees and dripping hedges and the remains of what might have been a graveyard.

Then she was waking, coming through some element that shattered around her, feeling sick, feeling thirsty, feeling halved, like a house fallen into the sea.

For the rest of the day Professor Stone caught glimpses of the figures, stopping on a street corner, entering the low doorway of a house, appearing in a room beneath eaves. They went on existing instead, in spite, because of her – she didn't know. And it was strange, this awareness, as if she was patting her head and rubbing her stomach, closing her eyes in a moving vehicle and imagining she was still.

The Poetics of Sound

Crossing the road from the hospital to Paddington Underground station, Professor Stone lingered on the kerb longer than usual: time had been returned to her and it would be foolish to spurn the gift. Sun winked in shop windows; cars looked sprucer than she remembered, pavements cleaner, people more friendly – she nodded to the man selling daffodils. The day was perfect and it was her own, had been wrapped and presented to her, and she smiled at the pleasing coincidence: the present, for once, being precisely where she found herself. It felt more like a resurrection than a remission; Lady Lazarus, that was who she was, albeit a bald one, though she did not hold with moribund female poets, particularly those who put their heads in gas ovens. Her wig itched and she adjusted it. The trials of the soldier returning to civilian life. But her hair would grow back, and the day was beautiful, 'fresh as if issued to children on a beach'. That was *Mrs Dalloway*, written by another neurotic woman – not a poet but she might as well have been for all the structure her sentences possessed; Professor Stone would dearly have liked to teach Virginia Woolf a thing or two about semicolons. But *Mrs Dalloway* was a masterpiece, undoubtedly. It was funny how great works stuck in your mind. And she must have a collection the size of the British Library in her own: the mind that less than an hour ago she had believed to be the cause of her irrevocable decline.

The train came with the sound of swords clashing and she settled herself between a nodding Indian and a woman in leopard-print leggings to 'the sleepy rhythm of a hundred hours'. That was T. S. Eliot, *Four Quartets*, whose 'Love Song of J. Alfred Prufrock' had come back to her only a few months before. Eliot was another great, though his status was a little more hotly contested than Woolf's; there were no skeletons in Woolf's closet but plenty in Eliot's, and yet – what was it? He stayed with you.

She had often tried to sum up the quality of greatness and after many years had come to think of it as memorability. 'It's as if we've heard it before,' she would say to her students. 'A poem is like a road. We set out not knowing where we're going and remember once we arrive.' It was the sound of words that elevated them, not their meaning. You could get all the meaning you wanted from a textbook, but a poem's form was as important as its content and at the level of great art, form and content were one. If her students pressed her further, she would say that great poetry separated from itself was recognition – which must mean that at some level something inside us chimed with its greatness, a universal database of consciousness perhaps in which all things were 'known' to all people. It was anamnesis, Michelangelo's account of love at first sight, 'La dove io t'amai prima', the shadow of the Argo passing over Neptune's head; something *felt*; indubitably yet inexplicably true.

She changed at Baker Street, got off at King's Cross and ten minutes later was standing in the echoing foyer of the British Library. She had been spending her days here since finishing treatment, not well enough to be teaching but hungry to be in contact with humanity again in however small a way. Walking to the locker room she passed a man dragging his foot, a moment later a woman in a wheelchair, and was alarmed once again by the amount of readers who seemed to be in some state of physical or mental disrepair; oh, yes, it wasn't just the physically disabled: she had twice seen someone talking to themselves, and once, outside the cafeteria, a man with a bandage on his neck, gesturing wildly in front of the bronze statue of Mr Punch. Was the life of the mind really bought at expense to the body? she wondered. Had her own brush with death been occasioned by such an imbalance?

She deposited her belongings in a locker and pocketed the key. What had the doctor said? Visit a friend, go on holiday (she had always had a distinct aversion to holidays, even the two-day kind at the end of each week), take time out. What a strange expression! Out of where? Of itself? A voice said: 'Time and the bell have buried the day'. And there, for the second time that morning, was Eliot.

She was breasting the top of an escalator a few minutes later on her way to the humanities room with a clear plastic bag, pencil and paper, when she stared, ran aground as the escalator steps disappeared into the marble, because there in front of her, leaning on an umbrella that was tightly rolled yet nevertheless tilted at a rakish angle, *was* Eliot – or at least a life-size cardboard replica of him. The bottom half of his body was turned slightly to the left but he was looking to the right, and he had the impish expression she had seen in photographs taken on the beach in New England when he was a child. Appearing just then, as he did at the top of the escalator, he had the air of an angel welcoming her to Heaven; or a demon, inviting her James Dean-style to Hell.

She was marvelling again at the number of poets Eliot had discovered when she saw, pasted to a piece of cardboard and looking rather dingy, a proof of 'Burnt Norton', the first poem of Eliot's late masterpiece, *Four Quartets*. The *Quartets* had reappeared in Professor Stone's life at odd moments ever since they had arrived thirty-five years ago wrapped in brown paper and smelling of tobacco. They had proved to be, in Eliot's own words, 'a familiar, compound ghost'. Inside the brown paper had been a letter:

As you know, I'm not a twentieth century expert but I do find Four Quartets *strangely moving – as an amateur, you understand – and I thought you might too . . . Now these are meant as a gift . . . you're not being tested any more, I'm just interested to see what you think.*

She had been consumed with fear, spent weeks composing a reply, finally spun some rubbish about time and timeless-ness, then gone around for a good many years denying the poem meant anything to her at all. She gave up on it again now and moved to the last display cabinet. Inside there was a photocopy of a handwritten page dated 1943, an excerpt from an article Eliot had written called 'The Music of Poetry', Eliot contending that we read Milton for the sound rather than the sense. She thought it strange she had never read this essay, having read virtually everything on Milton that had been published. Then she understood: the paper was in the Hyland Bequest in the archive of King's College, in the city where she herself had been an undergraduate. She had never known there was Eliot material there. He was talking about the cumulative effect a poem could have by means of sound and rhythm. '*[T]he senses are used to convey something beyond sense,*' she read. '*In reading* Pericles *I have a sense of the pervading smell of seaweed . . .*'

Professor Stone frowned. Then she rummaged in her bag for paper and pencil and went back to the cabinet containing the extract of 'Burnt Norton'. It was just an idea, it might be foolish but she had to try it out. She spread the paper on the glass and began scoring the lines, marking where the stress fell:

/   / _   _ / /
Time present and time past
_   /   _ _ / _ _ / / _
Are both perhaps present in time future
-   / / - / - - / /
And time future present in time past . . .

A few moments later she stopped. Her heart beat hard. There was a pattern; a faint one but a pattern nonetheless.

She knew that marking prosody like this was considered old-fashioned now, though it was something Eliot himself would have prioritised. After all, he had proposed the theory of the 'auditory imagination', a theory which he defined as a feeling for syllable and rhythm penetrating below the conscious levels of thought. The idea that the musical qualities of verse possessed greater power than their verbal counterpart was an old one of course. Milton himself discussed it in 'At a Solemn Music' and '*Ad Patrem*' where he spoke of 'Voice and Verse' as 'harmonious Sisters', capable in their 'mixt power' of endowing 'dead things with inbreath'd sense'. He believed that a return to the Golden Age (classical Greece *and* the Garden of Eden) could be effected through reuniting the divergent arts of music and poetry. One was reminded of the Grand Unification Theory of physicists, she thought, which claimed it was possible to recover the instant of the Big Bang through the discovery of a particle that unified gravitation, electro-magnetism, and the strong and weak nuclear forces.

Professor Stone believed that in general art forms degenerated when they attempted to emulate one another. Music could handle words rather well, as opera and even some types of popular music demonstrated, but words could not, on the whole, do music's job. There were successful examples, most notably parallels between the symphony and the novel, *Ulysses* being the first that came to mind – but not many. She had always believed that the *Quartets* were an exception, however; that they really did manage, in places, to come close to the effect music produced on a listener. What now occurred to her for the first time was that this might have been the reason they had made her so uncomfortable when she had initially heard them, the reason they had felt strangely familiar. Could it even have been the reason she felt she had understood the poem but couldn't explain what she understood? Could the music of the verse convey as much to a reader's imagination as words' literal meaning? she wondered. Could it convey *more*? A current flowing covertly, along the riverbed, along the sea floor; a pattern so subtle it might be missed completely, yet nonetheless shaped the movements above.

She put down the pencil and stood very still. Would it be possible to address the musical components of verse as an independent field of enquiry? The music of the verse working in conjunction with, or perhaps contrary to, the meaning of the words? Prosody had been studied for years but not with this intention, not as a language in itself. If she wasn't mistaken, it was nothing short of a whole new field of critical reference, an alternative template with which to evaluate poetry – possibly prose too. And wasn't that how poetry had begun? she thought. Not with a printing press or marks on a page but a succession of fleeting vibrations, through matter and air, flesh and blood? Declaimed aloud, endowed with rhythm and rhyme in order to be remembered? Was this what she had been looking for? The germ that would fructify? The promised seed? Not words but music – a poetics not of difference but of sound.

Her hands were trembling. It would be difficult; it might be impossible. She looked again at the paper. The starting point would be the *Quartets* and Eliot's ideas about the auditory imagination. That would be the template with which to evaluate other poems. She glanced again at the paper on Milton. It had been written at the time Eliot was composing the *Quartets*, not many years after he had evolved his idea of the 'auditory imagination'. She would have to see it. But that would mean returning to the city of books, a city she hadn't revisited for more than thirty years, the city where the reader dwelled who had said he would be watching her. It wouldn't take more than a week to inspect the paper – *if* she went. She would tell him that that was why she had come back; she would state it clearly in her letter to him, was already imagining how it would go. He would have to be notified: it wouldn't do to bump into him by accident; no, they would meet; it would be unavoidable – peculiar if they didn't after knowing one another all those years ago. She would stress that it was purely coincidental that her research had happened to bring her back, that it would be pleasant to meet if he was not occupied; indeed, she would value his feedback on the project; that he might be pleased to know she was finally bringing herself to write about the poem he had sent her, but she understood if he was busy. He must not feel obligated. If she got a reply, all well and good, if not it didn't matter. Perhaps she could not, after all, expect someone she had known thirty years before to remember her. But she hoped he would because then she could present it to him, her masterwork; and he would see that the wait had been worth it, that his hunch had been good.

She forgot about the humanities room, was on her way back to the lockers – and wasn't a trip to the country exactly what the doctor had ordered? Hadn't he suggested visiting an old friend? And what was Professor Hunt, after all, if not a very old friend? Though perhaps 'friend' wasn't quite the right word – words were such awkward commodities. 'Acquaintance', then. She wiggled the key frantically in the locker then realised it was open. The door clattered backwards and she retrieved her bag and mackintosh. Her hands trembled as she belted it – and no wonder. What a day it had been! The revelations of the morning eclipsed by the discoveries of the afternoon.

She walked quickly through the piazza, her shoes picking their way through the shadows cast by flagpoles and chair legs. At the gate some young people were bashing out

'When I'm Sixty-Four' on a black upright piano, one of many that had been dotted around the city this spring, as some sort of initiative by the civic authorities, the music as strange amid the blare of the Euston Road as an armchair in a ploughed field.

A Poetics of Sound. She knew as she stepped between the gate pillars that it was what she had been looking for. It would be controversial, it would be brilliant, it would be original. It would, indeed, be her masterpiece.

BOOK II

'. . . known, forgotten, half recalled . . .'

*

'Little Gidding'
Four Quartets, 1942

My Words Echo Thus, in Your Mind

It is surprising how quickly a face can be forgotten. Professor Stone had cause to reflect on this the next day when she sat down to write three letters. The first requested permission to look at T. S. Eliot's papers, the second to the archivist at King's College asking to be granted access to the Hyland Bequest, the third to the professor of poetry himself.

It wasn't easy to guess how old the professor might be. He had always had a timeless face; she couldn't remember it clearly, not even the eyes, which had produced such disconcerting sensations when fixed on her. Nor was it easy at such a distance to describe the effect he had had on her. Moments she had spent in his company, which hadn't seemed all that important at the time (a night when wind and rain came down, an evening at a concert, an afternoon of great light), in later years had come to acquire a resonance that could not be satisfactorily explained. The man was an enigma, what could she say?

That he sat in an armchair chain-smoking in spite of college regulations? That he tripped, often, knotted the laces of his boots three times, wore innumerable pairs of identical faded black jeans (or was it just one?) and shapeless jumpers? That his favourite word was 'fuck' and after that 'crap' and after that 'shit', and relished reading the Earl of Rochester to shockable undergraduates? That he loved Bach, held a book as if it was a living thing and breathed deeply when he read poetry? If she had had to pick one thing that captured the professor best, though, it would be his voice: gruff, northern, foreboding yet intimate; more sensation than sound. It was to this voice Professor Stone now addressed herself. The thing was to be professional, because that was what she was now: not a nineteen-year-old undergraduate but a professor herself. But although she drafted the message several times, she still wasn't entirely satisfied when she sealed the envelope. It was the second time in her life she had written him a letter.

The first had also concerned T. S. Eliot. Two weeks after her university interview she had found a parcel waiting for her when she got in from school. Her foster-mother was rolling pastry by the kitchen window. The day was dark though it wasn't yet four and the room unlit. 'Something for you,' the woman said, but Elizabeth had seen the letter before the bus pulled away in the lane outside with a wet hiss, seen it propped at the base of the salt-cellar like a glinting shard of meteorite. The vicar came in from his study, having sensed movement, and peered at her over the top of his spectacles; she seized the parcel and slipped past him upstairs, careful not to climb too quickly.

She had lived with the vicar and his wife, Rene, for ten years now, he a ruddy Church-of-Englander with meaty jowls and shining pate, and she an Amazon whose upper peaks were ensconced in herringbone and lower inclines in tweed and wool. They married late and fostered one child before Elizabeth, a missionary in Namibia, who wrote long letters littered with Khoisan phrases and accounts of the desert. Their current project was less pleasing: Shakespeare instead of the Bible, an eighteenth-century heretic instead of St Paul. But Elizabeth had never been theirs for the converting. She had come with a store of earthly treasure she had inherited from her mother, already partly consumed, though not by moth or rust but by damp, and a large quantity of bookworm.

The books were poetry mostly, acrid and dog-eared, sleek with age and grime, smelling of glycerine and rosewater. They sat beneath the eaves in piles on the carpet; there were no shelves and the room was small. When the cottage by the river seemed unbearably quiet, as it was wont to do on certain low afternoons, when possessed of an ache that nothing could assuage, she read aloud, imagining herself another, and there was comfort in the words, the way they dispersed the stillness, courted it and brought it within the circle of sound. She read in an undertone though not scripture; day and night, though that did nothing to reassure the vicar about the state of her soul. She read everywhere, with hungry eyes, a rapid blink, sharp exhalations, half-cough. She was one of those who felt a jolt of nausea if the school library was closed and spent break-times folded up with a book in some deserted classroom. When her English teacher suggested she apply to university, she knew it would cause a disturbance; at the vicarage, events acquired a magnitude they didn't elsewhere: if the sauerkraut boiled instead of simmered it was a disaster; when the heron ate the koi the vicar didn't leave his study for several days. But her foster-parents hadn't anticipated problems from her quarter.

She had always maintained a vacancy with them. It wasn't coldness; there was no agenda, simply absence. She was polite, evinced a mild apathy that could be mistaken for contentment, did not laugh or cry (the activity filled her with the revulsion others had towards vomiting), like or dislike. When she told them she wanted to study English, the vicar did not retire to his study (what that said about the worth of her soul relative to that of the koi, she couldn't decide). But there were reprisals. Over the coming weeks a chill settled over the vicarage; she was reprimanded for not saying 'excuse me', for biting her nails, eating soup from the wrong side of the bowl, pushing her feet into shoes without undoing the laces, reading at the table and spending too much time in her room. Moreover, if she didn't want the Church, the Church would return the compliment: 'God wants willing workers.' She now spent several hours every Sunday in complete solitude; chosen, not imposed as it was in school; unobserved and hence not shameful. So on that January afternoon, weeks after her controversial interview at a prestigious university, as she snatched the parcel from the kitchen table with a look her foster-parents had come to recognise, a look not easily described; incandescent, tenebrous, both trepidation and flickering delight; it was one more incident in a long line, drawing her further from them into a world of deception and error.

She latched the bedroom door as quietly as she could (the vicar was no doubt still listening at the bottom of the stairs). Her hands were shaking. She had never received a parcel before. Inside more brown paper was a plastic case containing a double cassette: 'T. S. Eliot: *The Waste Land, Four Quartets and Other Poems*, Read by Sir Alec Guinness', and a letter. She didn't know what *Four Quartets* were, had never heard of T. S. Eliot. The letter was written on a plain sheet of A4 paper folded into four, the words firmly dealt yet strangely wavering, the *es* half-moons, the *ys* reaching high, the *gs* ants, the body joined to the head by a tiny filament, a delicate antenna poking enquiringly from the top; there was, twice, a faintly coquettish trail of dots. She turned the page and her heart beat once, very hard; then she turned back to the beginning.

Dear Elizabeth,

I hope you're well. I just wanted to say again how good it was to meet you at the interview and how excited we all are about you coming. It was certainly the most interesting interview I have ever conducted and I'm greatly looking forward to working with you. Don't worry too much about the reading list, the important thing is to find things you enjoy.

We are all struck down with the flu here and looking forward to spring. This place can get pretty cold in winter so remember to bring warm clothes and stock up on vitamins. Regarding the tapes: now these are meant as a gift. You're not being tested any more. I'm just interested to see what you think. As you know, I'm not a twentieth-century expert but I do find Four Quartets *strangely moving and I thought you might too . . .*

She lifted the paper to her nose – tobacco, lilac and ashy, softened into perfume with distance, *'I'm just interested to see what you think . . .'* – then lowered it, her face very pale, her eyes very bright.

She closed the lid of a black Panasonic cassette player and leaned back against the candlewick counterpane. The wheels began to turn and a decrepit whirring wheezed into life, interspersed every now and then with an agonised squeak. She listened for several minutes to the sonorous baritone, breathing deeply and evenly, her face empty and cheeks flushed, then slipped down, so that she was lying on the carpet, and stared at the orange-fringed lampshade above.

The tape finished with a resounding click and all that could be heard was the wind over the river meadows, but that did not seem to be a sound any more so much as an amplifier of silence.

She was sure she had heard the poem before but each time she listened it got further away. The reply she finally wrote was scattered, Tippexed, laden with arrows and asterisks, and she knew even as she sealed the envelope that she had failed. It was a replication of the interview.

It wasn't the *Quartets* he had read that day but a sonnet. He knelt beside her and opened a book and held it between them. She hadn't known how to account for what happened then either, except words, spoken aloud, dropped one by one into an infinite and echoing well of silence.

The Word Spoken

The day was overcast. Hurrying banks of cloud filled the sky and the wind was cold. She turned left out of the lodge, beneath the battlements' stony faces, towards the river. It seemed to her that she was walking through the pages of a novel, a Brontë perhaps, a Hardy, a James. She hadn't known such places existed, such turrets, such arches, such windows, such spires. She passed through chained gates and entered a narrow path bordered by a small orchard where trees, cowed with cold-shrunken branches, touched tip to frosted tip. To her left was a medieval chapel, crudely hewn with a square bell tower, to her right a Gothic cathedral, whose arched windows glittered darkly; the whole place – the whole city – seemed to exist in a strange field of solipsistic demurral, things corresponding or failing to correspond with the quiet haphazard acquiescence of old neighbours. She passed through a turnstile and the river meadows spread out, lines of poplars swaying in the ghostly air, and beyond them the river.

She was running now, walking and then running again, and it was strange passing beneath those heavy clouds in such leaden cold, feeling light enough to blow away. She came back to the ghostly buildings in freezing fog and walked through the town as daylight faded and stopped in lighted shop doorways and stepped inside, wiped her spectacles and opened covers, stood for a moment and read a few lines, looked up the words he had taught her: 'Dionysian', 'esoteric', 'deictic', then went on again.

*

She has been in this city for two days now. By day she memorises words in an attic, looking on to a world of vanishing rooftops, accompanied by a heady and nameless longing that seems to be at one with the endless grey skies. At night she gazes at luminous stars stuck on to the sloping ceiling by the room's term-time owner and waits for the dawn. It is not that she doesn't want to sleep, it's just that sleep is a thing of the past now, something she used to do in another lifetime. Words prop her eyes open and will not let them seal over.

Once a day she sits at the end of a long wooden bench in the place insiders (mysteriously eliding the definite article) call 'Hall', surrounded by students who either ignore her completely or view her with the rightful disdain with which insiders view interlopers, she stares at silver bowls of potatoes and green beans, pushes peas around her plate, and when she has done this long enough attempts to extricate herself by walking over the top of the table. It isn't that she's not hungry, only that eating is a distant memory now. She cannot swallow: words are stuck in her throat.

She returns to the desk to memorise Hughes's 'A Sparrow Hawk', taut as a kite in high winds, and wonders how many others have sat there before her and looked up from the page, terrible in its pale immutability. The desk is just wide enough that when she stretches out her arms she can curl her fingers over the edge. She does so, often. There are three books on it: *Hamlet*, *The Poetry of Gnosis* and Hughes's *New Collected Poems*. The nameless authorities who invited her to this interview have asked her to bring a poem she is prepared to talk about and she has chosen 'A Sparrow Hawk', believing it to contain 'all', in the way *Goblin Market* or *The Rime of the Ancient Mariner* contain 'all', possessing depths impossible to sound and hence, hopefully, providing the answer to any question they care to throw at her; the advantage of 'A Sparrow Hawk' is that it is shorter than *Goblin Market* or *The Rime of the Ancient Mariner* by about two thousand and four thousand words respectively.

Her attention is drawn to a noise, half-gasp, half-sigh, and she realises she is making it. She tightens her grip on the table. Really, what is the point of it all – *Hamlet*, Hughes, *The Poetry of Gnosis* – only to arrive at the gates and not be granted admittance? To go back to the cottage by the river (the eyes of the vicar peering at her over the *bratwurst*, the broad and spacious tapered off, the penitent returned, chastened and malleable)? What is worse, now she is at the gates, she is not even sure she wants to enter, because they aren't so pearly close up but, rather, resemble the jaws that rose to allow the Christians into the arena – she thinks she knows exactly how they felt just now because it is all she can do to keep herself in the seat. But there is nowhere to go, only this moment, succeeded by another just like it. This is the portal for her rebirth. And she must be reborn: she knows this already, at seventeen. But 'A Sparrow Hawk' is not yielding.

Periodically she checks an enormous barley-coloured wristwatch. She found it in a box of miscellanea in the Army and Navy Stores at home. She has never owned a watch before and bought it for the interview, thinking that it would be hard to ignore. It is doing its job; the ticking is deafening; it sits before her on the desk like a great mechanical cricket, scratching its legs. Every fifteen minutes she measures its time against the chiming bells outside the window. They have been chiming all morning, removing her attention from the present yet simultaneously reminding her of its overwhelming importance. Don't they strike hours in this city, only quarters?

She puts her head in her hands, then jumps up, the chair clattering backwards. She must see where the chiming is coming from though every moment is priceless. She runs down to the street, her limbs a wickerwork of electricity, but cannot locate it.

For three more days she continues to believe that the sound is coming from the left. On the third day she realises it is in fact to the right.

Her first interview is with a tiny Chinese man with hands like a mouse's feet, a specialist in Middle English, whose skin is white, nails pointed, and mahogany voice deep, womanly and so polished she feels it an honour simply to be addressed. He asks her what the difference is between Old English and Anglo-Saxon. She racks her brain, comes up with nothing, and after a sufficient length of time has elapsed – time in which her heart beats so hard she feels sick, he tells her there is no difference at all: Old English is the name scholars give to the language spoken by the people known to historians and archaeologists as the Anglo-Saxons. She flushes, nods, looks at her lap. She does not get to talk about 'A Sparrow Hawk'.

Her second interview is with a beaming woman, who has long, ashen hair and appears to be eleven months pregnant. The woman asks her what she thought of the poems. (Poems.) That were pinned on the Junior Common Room notice board. (Junior Common Room?) She has not read the note on the notice board at the college lodge. (Notice board?) The pregnant one laughs. Never mind. Instead they talk about *To the Lighthouse*. She asks Elizabeth if she has ever considered Mrs Ramsay as a Virgin figure. (As in the mother of Christ?) She says: 'No,' thinks: should I? It appears that she should. They talk more about *To the Lighthouse* and she begins to think it was not such a good book to mention after all because the part she liked was where the house goes to rack and ruin, and the pregnant woman doesn't seem so interested in that.

Afterwards, standing once more in the corridor, she

realises she has forgotten again to mention 'A Sparrow Hawk'.

At lunch she toys with a pear, unable to bring herself to walk across the top of the table, and concentrates on dodging the crossbeams of eyes, buffeted by the rumble and swell of high-spirited conversation and periodically checking the moon-faced watch. She doesn't know how the first two interviews have gone. She doesn't know if the Chinese man is reserved by nature or his reserve was elicited by her ignorance of the fact that 'Old English' is synonymous with 'Anglo-Saxon'; she doesn't know if, despite the pregnant woman's innate goodwill, her failure to see Mrs Ramsay as a Virgin figure will count against her. But she does know the next interview is her last chance to secure a future here in this place; a place which has already, in fact from the first moments she arrived, seemed so strangely familiar, so intimately connected to her physical being that she would not be surprised if someone told her she had visited it when she was a child, or dreamed of it, or – to stretch the imagination to its limits – in another lifetime lived here, and been very happy, or very sad, because the feeling is not joy that fills her. It is heavier than that.

She checks her watch once more then bundles up her courage and turns to the girl next to her to ask for directions. The girl runs her eyes up and down Elizabeth, blinks, then says, 'I'm *sorry?*' as if asking questions was a quaint way to acquire information and it was taking her a moment to remember how it was done. She repeats her question, crimson-faced, aware that she has violated some unspoken code of conduct but ignorant as to what it is. '*Oh.*' (The girl remembers.) 'Yup, it's in New Quad,' she says emphatically (everything about the girl is emphatic: the thrust of her bosom, the timbre of her voice, the blood in her cheeks, the rigorously messy chignon) and unnecessarily loudly, as if addressing a small child. 'Through the vestibule, past the fellows' garden, under the tunnel and it's the building on your right?' she says, with a curious rising intonation that suggests she is the one asking the question. Elizabeth reaches for a napkin to write down the directions but has no pen. She turns back but the girl is already rising with her emphatic chums and walking across the top of the table. Astonishing.

Some time later she finds New Quad. She finds the vestibule and the fellows' garden but cannot find the tunnel. Nor can she find anyone to ask directions because the college is suddenly deserted. As she races back to the lodge she feels she is levitating. Surfaces have become terrifying – the grit of flagstones beneath her feet, the lead sills of lattice windows, the bowling-green grass; smells, sounds, sights are all unbearable now. She presses a brass bell, waits at a wooden counter, and a man with rosy cheeks and eyes that slope gently downwards comes into view. His face appears to be subsiding and, coupled with his smile, gives him an expression of innate kindness. He says: 'Yes, Miss, how can I help you?'

She shows him the letter of acceptance, explains about the interview, the time, the tunnel.

'Oh, you're an interviewee,' he says. 'Well, there's nothing to worry about. Professor Hunt's room is diagonally over the next quad and through the tunnel by the laundry rooms.'

He is very kind. Her face is suddenly filled with heat. Her eyes prick, her jaw aches.

He peers more closely at her, then beams. 'You're not nervous, are you? Don't be nervous. Professor Hunt is a lovely man.'

She has to make do with nodding thanks because her throat has constricted. She goes up the ramp into the quad and he calls: 'Have any problems, come back and see me – ask for Albert.' She nods, chokes back tears, and some minutes later finds the mysterious tunnel – source of many an interviewee's bewilderment, she imagines – goes through it and emerges on the other side of the street. Suddenly the city is reversed. She is now standing on the same side as the bells – she can hear them nearby – they have finally met. And there is the church, thirteenth century with double façades, crenels and spirelets. There is the clock too, but for once she forgets to check it.

She passes through an iron gate and finds herself in another quad, lovelier than the first, and in the corner, next to the railings bordering playing fields, beneath a large horse-chestnut tree, a seventeenth-century building with lattice windows. She follows a path to stone steps leading up. There is a double door, and beyond that another. The smell of polish and wood and something else: the concentration of time in public places, which, unlike that in private ones, accretes itself with a cool disinterest. She passes along a corridor, one side of which is walled in glass. The glass is old and uneven, the scene beyond of a rose garden. The garden is emerald in the grey light and everything is dripping. The lawn has been rolled light and dark but the bushes are bare. Halfway along the corridor there is a door with white metal edges, uneven after so many coatings of paint. The handle, a dropping, bronze affair, looks loose.

In spite of the importance of continuing she stops. Perhaps because she is feeling peculiar, fizzing yet numb, stationary yet pulsing. Perhaps because the garden is set behind this old glass, which is warping it in places and not in others, so that the image has the quality of a mirage. But it is not hot today, it is solderingly cold, and the cold has imbued the garden with a stillness that is mesmeric, has blanched it; there is dustiness in the air; a sediment is suspended between her and the world of form. Perhaps it is not even that which arrests her but the way the window is framing the scene, so that it appears to be displayed in a book, and she is standing at the fulcrum – if this were a book, where the covers would meet the spine, where the spine closes, at the epi – the very – centre. Or perhaps she stops simply because she has never seen a rose garden in winter before, and it is shocking, emaciated, lost, soil peeping through grass like a blackened scalp, bones of a pagoda visible, branches of rose bushes sprouting gracelessly, butchered, truncated, pitiful, like a drenched cat, or a bird with oiled feathers. Yet it is none of these things alone that arrests her but something invisible, something enduring, something extreme, perhaps even immortal about the scene. And it is held by the most fragile of frames because the glass is ancient and the frame peeling. A plume of cold air brushes her legs and she hurries on.

At the end of the corridor she passes once more into darkness and comes to three oak doors. The one nearest a flight of stone steps reads 'Professor E. G. Hunt'. Beyond it there are voices. She checks the watch, then leans against the stone wall and covers her face with her hands. She has made it. There is nothing more she can do now; in a sense it is already over. The course the future will take has already been decided, and it is a relief after waiting so long. Yet even as she thinks this she feels the flutter of a veil, a knowing before knowledge rises like wind in treetops a moment before it is felt on the skin. She pulls back her sleeve. The second hand is jumping.

She stares at the watch. She puts it to her ear. She tears it off and hammers it. The second hand continues its mad twitching. She closes her eyes and begins to fall from a very great height. It is not possible, after so many months, after such careful waiting, watching, winding. How did it stop? How late is she? Should she knock? She raises her hand, then lowers it. No, she should wait.

She is floating now, back down the corridor. This time she has the impression the garden is watching her and its stillness is an indictment. She goes through the door at the end and a bird rises, calling.

She finds herself in a small kitchen. She will not let herself think about what this means yet, about what she has lost. She will wait for the 'lovely' man; some corduroy-clad professor, no doubt, with a crisp English accent, cheeks like Red Delicious and masses of curls, who will take one look at her and send her right back where she belongs; she belongs nowhere but he is not to know that.

She hears a door opening and voices, then footsteps coming towards her. Her heart begins to beat fast. The footsteps pause for a moment, then come nearer. A face peers around the kitchen door, a face whose years are impossible to number, in which bright, black eyes peer out beneath baby-soft hair that sticks up in unbiddable tufts. The body beneath is clad in denim jacket, jeans and jumper. A rock star. Replete with Vans trainers. The cleaner perhaps. A mature student. But he says, 'Elizabeth,' and it isn't a question. And before she can answer he says: 'You're late.' The chair scrapes as she rises. He says, 'Follow me,' as if she would be wise to do so, but she should be prepared for the consequences. So she does, back down the corridor, like a sorcerer to his cave.

And indeed the room into which he shows her, tripping slightly on the carpet-stay, is cavernous; a kaleidoscopic jungle of Bach and New Order, masks and playhouses; ashtrays, photographs, kettle, mugs, a number of pot plants in varying stages of despair. A Fender, toaster, coat-stand; in the corner sink, razor and toothbrush; a rug of intricate and threadbare design – and books. New, stiff, bent, stained; coverless, ravaged, unsullied; sloping fraternally and amorously interleaved, rudely splayed or tightly bound, towering ambitiously and fallen; regimented, strait-jacketed, whispering, confidential; slanting towards and away from one another, spine to secret spine.

'Take a seat,' he says, and drops into an armchair that has seen better days. She perches on the edge of a sofa. She doesn't notice how uncomfortable the springs are. He taps a cigarette from a packet and lights up, fixing her all the time with small black eyes – eyes of a bird, she thinks, in which, unless she is imagining it, she sees a hint of pleasure now, diabolical, incendiary. The eyes seem to know something she does not, and presently, when they have drunk their fill, he pushes his hair up at the front of his head, a curious womanish gesture he performs with the tips of his fingers and squinting as he takes the first drag, says: 'So tell me what you've been studying.' Perhaps not the cleaner. Who then? An assistant? Some sort of stand-in? This cannot be Professor Hunt. The room isn't exactly as she had imagined either.

She decides against *To the Lighthouse*, says: '*Hamlet*.' She thinks she says *Hamlet*, but when she looks up he is still looking at her expectantly. 'Take your time,' he says, a little sarcastically she thinks.

'*Hamlet*.' It is no use. Her throat has been cut and only air is escaping.

He is turning, searching for papers, perhaps giving her time, pretending not to notice, perhaps telling her he has things he could be getting on with.

She loosens her collar. '*Hamlet!*' The word is no more than a whisper.

He looks at her. 'And what do you think of *Hamlet*?'

'He's riding a wave,' she says. 'The play reaches high and then tumbles down. Hamlet knows where he's going but can't do anything about it. It is as if he's writing the play he's in.' She says all of this and more but none of it is audible; the words are a light breeze passing on its way elsewhere.

He taps the cigarette and sniffs. 'I see you've got something there.'

It is 'A Sparrow Hawk'. Finally someone has noticed.

46

But what is the use now? She cannot speak. She tries again. Her breathing is getting laboured.

He stubs the cigarette out and says with some finality: 'It's OK.'

The words hang in the air along with the smoke. She swallows them and is grateful. Her body slackens, her hands rest in her lap.

They sit in silence for a minute and she can see herself, her feet amid the swirls of the rug, her hand against grey skirt, as if she is looking at a picture or an engraving. Then he is getting up, saying, 'Have you read Shakespeare's sonnets?' fetching a large volume and leafing through the pages.

A quietness has come over him now as if his moment, too, is past. Perhaps he is relieved to have got the interview over; an easy one, no doubt; no hard decisions here. So she doesn't understand why he is keeping her there, or why he comes to her side and kneels beside her, holding the book open, but she sees that it is beautiful, decorated with beasts and cherubs and creeping foliage: 'SHAKE-SPEARES Sonnets', say black curling letters, and beneath them are others:

To THE ONLIE BEGETTER OF THESE INSUING SONNETS MR. W. H. ALL HAPPINESSE AND THAT ETERNITIE PROMISED BY OUR EVER-LIVING POET WISHETH THE WELL-WISHING ADVENTURER IN SETTING FORTH . . .

His hands are trembling. She is surprised: he doesn't seem to be the sort of person who would tremble. It is the first time she has noticed his hands: blotched, swollen, womanish; hands that look as if they have just been taken steaming from a bowl of hot dishwater. The hands are barely touching the page, just supporting the edges. When he turns it, it is as if a breeze has lifted it. Something flutters against her, something she has forgotten. Then he begins to read:

> *'Not from the stars do I my judgment pluck;*
> *And yet methinks I have astronomy,*
> *But not to tell of good or evil luck,*
> *Of plagues, of dearths, or seasons' quality*
> *Nor can I fortune to brief minutes tell,*
> *Pointing to each his thunder, rain, and wind,*
> *Or say with princes if it shall go well*
> *By oft predict that I in heaven find;*
> *But from thine eyes my knowledge I derive,*
> *And, constant stars, in them I read such art*
> *As truth and beauty shall together thrive . . .'*

Elizabeth doesn't 'do' love poetry. Of all the types of poetry there are, this type she does *not*. The comparisons to summer days, food and drink, music, topless towers, ever-fixed marks, silken lines, hooks and wandering barks are all lost on her. She does not believe in the insubstantiality conveyed by the beloved's kiss, that hearts can break, contain treasure or possess keys. She doesn't know, beyond the double-entendre, why the metaphysical poets liken love to death. But now she sits in complete silence, the words a light graze upon her skin, and she is created, set in motion, slipped off something; someone has removed an invisibility cloak, and when he finishes and looks at her she thinks she has been in some other place – and perhaps he has too, because his eyes are so dark and so bright.

He says: 'What do you make of that?'

And she says: 'He doesn't love her.'

The words are perfectly audible though she doesn't know where they have come from.

'What?' he says. She has struck a match and his eyes flare with it.

She flushes. Now she will have to explain herself and she doesn't know how. 'I—'

'Go on.'

'I don't think—'

'Yes . . .'

'I don't think he's in love with her.'

A pause.

'What d'you mean?'

'I don't know.'

'You don't know or can't say?'

She feels dizzy. 'I can't say.'

'Try.'

She is back-pedalling, has exposed too much, but he has caught hold and won't let go. 'I felt it.' An absurd reply. 'It's clever, but it's not – real . . .'

His eyes glitter. 'Have you ever read a poem that was "real"?'

'Yes – that one by John Clare, "Little Trotty Wagtail". . .'

She is furious with herself – what became of 'A Sparrow Hawk'? Who cares about 'Little Trotty Wagtail'?

He is wrestling with something that looks like a smile. The smile appears to be winning. It is interesting to watch.

'But it's beautiful,' she says. 'If I could write something I would write it like that. Cold, clear . . .'

'Would you?'

'Yes.' She looks down.

He gazes at her a full five seconds, and during that time she doesn't feel she possesses clothes or skin but only internal organs. Only knows that no one has looked at her this way before and is sincerely grateful they have not. Then he begins to read again, and she begins to float. And whether it is the effort to concentrate or the stillness of the room or that he is now resting the book on her lap, the words begin to stretch themselves across the room – or it may be a firmament and the words spheres, because music is a better way to describe the sounds that are lapping around her now, throbbing multitudes. Spheres, words and room are swimming together; his voice dark, the paper pale, the letters flesh – or is the flesh letters? He is speaking, going ahead, or is it she who is speaking and he coming behind? She is prostrating herself and the words are pattering like raindrops in a wood. Then she hears a voice say, 'Are you all right?' and he is propping her up.

The words collect themselves, the firmament vanishes, there is humming in her ears.

'You passed out!' he says.

'I – I haven't eaten.'

He shuts the book with a snap, goes to the sideboard, comes back and sets a tin of biscuits in her lap. He says: 'Eat.' He goes out and she hears him striding down the corridor. He returns a moment later with a plate of sandwiches, which he places on top of the tin. Then he goes back to his chair and lights up, his leg swinging. 'Eat,' he says. She eats.

The blackness is back but with it something else. His eyes look as though they might want to smile but they don't yet. He seems about to speak but thinks better of it. Finally he says: 'What I was going to ask, before you swooned so dramatically just then, was did you know that the object of Shakespeare's desire wasn't a woman but a beautiful young man?'

She stares at him, then shakes her head.

The leg swings higher, the mouth is twitching again, but she still cannot see anything to smile about. He looks out of the window. 'Did you know that the circumstances surrounding the printing of the sonnets, the dedication to "Mr W. H.", the reference to the poet as "Ever-Living" and the fact that the name "Shakespeare" is hyphenated all fundamentally alter our understanding of the historical figure that is William Shakespeare?'

She shakes her head; ignorance doesn't matter now, whatever she does or doesn't say.

'Well, that's the sort of thing you would be studying if

you came here.' He ruffles his hair, taps the cigarette, crosses and re-crosses his legs. 'Would you like to do that?'

Her heart understands if she does not. Her heart is murdering her. He shoots her a look and she catches a whiff of the infernal smile. He is grinning, and it is diabolical; he is not making sense. 'You're in, Elizabeth!' he cries suddenly. 'Well, what were you afraid of? Your submission essays were extraordinary. I knew I wanted you from the very first lines. It was as if they were written by someone with a very thin skin – someone who felt the words rather than read them. We don't usually let people know at this stage of the process but I had to make an exception in your case.' His leg swings even higher. 'Well, what d'you think of that?'

She opens her mouth, and gulps.

'Don't choke.'

She coughs, removes her glasses; gasps and wipes her eyes.

'All right?'

She nods.

He is leaning forwards. 'There's more to you than meets the eye, isn't there, Miss Stone? Volumes more. I've got a hunch I haven't seen half of it yet.'

She replaces her glasses. Her heart is still hurting. She shakes her head. 'I don't—'

But he says: 'Yes, you do. You understand very well. You understand a lot more than you let yourself believe.'

She doesn't know how he knew what she was going to say. She doesn't know how she has won a place in this temple of learning. She still does not absolutely know who this man is. But for once she will bask in ignorance. She looks out at this stillest of December days and the day takes on a warmth, an easiness, a co-operation she hadn't noticed before but sees now was there all the time. The roofs, lawn and horse-chestnut tree glow into new life even as she looks at them and speak of alien, scarcely possible other worlds.

He is beaming. 'So are you going to come?'

She says, 'Yes,' clearly this time. Then: 'Please.'

He slaps his leg. 'That's that.'

He stands and she does too, and he grasps her hand in his own, which is clammy and hot and he says: 'I'll see you when you come up.'

'Yes.'

'Have a good summer.'

'OK.'

'Don't work too hard.'

'I—'

They look at each other. Then he lets go of her hand and she goes to the door. But there she turns and says, 'I was late because it stopped,' and she pulls out the moon-faced watch.

He laughs suddenly, a loud 'Ha' like a shot. He seems to be considering some violent action or other but in the end he has to make do with a paltry 'Take care of yourself.' She tells him she will.

Eighteen months later he becomes her tutor. She sees him twice in that time, once she is sure of and once she is not. The first carrying a bag of shopping through the town, harried, tripping as he seems wont to do, his legs at some variance with the rest of his body. The second deep in some tome in the Upper Room, spectacles perched on his nose, a look of absolute contentment on his face.

The second time she stands, wondering whether to approach. In the end she does not. The spectacles throw her. If he had spoken she would have been sure, but the apparition is silent.

His voice she remembers, his face she forgets.

The Art of Detachment

Professor Stone had had more than one occasion in a career spanning thirty years to note that the key to writing well could be summed up in one word, namely: 'detachment'. Detachment was the *sine qua non* of the academic's work, the paradox being that while poems were full of tempests and swelling breasts, fits of passion and fevered brows, they demanded the utmost clear-headedness when responding. Poets liked to fool you: their lines were mellifluous, their rhythms sensual; however, if one was for a moment lulled by the cadence of Eliot's 'evening', spread out like a patient on a table, one might forget that such an evening was also maybe bloodied, moribund, open-mouthed, perhaps even dead. When constructing a critique of poetry therefore it was imperative not to become involved: rapture could lead to complacency, high-spirited approximations, sugary vagueness; who knew how many promising essays she had penalised because the writer was too involved with his own argument, or how many examinees hamstrung themselves before they had even begun by over-zealous use of the first person singular?

Professor Stone didn't think she was conceited in believing that detachment was the quality most apparent in her own writing – and, she hoped, her life too – because there were many 'slings and arrows of outrageous fortune' and it was best to be indifferent to most of them. To be a 'wandering bark' on the sea of life was to pray for shipwreck. She had occasion to test the truth of these beliefs again when, ten days after she had posted her letter to

Edward Hunt, she received his reply. It was waiting for her in her pigeon-hole and she knew it was his immediately. She recognised the half-moon *es*, the arch trail of dots; she thought she could discern the advancement of age in the tails of the *gs*, though the *ys* were as ambitious and un-giving as ever. She slipped it inside her other mail and waited till she was alone in her room to read it. Then she sat down and held it for a minute, with both hands, before opening the envelope.

After she had read it she remained sitting for some time. Presently she got up and said: 'So, that's that.' She stood still for a moment, then walked out of the room. The letter had been courteous but to the point: Professor Hunt did not see the need to meet.

As she went about her day – as she went about several days after that – it did occur to the professor that it might have been better not to state quite so plainly that it was on professional and professional business alone she was returning to the city of books; she had been seeking to put Professor Hunt at ease, wishing to make clear he should not feel obligated, but his wording ('Thank you for your letter', 'As you say, there is no need to meet', 'I myself will be very busy at that time in any case', 'Good luck with the project', 'Best wishes') suggested that the wording of her own letter – the letter she had taken such care over – had been ill-judged. She wrote back, attempting to clarify things, but screwed the letter up before she was halfway through, suspecting it would only make matters worse. She couldn't help but notice that he had made no mention of her idea for *The Poetics of Sound*. And this, if she was honest, troubled her most.

She buried herself in work and there was much to be done. There were huge amounts of philosophical, linguistic and musical papers to read in the British Library, and familiarising to be done with the rules of metre and scansion she had learned as a student. She had already begun to unearth an alternative poetic tradition stretching from the Anglo-Saxon Scop through to Chaucer, Spenser, Shakespeare, Milton, Dickinson, Hopkins, Yeats, Thomas and Eliot but she was careful to pace herself, a thing she had never done before, setting aside an hour for lunch and half an hour in the afternoon for a walk.

The project ahead loomed large and glittering; she could feel the current quicken, hear the grand sound of its distant thundering, and was buoyed by it. Though sometimes towards the end of the day, when the clock in the humanities reading room became human and the stillness portentous, she would raise her head and look around at the bowed heads and pools of lamplight and it was not clear then, to anyone who happened to be watching, whether the brightness was due to excitement or some other emotion. She would walk past the library attendants and go to drink at the fountain – cup after cup – her mind full of the work that awaited completion, and when she went back to the desk her heart beat strangely. So that for all the straightness of her shoulders, the neatness of the words that appeared beneath her hand, the mouth pursed in concentration, the bright eyes and determined flare of the nostrils, she may have appeared, to someone who didn't understand, a little like one possessed.

The day of Professor Stone's journey dawned clear and bright. The Thames glittered bluely, there was a haze over Regent's Park, doves above St Paul's and that freshness London sometimes dreamed up on summer mornings like this one and laid like a newly laundered cloth upon its grimy table. Before she left her flat, she inspected herself in the small mirror beside the front door. The face that peered back, unlike the city, had no means of concealment, or perhaps merely chose to deploy none. It was the face that appeared on the flyleaf of her latest book, a face with glittering eyes, sharp nose, and a mouth upturned only at the corners, as if the owner had decided it was judicious to distort the lips just so far. The chin tilted now, too, as it did in the picture, so that the viewer was a little higher than the viewed, the head held back in dispassionate reserve, though there were also some changes: there was a hollowness to the face in the mirror that the other face did not possess, and the darkly burnished hair in the flyleaf, coiled in a bun, was now shorter than a boy's and clustered around her face in fine wisps.

The face in the mirror sighed and lapsed into weariness; Professor Stone did not like making forays into the world. The world had a habit of throwing one into the present, where it was easy to fall, breaking on the shores of oneself, as Joyce put it, or words to that effect. For this reason she always had two things to hand: a pair of earplugs (sounds being harder to ignore than sights) and a good book. She checked she had both again now before setting off.

Three-quarters of an hour later she opened the book in a carriage at Waterloo. It was written by her favourite critic, Christopher Worthing, and was titled *Vigorous Most When Unactive Deem'd: Classical Heroism in Paradise Regain'd*. She had opportunity once again as the train filled to consider what a great writer Worthing really was. Reading him was like settling back in a chair of great quality, firm yet accommodating, stylish yet comfortable. She allowed herself once more to be swept along in the great river of his pellucid prose.

Doors were banging. A whistle pealed. They were off. But the carriage, she now discovered, was not as quiet as she had hoped. In fact, thanks to a group of teenagers intent on procreation, a mother and baby, and a business-woman with a mobile phone there was a positive cacophony. Moreover, as they began to move she realised she was facing the rear of the train and would soon feel sick. She couldn't change places because the train was so full so she dug herself further into the seat and raised the book. A burst of laughter snagged the professor's attention. One of the teenage boys was pinning a girl to the window; the girl was laughing helplessly and throwing something – Professor Stone didn't like to think what – to her friend at the other side of the carriage. She adjusted her glasses and raised Worthing higher.

At half past twelve, thanks to the din, her position and the sunshine, she was no further along with Worthing but much further along with the nausea. She forced herself to eat a croissant from the buffet trolley and drank a hot chocolate slowly, regarding the watery liquid with some distaste, then sat with her eyes tightly closed, running her fingers absently along the jagged scar in her hair.

The nausea lasted till half past one, when the train must have changed direction because the glare of the sun lessened and, joy of joys, the group of teenagers, businesswoman and mother and baby all got off and she was able to reseat herself facing the other direction. She had just picked up Worthing again when a voice said, 'D'you mind if I sit here?' and she looked up to see a portly man, perspiring heavily, dressed in a black jacket and white shirt, the sleeves of which reached down to his knuckles.

'No,' she said. She pulled the hem of her mackintosh off the seat.

'Nice bit of weather we're having.' He was a little wide-eyed.

'Indeed.' She smiled briefly, reinserted the earplugs and returned to her book. But he was rustling in the bag at his feet – she could smell his aftershave, see the top of his bottom.

'Going away for a few days to see my family . . .' He came up again, his face red. 'Just checking I got everything.'

She nodded, smiled faintly and raised the book higher.

But his movements, the smell, the jolting of the seat were distracting. From the corner of her eye she saw him unscrew a soft drink and look around the carriage. There was something not quite right about his face, she thought. It looked soft, as though it had been pummelled; the eyes were watery. She sat up straighter and, with some difficulty, returned to her thread:

The retreat at Horton, and the retreat of his blindness are alike considered in relation to a classical heroic scheme.

III. He grew up in the privacy of his own family, and till his age was quite mature and settled, which he also passed in private, was chiefly known for his attendance upon the purer worship, and for his integrity of life . . . he was a soldier above all the most exercised in knowledge of himself; he had either destroyed, or reduced to his own control, all enemies within his own breast – vain hopes, fears, desires . . .

Yes, she thought. Conquering the self, that was the thing; the world was easy in comparison. It was a constant theme in Eliot too, desire and its manifestations – 'undisciplined squads of emotion', he called it in *Four Quartets*. The romantics valued overpowering emotions, making them central to the achievement of art but the Modernists and Eliot (at least nominally) opted for objectivity, impartiality and disinterestedness. Unlike some poets, whose work was read in conjunction with the tawdry and sensational details of their private lines, Eliot's was committed to impersonality. She liked that, the stringency, the classicism, control, marble-like gravitas, even if it did become a little laughable at times: 'or even a very good dinner'; only Eliot could have inserted that line into a masterpiece and got away with it.

A 'pop' startled her. Her neighbour withdrew the bottle from his lips and screwed the top back on, belching into his fist, then settled himself back in the seat with what she considered to be unnecessary vigour, letting down the armrest with a bang. 'Oh, sorry,' he said. He pushed it back up and grinned sheepishly. 'Got to get comfy, haven't you?'

She didn't answer. She was beginning to feel bewildered, though nothing betrayed her confusion except the beginnings of a rash on her neck. She pushed her spectacles up and turned the page.

'Anything interesting?' He moved his hand up his leg, smiling nervously.

He repeated the question so she removed an earplug. 'I'm sorry?'

'Anything interesting?'

She smiled tightly. 'Not really.'

'Looks too clever for me. I like a good blockbuster, I do.'

'Ah.' She turned back to the book.

'What's it about, then?'

Dear God, she thought. But she turned the page with a look of innocent absorption, her eyes travelling unseeing over the lines, and after a moment her companion's smile faded; with some coughing, he followed suit, taking out a newspaper.

The rattling was astonishing. He didn't seem to be reading the newspaper but looking at the pictures, which she saw from the corner of her eye were many and graphic. She peered about surreptitiously but couldn't see any free seats; besides, it would appear rude to move now. The pages went on rattling at a furious rate and when he had finished she saw with dismay that he went back to the start and began again. She took off her glasses and pressed her eyes.

'Headache?'

She removed an earplug.

'I said: got a headache?'

She smiled as one would at a small child. 'Just resting my eyes.'

'P'raps they need changing.' He indicated her glasses. 'I got a great pair of reading ones the other day. Supermarket. Tenner.'

'Really.'

'Aye.'

His breath was audible and smelt a little. He folded the newspaper into the put-away table and stretched his short legs in front of him, shuffling his ankles, apparently pleased that she was no longer reading. The professor replaced her glasses, moved imperceptibly closer to the window and raised the book. There must be something wrong, she decided, a disability of some kind, unnoticeable till at close quarters. Well, it wouldn't be long now, another half-hour.

A jolt returned her attention firmly to the present. Her neighbour, having bent down to his bag, came up and pinned her mackintosh to the seat. She closed her eyes, counted to ten, then opened them and said, in a crystalline voice: 'I'm sorry, but would you mind moving? You're sitting on my coat.'

'Oh. Sorry.'

A vein was jumping in her temple. She said, 'Not a problem,' and smiled ferociously at the book.

He cleared his throat and brushed something vigorously from his trouser leg, while she returned to Worthing. All was quiet for a moment. Then he said:

'Where did you get on, then?'

She inhaled, a moment later removed an earplug, and turned to him with an expression of innocent surprise.

'I said: where did you get on?'

She blinked several times, then said brightly: 'London.'

'Oh, yeah?'

What on earth there was to say about that she didn't know but he seemed to expect her to find something. She said: 'I live there.'

'I got an uncle who lives in Shoreditch.'

'Really.'

'Used to go and see him when I was a kid. Where'bouts are you?'

After a moment, in which no other option appeared to present itself, she said: 'Bloomsbury.'

'Oh, very nice. You a teacher or something?'

'Yes.'

'Thought so. You look like a teacher. Going far?'

'No.'

'Business or pleasure?' He gave an over-eager smile.

A muscle flexed in her temple. 'Business.'

'Still, beats stayin' at 'ome, doesn't it?'

His voice was jocular but his eyes were watery. She couldn't make him out. 'It certainly does.'

She heard him swallow. 'I got a bit of business to attend to myself, yeah.' He laughed half-heartedly. 'Life's a funny old thing, isn'it? You don't see the big things coming, it's just bang, wallop.'

She put the book down and looked straight ahead. In a voice higher than she intended, she said: 'I'm sorry, but would it be possible for you to stop talking to me? You see, I've got a lot of work to do. I have to finish this book. I don't mean to be rude but—'

'No. Course. Sorry. Didn't know it was' – the strange gasp again – 'important.'

'Thank you.'

'Sorry.'

'Not at all.'

'Didn't want to interrupt—'

'It's all right.'

'I'll leave you be.'

Oh, God. She picked up Worthing again and began to read at a feverish pace. His leg was jostling; he was scratching his head; his hand dropped to his lap, pulled up his trousers, dropped to his lap again. Oh, this is unbearable, she thought. What is wrong with him? She was about to ask him to excuse her, because sitting outside the toilets on one of the fold-up seats would be better than this, when she stiffened. He was rummaging in his pocket, sniffing, wiping his face.

Professor Stone was breathing shallowly and fast. She sat very straight, her eyes fixed on the seat in front of her. The man said, in a thick voice: 'You haven't got a tissue, have you? I don't want to get up like this . . .' She didn't carry tissues. She scrabbled in her bag and handed him her lawn handkerchief.

'Thanks.' His hand closed over her own. It was clammy. She sat back, blinking.

He refolded the handkerchief and handed it back to her.

'No,' she said breathlessly. 'Keep it.'

He sighed, and she felt his body slacken. His nose made a squeaking sound as he swiped it. 'My mum,' he said. 'Just passed away. Cancer.' He gave a shuddering sigh. 'Just comes over me every now and then. I try and stave it off, like, talk to people . . .'

For the next half-hour he continued to sniff and wipe his face but eventually he became quiet and turned his attention to the view beyond the window.

Professor Stone and her fellow traveller did not exchange any more words. When he got off he didn't say goodbye and she did not watch as he walked away. She didn't move at all, in fact, for the rest of the journey but sat looking straight ahead, Christopher Worthing in her lap, her face very pale, her eyes very bright.

City of Books

A girl with long limbs, large glasses and hair the colour of new chestnuts is standing on a flagstoned landing looking out of a deep-set window. Bells are chiming, weathered, archaic, icy, discordant; toppling over and under one another. The sound comes from nowhere and then it departs and the hour remains, though it, like the sound, is invisible. She hasn't seen any of the bells yet. Perhaps she should look up. Perhaps in one of the towers, at the top of a steeple, she will see them. But she prefers it this way: to see the timekeepers as well as hear them may not be bearable.

The library in which she is standing, like the city, is steeped in time. Time has been distilled here, filtered like a spirit, and the city is purer for the transmutation. Walking beneath the shadows of its walls, stepping from doorways into light, gazing from roofs upon ramparts that in places still bear the scars of arrows and cannon-fire, witness to the attrition of centuries, the corrosive yet calming tax the elements exact, it is possible to believe that the currents of history have been made peaceable by the clamour of rain and wind, the ardour of the sun's heat; looking out through windows where light illuminates the scenes of antiquity in many-coloured glasses, that its essence has been extracted for safe-keeping.

The city began with this library, or so they say. A sage came to the river-plain with a collection of scrolls. In time a settlement grew around him and a building was made to house them. The sage lived almost two thousand years ago. This means the city had its inception at the same time as

Christ. There is something fitting about the Word and words beginning together, the name that cannot be spoken and the inception of a debate about words that has continued till the present moment. The inception of Time too; of Christ, who gave his title to the Common Era, and the beginning of another sort of time – a new dispensation – altogether. Would eternity itself have meaning if it weren't imagined in light of man's embroilment in history? she asks herself. In her studies she is discovering that attempts to gain perspective on history are usually doomed to failure. That is why Art is needed, she has decided, to elevate from the temporal – to enable truth to be spoken, even if elliptically. The challenge she faces each week is to translate that truth (the truth of Art) back into words (or, at least, that is what her tutors expect), though it is impossible: the return to the element in which words move warps truth and renders it unreadable.

This library, however, is undaunted by Time; it wallows in its ancientness, flaunts it like a fur, sits impenetrable beneath crumbling battlements and riven turrets. It has floors warped with time and walls weathered by it and ceilings carved with its chisel. It has books too old to consult and books too large to lift down and books so precious they are chained to the shelves, the covers padlocked. It has a square in the centre with a bronze statue of its founder, whose face gleams dully while clouds pass like spirits in the dome of his forehead, and private gardens beneath windows narrow as arrowheads where aspens shiver. She comes here every day, arrives at nine and stays till ten at night. She shows her card to the attendant; a wooden gate opens, she turns into the dark of the stairwell and begins to climb creaking steps. She stops on this landing between the fifth and sixth flights because from the window she can see the whole of the city, and if she looks hard enough, down by the river, the college of the professor of poetry. She has walked there sometimes, through the orchard, and stood by a chained gate looking on to a rose garden. The view it affords of his window has become so familiar that it seems to belong to her. She has thought about meeting him so often it has lost reality and faded, as the college does now behind rainclouds. She has read the poem he sent her till, like a scent, it too seems to be fading. She thought she remembered it but each time she hears it she understands less. She hopes the poems he will set for them next year will not leave her in such darkness. After all, he is waiting for her to impress him. He said her work was different. He said there was more to her than met the eye. He said volumes more. No one has ever said that. She runs up the last flight of stairs and pushes open the curmudgeonly spring door. The room she enters has large windows of many panes, white bookcases lining the walls, brown high-partitioned desks and a parquet floor. It stretches the entire length of the building. When you reach the corner it stretches down the other side, and when you reach that corner it goes on again. This means that from the windows you can look across to the same room opposite; that the room is self-enclosing; its own sphere of reference cut adrift on the currents of thought. You can look across on three sides but on the fourth there is only darkness behind the panes. She doesn't know what that room contains: it is close and it is distant, like the dark of the moon, the inside of an eyelid.

The library, especially this room, reminds her of a ship, a tier of decks and ramparts. Lulled by the scratch of the moon-faced clock, you can look out at the clouds and it appears to be sailing, the windows those of a galleon, and beyond them a rigging of rooftops and masts. She has become friends with it now, feels a magnanimity towards its foibles and idiosyncrasies, its smells, moods, foolishness and sadness, that she doesn't feel towards people. There are as many moods of this library as there are rooms, and rooms exist here as cells in a body, small cavities, industry and conversion, creation and transportation, and between them all runs an intricate arterial network of corridors, pulleys and lifts. There is Sir Godfrey's, dark-ceilinged, filled with the smell of pencil lead and warm wood, pierced by needles of light that fall from narrow windows across the floor of a vaulted tunnel of narrow bays leading through the proscenium to an inner sanctum – a Holy of Holies – chamber of staircases, balconies and ladders unfurling height upon height of still more books; a magician's tower, an Aladdin's cave, where coloured light from jewelled panes falls upon pages not to be touched with bare hands yet pored and wrinkled and smelling like skin; upon letters written by men so long dead their tongues have become obscure and strange-sounding, but are themselves illuminated and stand up quick and brilliant as if the ink hasn't yet dried.

There is a round sandstone building – a single room, and above it another – beneath a blue dome, where on winter mornings sunlight falls in golden slabs across burnished walnut and at evening each desk is a honeycomb around which galaxies pivot and coalesce; where, when sitting by the barred window and looking out, the lamps appear to be globules of light in deep water, suspended on chains from untold fathoms above. There is the Aeolian, encircled by winds, with its gold swing doors, marble pillars and red carpet, view of white city hotels and passing traffic. The faculty, with its anodyne blond bookcases, new-fangled flooring and low ceilings papered with lost sunlight. And there is the cold, concrete underworld of pipes, alleyways and trundling bookcases that comprises the intestine of this magisterial corpus.

The basement is the only place she doesn't visit unless she has to. She does not want to see the workings of this organism for, unlike a real body, the insides of this mega-lith are silent, except for the tinkle of a fluorescent bulb. Who knows what noises of one's own might arise in such emptiness?

This morning the Upper Room is filled with bent heads, rustlings, shufflings, small coughs. It is bright and lurid because the day beyond the windows is grey. On fine days it is a different story, sunlight broaching the barrel of each high-sided desk, chairs shockingly cool beneath bare arms and legs, motes drifting in currents from open windows.

She goes down an aisle bordered by bookcases on one side and chafed pine desks on the other. At the end she turns left into a bay where she collects the books she ordered yesterday and notes with satisfaction that the pink slips are still in place. To be greeted by these tightly wedged strips each morning is immensely reassuring; to discover they have been shuffled a disaster, for they are her markers in a sea of pages, groynes against time's constant thumbing. She walks to her seat beneath the row of small suns, surveyed on either side by a border of luminaries, faded heads, ancient leaves, cracked cornucopias, furling scrolls – for this is also the home of the gods: masters, poets, philosophers, 'auctors' all, who studied here before her and whose works now fill its shelves. The eyes of the gods follow her. 'What about this one?' they mutter. 'Will she have something to say?' They stroke hoary chins. 'There is possibility,' they say, 'but there is also doubt.'

She begins reading the moment she slips into her seat, thumbs in ears, hands blinkering the world out. She is made supremely aware that she must not waste a moment because while this is a city of books it is also a city of bells. In order to maximise the efficiency of her working hours she devotes three hours a week to leisure. She has made her Sabbath a Sunday, not because of convention but because that is when the library is closed, procured a guide-book and visits a different point of interest each weekend. Last weekend she saw a clock that speaks the hour aloud. This week she will see a printing press that legend has it is possessed by a 'black art', inserting ghost letters at random intervals. There is a book it printed in 1776 in which ghost letters appear twenty-one times. No one knows why.

She does her sightseeing on Sunday mornings. On Sunday afternoons, she goes to the supermarket. On Sunday evenings she reads for classes on Monday and does her washing in the basin inside her wardrobe. Then, over an open book, she feasts on tinned sardines, toast and fruitcake. The rest of the week she lives on bread, spread and tea. She is the happiest she has ever been. No, not the happiest; the most purposeful. She is so full of purpose she thinks she will die of it. Her goal is simple but elusive: she intends to attain the highest marks in the university exams at the end of the year so that Edward Hunt will hear of it. She knows that in order to stand even a chance of doing so she must abjure ordinary life and its distractions – not that she has ever known how to conduct herself in that sphere anyway, but time can be wasted easily, anywhere, reading second-hand novels in the covered market, sitting in the roots of trees on the banks of the river, watching fellow students from the crack in her curtains; so for six days a week the world has contracted to this room where people read, fall asleep, fall in love, make friends, make enemies, have panic attacks, have epiphanies, contemplate suicide, and make the discoveries of their lives. So she exists on a tissue of minute-by-minute human interchange, the fractional move-ments of arms and of legs and of heads, breathes currents like weather fronts, swathes of heat and light and electricity and, so far, it has been enough. She is the one that remains through the day, she and a few other hard-core questers. One by one the mortals depart. She has seen them, these other voyagers in the long afternoons, leaning their heads in their palms or sitting up straight. Their eyes do not surface long; the pressure pulls them back under.

She has almost learned to love this struggle now between clock and page, the ceaseless movement of one, the continual consumption of the other, but when the phases of the clock become too onerous, when words drip like treacle, she goes out and walks the city, gazing at contorted stone faces, the airy black heights of cathedrals. She is in love with these streets, with the dappled echoes of cobblestones, the way crumbling stone inches out of shadow and alchemises in sunlight. When the bells ring out again, she returns.

Sometimes she feels an unnerving desolation when someone leaves who has sat beside her all day, or when, having conducted herself under the field of an imagined gaze, she surfaces to find the gazer oblivious, or insentient: a chair, a coat, a bag. She goes back to the company of books, because there is company there, but it takes will to find it, and you cannot be in its presence and be aware of its presence at the same time. You can only be aware of its loss.

When it works, she experiences a nearness, a voice heard in an adjoining room. She meets someone but she doesn't know where, someone speaks but she doesn't know who – and the interlocutor is able to break off contact without notice because reading is a longing never to be sated, at one with older longings that cannot be verbalised. The longing becomes one with the loneliness and together they modulate into something new. She moves in a current, a small, transparent, wondering fish – her aloneness transmuted by its very concentration into something rare. A thing at the edge of others. A palm tree perhaps, at the end of the mind.

From time to time she doubts she really will succeed in impressing Edward Hunt. At this moment, for instance, she is translating an Anglo-Saxon poem. The line has taken half an hour and is eight words long. She has never yet received full marks for any of her translations from the tiny Chinese man, who seemed surprised to see her among the chosen few. The other tutors are pleased enough with her but she still cannot construct an argument well. She knows now that writing is a homely art, no flourish and dash to the finish line but a task that requires long hours and rolled-up sleeves; that before illumination, if it comes at all, are hours of preparation, searches with a fine-tooth comb, acres of loosening and teasing apart. What is more, the materials she must use are humble and rough-hewn because time has not invented any other way of reading than the eye, or of scanning than with pencil and paper, or any better way of measuring words' music than reading in an undertone.

She has heard of a painting in the church across the square of the music of the spheres. It is by an Italian called Guardi. She wants to see it because she cannot bear music. This is her secret. She has read of a rare condition in which people cannot physically endure music; her affliction is not that severe, but the discomfort is enough for her to exit a shop or cross to the other side of a road if she is able. She wants to see the painting to find out whether she experiences the same fear looking at a visual representation of music as hearing it. She also wants to see it because she doesn't think such a thing can be done – to render sound visible seems to her impossible, akin to depicting the face of God, and so, perhaps, similar to what she finds herself doing each day: attempting to put words to what cannot be expressed, to that which, when articulated, dissolves in front of her. And there is a third motivation for seeing the painting: she is hoping for a cure. If she cannot appreciate music perhaps she is insensate and will never be able to respond properly to poetry, which is, after all, verbal music. Perhaps then, by visualising the object of her fear, confronting it in a different medium, she will overcome it.

She goes to the church one Sunday but the painting is being restored. It will be for several years, the attendant tells her. When she raises her eyes to the ceiling all she can see are white drapes.

The days have been getting darker; upswept clouds line skies vacant with cold. She was brought to life this autumn, disquieted by the fragrant chill of russet afternoons, the paradoxical renewal in the glittering mornings of the world's fall. She had never felt such unease, or if she had it was too long ago to remember. She doesn't know if it is a good or a bad thing. She doesn't know how it will turn out. All she knows is that there have been moments: at midnight alone in her room, a night in the Upper Room when the fluorescence was unreal, a morning in the Round Room when frost and fire whitened the square; an evening when in the windows' reflection bicycles sailed past reading lamps and passers-by through avenues of bookshelves beneath crenellated arches of pine and of teak, while readers, in a subaqueous dream, rotated on a merry-go-round of books; a moment when she ran down steps to the square and the clocks struck the hour and the steps reeled backwards – upwards – were snatched from under her like a carpet, caught away and ascended; moments that are incendiary, one after another. In blackest night, in sunshine, in wind – on days when the city rushes like the sea, and days when it is laid out in mist like a shroud. Moments in which she is sure she has touched something. Something rose and she stepped outside the normal rhythm of things and the cloud-capped towers, the gorgeous palaces, the solemn temples really did threaten to dissolve, thaw and resolve themselves into a dew, while words broke ranks, assailed the air in throbbing multitudes, promised to convey her beyond themselves, to the dark lands at the world's edge, and, perhaps, over its rim.

71

So she gets up and sits down, takes off her glasses and puts them on again; bites her nails, twists her hair; rocks, writes, reads; while words tug at her sleeve, outrun her, scamper in every direction, overflow her eyes and her fingers and tongue; does things of importance and of no importance at all in order to come back to this room and this desk and this chair and master again the art of saying satisfactorily what cannot be said.

In order that when they meet, she and the elusive professor of poetry, one afternoon in the ever-present future – an afternoon perhaps not unlike this – he will see that his wait has been worth it and his hunch has been good.

Written on Skin

So. They wouldn't meet. It was probably for the best because anything else, no matter how small, would distract her from the work at hand. Professor Stone raised her chin with the air of a general surveying his troops and finding them satisfactory.

She was standing at a window looking over river meadows. The sill beneath her was white and so were the sashes, the glass the old type with imperfections. The building was stone, sun-warmed, rain-pitted, wind-crumbled and covered with ivy. Below the window an assortment of roses clung to dark railings, and beyond them young men played cricket in the afternoon sun. Further off, a line of poplars rose in shimmering columns leading down to a river. The view reminded her of that from another window. There was the same feeling of troubled sky and fallen sea and interminable open spaces, though there was no one thing she could point to in particular and say, It is this or It is that, only the general aspect of the scene that chimed with the earlier. She opened the window now and the wash of the afternoon came in, and this, too, was familiar.

It had been more than thirty years since she had walked these streets. Looking at her reflection in windows on the high street this afternoon, she had wondered if she had stood in precisely the same place decades before, marvelled at the unchanging quality of glass and of stone in comparison with the transfiguration of flesh and blood; all those fingerprints, footsteps, molecules bequeathed to glass and concrete and stone. She envied objects' remove from the palpable, this afternoon would have welcomed imperme-ability, because even the soft gusts in the horse-chestnut trees tugged at her stomach and made her shiver though the day was warm, and there was an aching in her chest that she couldn't shake loose and returned her, moment by moment, to the present.

She came away from the window, hung up her mackintosh and unzipped the holdall. It was strange, she thought: she hadn't felt anything as the taxi pulled over the plain, except how natural it was to be back, as if she had just slipped away for a minute. Thought only that the place was greener, smaller, darker than she remembered, the high street more tawdry. She laughed at how imposing the city had seemed – there was nothing golden about these walls – and the spires didn't seem to be dreaming so much as bored. The only constant was the homeless, still omnipresent, still torpid, quietly acquiescent to their fate. She had felt nothing. Perhaps this was how life was: the things we expected to mean a lot meant nothing at all and the small things caught us unawares. It was rather consoling. And then she heard bells.

She said to the driver, 'Here, please,' though it was too early, then she was walking, running a little, through streets belonging to feet and to bicycles and the smell of dinners from college kitchens, past lawns and gardens and walls and gates, beneath spires that travelled with clouds that sailed in a sky glazed white and gold like a china cup, while notes broke around her in heavenly cacophony as more and more bells rang the hour. So that when she came up to this little room with the sloping ceiling, fake-wood furniture and knobbled walls (the college was not so pros-perous on the inside), she was blown out, as if she had been down by the sea all day and the wind and sky had left her empty; empty, and then this aching. He had said that her submission essays were written by someone with a thin skin, she thought, as she hung up her clothes – but it was best not to be thin-skinned, particularly if one didn't have means to express the sensations experienced; what was the point of feeling if not to extrapolate meaning from the flux of experience? Then the bells pealed out again, saying everything effortlessly as they always did.

Perhaps the sensation of unease was simply due to weariness, she thought, as she placed her laptop on the desk; the simple break in routine had tired her. Yet she remembered her nineteen-year-old self feeling the very same shifting, and towards evening the incipient chill. Perhaps the sensation was reserved for this city then, the city where she had come to squeeze the universe into a ball and roll it towards some overwhelming question. Well, she had rolled it for three years, and with each day the ball had got bigger. Then she and the ball had stopped, teetered, tipped, and begun to descend with sickening suddenness. The end of it all was a marble staircase leading to a hall where an enormous clock kept implacable time and the contents of all the books and all the papers and all the thoughts of three whole years must be poured out in two weeks on booklets of wide-ruled paper. She had poured it all – wasn't herself for some time – but she wasn't sure even now if she had answered the overwhelming question. It was that time of year again; there had been glitter and floss on the cobbles outside the college gates this evening.

Professor Stone filled the kettle at the little sink in the bathroom. Thin-skinned, he had said, but this afternoon she had felt as if she had no skin at all and was not sure if the ghostliness belonged to her or to the city. Was that why it gnawed at her skin? To invest itself with her own? She and the city were alike in this respect, knew only each other, only the passing of buses in violet-ochre night, only ink above the river after the sun had set, blind tossing of poplars in darkness, glitter of lamps at dining tables, chink of heavy cutlery and hubbub of dinner-talk, the unending noise from air vents, gargoyles' leer in tangerine streetlight, coloured pictures that settled like scenes from a lantern on desks and on chairs in rooms where the anointed dined on words of the spirit, where tongues of flame illumined heads drinking deep from the chalice, a silent fellowship looking on to a blue midnight land. She and the city knew only wind on battlements, twilight ringing, the rushing of evening, the infinite emptiness of dark rooms beneath eaves.

She squeezed the teabag against the side of the cup. Of course, the ghostliness might have nothing to do with being back, might be attributable to what had occurred on the train. She hadn't expected it; that was how life was, the armoury of Worthing not always thick enough. But the view, she thought, going back to the window, really was so like the view from that other house, the room too, the way the light entered it. Perhaps that was the reason then for this insubstantiality, this aching. For the house by the sea had been a place of books too – and what were books but ghosts, intimacy by proxy with things long dead or that never existed, approximations of presence traversing time and space?

'Bring a book,' her mother had said.

Elizabeth's mother did not play, plait hair, hug and offer kisses. She said: 'Bring a book.'

In the beginning was the voice. It is acknowledged that sound is the most emotive stimulus; was that to do with the fact that, everything being on one level essentially vibration, sound, being purely vibration, was by one definition the manifestation of matter itself? She didn't know, but her mother's voice was peculiar – beautifully peculiar: low, musical, husky. Her words traversed the delicate hair follicle, the hollow where the pulse beat. When her mother read, Elizabeth thought she saw angels' palaces in the herculean heights beyond the window.

Her mother's voice was of the heavens but her hands were

of the earth: mottled and ruddy, fingers swollen, hands that looked as if they had just been taken steaming from a bowl of hot dishwater. Hands; like other people's, and not like other people's at all. The hands were cared for by glycerine and rosewater, a bottle sat on her mother's dressing-table, and the scent made its way into the pages and pressed itself there, watery and unsettling. The hands didn't hold the child's, they held the pages as if they were living, barely touching the paper. But the arms, in holding the book, came around the child also, and leaning back she could feel her mother's chest rise and fall, smell her hair and, if she turned her head, hear the watery caverns of her heart.

The books creaked when they opened, gave off soft plumes of mildew and sharp whiffs of damp, the muskiness of smoke, savouriness of skin, of things that have set up colony, meant to go elsewhere and found themselves here instead. The pages were furred and they were patterned; sometimes they were lacy, like the bubbles left by the sea when it retreated, sometimes scribbled like the sand at high tide, and sometimes they were wrinkled, like the bay when it lay so long with the water it came to resemble it, as lovers, after a lifetime, come to resemble each other.

In the beginning was the voice, and the voice moved over the face of the deep, and the deep veiled and unveiled itself, and her mother's face was also shrouded; she did not remember it. She remembered her hands' blotched frailty, the slender knuckles, the milky half-moons. She remembered her hair, coiling and muscular, feral and sharp-smelling. She remembered the long lines of her body folded on the threadbare divan or in the window seat, lines so faintly drawn they appeared to peter out altogether at points. But her face was a mystery.

Her mother read aloud, to Elizabeth or the air she was never sure, and for that time she was taut, like a kite on a string. She was borne on high. She was woken. Her body was warm and her body was light; she could not hear people passing or children or dogs or cars or the wind or the rain or the gulls, and on the coldest day felt nothing but heat all around her, this charge, and for that time suns rose or set, meals came and went, clocks chimed, the sea churned or glittered or sighed or spat, but they were steadfast on their rock and unmovable. These were the moments other things clustered around, when life stepped out of its rhythm and lingered a while on the shore. At last the words gave way, too, and became merely a pattern taking place within something larger, in which dark and light, day and night were portions of a day longer and more elaborate than most people ever know.

The woman and child read in a bay window seat, looking over the beach stretching for miles one way and miles the other. To the left a road wound uphill past walled gardens to a church on the cliff; to the right a path led down to the beach. The sill was white and so were the sashes, the glass the old type with imperfections. Draughts of salt air shuttled through; the panes rattled, sometimes they spluttered; and in summer they stood open to the wash of the day. The bay of the window framed the bay of the sea, arranged it, changed it, opened it each morning and shut it between covers each night. There was nothing to be seen then but the itinerant headlights of a car, the eyebeam of the lighthouse or the moonlit edges of furling water. The picture opened and shut, the window lightened and darkened, but the books, taken up and put down, did not really end or begin but like the sea below, erasing the sand only to inscribe it again, only appeared to; the words could not die because they were patterned and hence endlessly memorable, thumbed in the child's mind like a rosary of hope.

'In the beginning was the Word and the Word was with God and the Word was God': they read that in one of the books, not a book of poetry, but it might as well have been for the rhythms it possessed. Words were a god the woman and child prayed to; words wrapped them, buoyed them, accompanied them by day and navigated the night; saved them from silence and stillness that seeped like seawater into the house. In the nave of a church on the rocks above was an effigy called the Word. He was a baby there, held by a woman. The Word made the earth, her mother told her, and everything in it and when 'The earth was formless and waste . . . the Word was moving across the waters.' When He was grown He came to earth to speak to people. He calmed the sea and walked upon it and opened it for a tribe of people to pass through. A corridor of dry land had appeared between walls of water, walls as invisible as sheets of glass. At night the child imagined the Word walking over the sea on the path made by the moonlight and she prayed that the Word would protect her mother, from the silence and the sea and the stillness of the house.

Years passed, pages turned, waves rolled over. The sea watched and waited. It possessed mnemonics of its own, rhythms it would teach in good time, scores to orchestrate and to settle. In the books they read there were stories of adventurers who set forth on the sea, and did or did not come back: Aeneas, Ahab, the Ancient Mariner, Pericles, Sebastian, Viola, Odysseus, and the child journeyed, too, because the books were not meant for her. There was no concession to age, the words wove a web of sound only, were stepping stones, drawbridges, cords leading to clear, shining spaces. Her favourite had a red cover and a picture of a woman with long, burnished hair sitting on a white horse. A knight in chainmail leaned towards her. The knight pledged fidelity to the lady and the lady pledged truthfulness to the knight and the knight went journeying to the dark lands beyond the world's rim. The child did not know where the dark lands were but she thought they might lie beyond the lip of the sea, where it curved slightly at the horizon. She often found her mother watching that line but when she asked her what she was watching she said nothing. On clear days the child felt she could touch the curve. But her mother said that even if you sailed for ever you would never reach it, it would just keep getting further away. It was a brave thing, then, to journey there; and this was what love did: it made people brave.

Sometimes it seemed to the child that her mother went to the dark lands though they were sitting side by side: her eyes dimmed, she did not hear or see her, she saw something else. Her mother could disappear instantly, so each sentence, each page, was a marvellous thing; her face could cloud as suddenly as the water in the bay, so when she read, the child was as quiet as the grave. Though the sea below took great breaths and so did the night and came rushing around her at the moment she slipped into sleep, lifting her up.

When she was older she tried to read to her mother but she read in fits and starts, wrecking the music and breaking the line, weaving a spell but as often as not unravelling it again. Sometimes her mother returned from the dark lands to sit beside her again, but more often she couldn't keep the bobbin humming, the line taut. The child looked on then at what she had done; could not do. The knight must go on alone, then, and the lady stay behind, an aching in her chest, the thread tugging with each step.

The professor pushed these thoughts away as she pulled the armchair to the window. She knew how to get the better of words now, had done battle time and again, dredged them up cold and inflexible from dry, dusty places; pieced them together and set them humming. In seven days God created the world; well, she had twice that to create her masterpiece. The ghostliness, the aching merely reminded her that time was passing, that words were waiting, that she must begin.

She stretched out her legs and removed her glasses. Just before sleep took her she thought she heard the sea rushing again. Beyond its rim the dark lands lay, infinitely close and yet infinitely distant, not meant for her and meant for her alone. But for some reason, whether because the journey had never been quite so momentous, or the prize quite so glittering, they did not appear to be dark any more but, on the contrary, filled with remarkable light.

What the Sea Said

Words stayed, sometimes a lifetime, but Elizabeth's mother left shortly before her seventh birthday and did not leave word of where she was going or when she would return or what to do in her absence. The child left the house by the sea then to live with strangers, and the people continued to be strangers though she knew their names, and the house on the cliff continued to be empty, although it was occupied, and her mother continued to be missing, though she had gone long ago. Later she thought she should have seen what would happen, as storms could be seen out at sea days before they arrived; there had been signs. But the signs accumulated only to dissipate again as the sea clouded and seethed, then transformed itself, sometimes hourly, into sheet glass.

It wasn't easy to read things by the sea because everything was continually in motion. It wasn't clear whether anything really happened or only appeared to because things were constantly changing. Houses fell, cliffs crumbled, boats, animals and people were there and then gone. And if things changed they also endured: the rocks below the window were eternal, the shoreline set from time immemorial, and whatever confusion the sea and sky fell into was resolved just as easily into a line as uninterrupted as the seam of a closed eye, because the sea was nothing and everything, uniform and variable, constant repetition and continual repose, all time, an instant and no time at all; black, white, a beam swinging in circles and line of moon-lambent light. Shallow, fathomless, the blare of a foghorn and the sputter of wet sand; the bip of Morse, trickle of voices laced with radio static, creaking of metal, shuddering of masts, shriek of gulls, reek of surf, slap of hulls, tolling of bells, mulling of swells, dwelling of souls in gulfs deeper than sleep, manifold sound and silence many-folded; between waves, between days, between rain, between sleet.

Even vegetation and elements were enfolded in one incestuous whole in the rocks beneath. There were animals that looked like flowers, and plants that were animals, shells that scuttled sideways, stones that were living and combusted when trodden upon, exploding in showers of powdery spore; there were creatures made of mud and those which resembled glass phials and those which appeared to consist solely of etheric phosphorescence, brimming saucers of light in the darkness. Past and future coexisted cordially in the rock faces below the house and in the seabed, which were laden with trilobites, asteriacites, ammonites, belemnites – tribes who had paid for their ungodliness with extinction, yet petrified, were beautiful; encrusted, entombed, inlaid, overlaid – and, if you looked out to sea and were inclined to believe in universal entropy, the future winked gnomically from the dawn of the world, foretelling the subsumption of all that was in the very element from which it arose, in mile upon mile of uninterrupted water.

Watching the sea from the window, walking at its edge, hearing its thunder, the child discovered a thing done, undone and redone in an instant. A ravelling of nets and travelling of squalls, a short volley then a long shot, a line of breakers that turned at the end and began stitching the next, a thing that never arrived but continually promised arrival, a limpid caresser of ankles and toes, and a dasher of boats, brains and beliefs against rock. The sea's moods cancelled each other; its rhythms made a mockery of here and there, now and then, once and always. Too self-conscious to remain in one style for long, it blustered one day and beguiled the next, was by turns anapestic, dactylic, alliterative. Even at its most prosaic, the patterns it wrote at the edge of the land made the stolid stone sentences of the houses appear dull. Sometimes, provoked by their unremarkableness, it swept one or two away altogether, or left them dangling half on and half off the page.

The child had seen one of those houses with her mother, seen wallpaper sawn asunder, trelliswork obliviously going about its regimented business, a child's cot, the blanket still inside it, a wardrobe with one door ajar, cables and joists dangling like tendons, beams and staircase jutting shards of bone. 'What happened to the people?' she asked.

'They got out,' her mother said.

But how did her mother know? How did the people know before that moment when everything was lost? She and her mother lived further down, near the seafront, with the hotels and rock gardens and railings and cars, but in her dreams the front of the house sometimes gave way and she woke scrabbling at bedclothes, suspended above waves which reared with open jaws, trailing ropes of salty saliva. So the child learned that the sea took what it wanted and, in its contrary way, sometimes returned it – as often as not the things people most wanted to forget. They were found days or weeks or years later, bloated or blasted, piecemeal or peaceful, insensate or in sleep.

The sea was invincible because it had no sphere of reference but itself, which it was forced to speak over and over. Subject, object, it could not be definitively spoken about – was not even solely itself, transforming once or twice a year into great inland vats that appeared to the east of the town and at other times retreating so far it seemed to disappear altogether, leaving in its place long stretches of blinding flats. You could not say one thing about the sea before it became another; it was eternity and a happening over and over; it was an instant, eternity asleep. 'Again,' the sea said, as if time was all around, but it also said, 'Now,' as if there was none. It said: 'For ever,' over and over, but that rendered 'For ever' redundant, because didn't it mean 'always'; mean 'over and over and over'? The child could hear eternity in the space between the dying of one wave and the rising of the next, silence encircled by sound, stillness cupped within the ogee of movement. Finally everything was numbingly one. Her ears were sealed up by its whiteness, its sameness, by a richness of sound that spanned the whole spectrum, an oscillation of matter so minute yet of such magnitude that each movement became one of degree only, nothing and everything, and in everything, peace.

Life in the house on the cliff was equally indeterminate. There were no events, nothing you could put a name or a date to, no birthdays or holidays, workdays or school days, days set apart for one thing or the other; not even days of the week. Sometimes the division of day and night itself became arbitrary and time was designated not so much by clocks as by place or by mood or by weather. There were fine days when they went down to the beach, there was the time of great light (owing to the weather or her mother's mood, the child was never sure) when they climbed the cliff and lay down in the heather. When the wind blew they donned ill-fitting coats from an assortment her mother kept on a line of hooks by the back door and climbed right to the top, where yew trees grew and dripping hedges, and a number of graves, sprouting through the rough grass like molehills, surrounded a stone church, which on misty days was obscured by sea-smoke, and which tolled the deaths of the men who were scattered upon the waters and didn't come back – 'To take the air,' her mother said, though you couldn't breathe for the force of it.

When it rained they read in the bay window or made things with cardboard and flour and paint or put on wellingtons and ran laughing up the seafront past the windows of all the upright, respectable women, who looked askance at the tall woman and the untidy child, at their wild hair, their clothes that might once have been good but were now old. And there was the time of great stillness when the sky was leaden and the rocks statues, and seals came to the bay, sleek-haired and glistening, all whiskers and black-eyed brilliance, and they watched them from the attic. The first time the child had not been able to believe it was animals she was hearing, though her mother said that it was, and that they were quite content though they mightn't sound it. Still the child had to remind herself, stared hard at the silky heads, the curved bodies that looked human, at the silver coils which spread like oil on the water and went on spreading, like hair, that looked just the way her mother's hair did when she swam in the sea. When there was a storm they lit a small fire in the front room with driftwood or whatever coal they could afford and listened to the radio, while the sea, shut out of their idyll, hurled itself at the rocks. But if there was a storm her mother might just as easily decide to go down to the breakers with a book, declaiming aloud like some beautiful Lear; on sunny days she had been known to light a fire and sit shivering beneath a blanket – and on days when it rained she might run with her along the sand, laughing. And it was raining the day they found her mother's body and brought it up to the little church on the cliff.

It made the child sick wondering what sort of day it would be. But there was no way to forecast because inside and out, cause and effect, were not that easy to distinguish. Did the sky cloud over because her mother's face had the moment before or had it been going to anyway? Did her mother brighten because the sun returned to the bay or would she have been just as happy if it had rained? Was the strange moaning in the wind a portent for the stillness that overtook the front room that evening or did the two things have nothing to do with one another? Whether the currents of life in the house on the seafront were occasioned by the ceaseless dialectic beyond the windowpane or by a movement of energy or heat or moisture less easily pinpointed, present, perhaps, in the house itself, or passing between her and her mother, remained uncertain.

She found herself watching the sea as often as her mother. It was easier to estimate; she felt the flutter of a veil, glimpsed the fumy funnel of a coming storm, heard the scratch of the burrowing crab; a gull swooped low and stopped on the windowsill, looking in at her with its yellow eyes. When the storm did arrive it was still hard to say afterwards what had happened. Her mother became quieter, moved more slowly; the air seemed to become denser; a recurring sensation was that she was moving through deep water. But none of these things could be rationalised or spoken about. It would have been more accurate to say that her mother retreated from the everyday world by a process of not-being, not-saying, not-doing. The summer her mother disappeared she filled a small notepad. 'Mother didn't get dressed', 'Mother drank from the milk bottle', 'Mother laughed for a long time', 'Mother was watching me when I woke up', 'Mother couldn't eat her toast', 'Mother pulled my jumper on too hard and hurt my ear', 'Mother said sorry too many times.' Was something really happening or was she imagining it? Did these things matter or not? So she looked for patterns, so she waited and watched. And all the days filled with nothing in particular, and all the days she willed the particular to manifest – because it was better to have lightning than listlessness, waters churning than dead – the nebulous grew and reached out tentacles, ensnared this and then that, until everything seemed to presage disaster. So she slid down the banisters, balanced on kerbstones, ran across the road, jumped from rocks, in order to see the look of reproof in her mother's eyes that she loved, in order that for a moment the nebulous might come within grasp.

The sea taught the child that pain takes place only in time, that it was impossible to hurt and be truly occupied, but if your hours were empty, pain could be felt very clearly indeed. Pain had much in common with the sea. Both ebbed, both went unnoticed for hours on end, then reared up and took your breath, and neither pain nor the sea was ever completely at rest. When silence pressed too close in the house on the cliff, the child put herself elsewhere; when the hours dragged, the child filled them with chatter, with questions, with plasticine, inventions, gifts for her mother, amulets to keep her safe. If all else failed, she brought a book. A poem could usually be counted upon to shatter the quiet, carry them through the wilderness and bring the knight back safe.

This is what the sea told the child: that nothing ends and nothing begins, nothing can be saved because nothing is lost, that each moment, each movement, was one of degree only; was nothing and everything, and in everything, peace. But afterwards she thought that the sea had lied. All moments were not alike. Some were lost. And there was no peace in it.

The First Day

Professor Stone stood at the window while the kettle boiled. Light was raking the river meadows, poplars emerging from a sea of mist. The playing fields glittered bluely. She could smell honeysuckle, see a mower crawling slowly over the cricket fields, hear the jetting of a water sprinkler. The day could not have been more perfect but the night's sleep had failed to dispel the aching in her chest and there was now in addition a heaviness that felt like the ghost of an old pain, though she couldn't identify it.

She turned away from the window and washed and dressed, gathered freshly sharpened pencils, papers, her copy of *Four Quartets*, and went down the steep black wooden stairs. She couldn't detect any sounds from the corridor below. Students weren't the earliest risers but at this time they were probably revising for exams. It was strange to be living among them, even if only for a few days, and for a minute she was almost persuaded that no time had passed and she herself was a student again.

The corridor was lit by windows that looked on to a quad at one side. It smelt of polish. The carpet beneath her feet was thick and cream. It felt as if it had been laid over another. Beneath, floorboards creaked with each step. She turned again at the end, to descend another staircase, wider this time, of black oak that clattered theatrically, and paused at the bottom to pass her hand over a carved banister varnished to a dull lustre by centuries of dust and palm oil. It dizzied her, the past laid up in this place; the films, the coatings, the layers. It was the layers that kept it together, she supposed; too old to brook subtraction, things could only be added. 'All is always now,' Eliot had said in the *Quartets*; she was surprised to find that she didn't like the thought.

She was walking through cloisters now and there were others, students, tutors, fellows, sometimes it was hard to tell. She crossed a quad, passed a chapel, a lawn not much bigger than a king-sized bed surrounded by firs and flower-beds, enthusiastically named 'The Deer Park', then climbed stone steps beneath gargoyles to the dining hall. It was as she remembered: panelled, cavernous, decked with portraits, shafts of light falling from tall windows, above High Table the college arms and regalia. What was different was the buffet bar at which she queued for grapefruit and yoghurt; that and the immigrant caterers.

She sat at the end of one of the benches, glad she knew no one. Among the few students breakfasting, she thought she could distinguish which still had exams to sit. The rest bore the look of survivors, the tension of the past weeks erased from their faces. It was like coming back from the front, she thought. She had been lily-white, eyes ringed, ethereal with months of study, a breath of wind enough to blow her sideways. She felt a camaraderie with these escapees that she felt for few humans; but it doesn't last, she could have told them. The bliss gives way; the torment is simply replaced with another you cannot imagine yet.

She wondered which of them would eschew the world of action in favour of the life of the mind, and thought she could identify the hard-core academics. There was an energy about them, a simultaneous alertness and oblivion, a clumsy youthfulness, which adhered like a puppyish lollop well into middle age. They were eternal teenagers, dimly aware of the fact and perpetually uncomfortable; 'virginal', she supposed; that was the word she was looking for. And when that virginity lasted many years it became a freakish quality, like all things unnaturally preserved, a parody, a spectacle.

She sat a little straighter. But for Keats, she reminded herself (granted, an example of premature demise rather than perpetual arrest), unheard music was sweeter than that which was heard, the life unlived more enduring than that which was tasted. Which was it, then? She watched a boy with a cow's lick and a milky complexion begin to laugh. The noise came in spasms, like jets from a water fountain, his body buckled, face contorted; his eyes were terribly bright; he seemed to be in the grip of something he was only just mastering and embarrassed by the knowledge. Professor Stone turned away. Had she looked like that? Did she still?

A line of sweat slipped between the straps of her bra and she removed her cardigan. The heat was accompanied by a flicker of nausea. She watched a waitress move down the table, arranging plates along her arm, her face sealed over with the self-absorbed content of pregnant women. It was a sort of abstraction, she thought; she experienced it herself at times, when a paper was working. What must it be like to produce a living creature instead of one made of paper and ink? A creature that became a real entity, no longer merely an appendage to its creator. But that was what happened with great work too, she reminded herself, with a work that influenced others: it took on a life its author couldn't have imagined and outlasted them.

She finished the yoghurt but not the grapefruit. She was still feeling a little nauseous and, prone to mouth ulcers since her therapy, didn't want to court trouble. She went down the steps, across the quad towards the lodge. Breezes lifted the hairs on her arms playfully, bells greeted her in joyous midsummer tumult, but her stomach was awash with unnameable jitterings and her body felt as if it had been filled with wet sand. Summer sickness. She had felt it years ago in this city. It was one with heat on playing fields, prisms of cloud in morning skies, the knowledge that work of critical importance awaited completion.

She stood on the kerb opposite the church that held the painting she had wanted to see when she was a girl. She did not remember the painting now and passed into the square, which was already full of tourists. The blue dome and the spires of twin towers ascended into blue haze. She passed through the shade of King's gate-tower, through the first quad and, in a flagstoned passage leading off it, found the stairs to the archives. At the top of the stairs she buzzed a heavy wooden door and showed her letter to the archivist, a young woman with dark eyes and dewy skin, who led her down a short corridor. A second door closed behind them with an aged clatter and she found herself standing in a small room with four tables; the walls were lined with books.

The room was dark except for light falling from four narrow windows that looked on to the square. Red carpet that ran like a tongue between the tables absorbed sound, and the panelled walls reverberated it flatly and decorously. The room smelt dim with age and with wood but mostly with silence, because silence was a smell here, colder than air, and thicker, like smoke. There were only two others, a young man with blond hair and pale skin, skin so pale and so delicately flushed it could have been a girl's, and an elderly man, his hair a white nimbus, his back so bowed his nose was not suspended many inches above the magnifying glass he was holding. The young man looked up briefly but his companion didn't notice her arrival. She thought perhaps he was the young man's father because there was some resemblance between them, their paleness perhaps, because they were both as white as the papers they bent over. Appearing as they did just then in a wash of early-morning sunshine they seemed a little other-worldly.

She settled herself by the window looking down on to the square. The archivist reappeared, carrying two grey boxes bound with elastic bands, the sum total of the Hyland Bequest, but for a moment the professor didn't open them. She sat looking down at the square, at the burnished dome, the sunshine drenching the stones of the church with liquid light, the blue shadows buttressing the walls like attentive lovers, slitted windows where, for no more than an instant yet nevertheless completely, a shiver of jet erased all trace of the light. She was breathing lightly and evenly in an attempt to contain the pain in her chest, which had quite suddenly become overwhelming, and in spite of having the moment she had waited for here in her hands it was several minutes before she lifted the lid of the first box.

She reminded herself that in one of the boxes would be the paper on Milton in which Eliot observed that the effect of poetry was like music, that '*the senses are used to convey something beyond sense*' – a small sentence in which lay the seeds of her own grand idea. Inside there were lectures on Scylla and Charybdis, the aims of education, 'Annual Lecture on a Master Mind', and a First Day Address at the Methodist Girls School of Penzance, all written some time in the thirties. There was the cover of the *Saturday Review of Poetry*, 12 March 1949, with Eliot beaming uncharacteristically and rather ludicrously and the quotation 'His whole life has been a continuing search for order in an appallingly disordered world', which struck her as rather funny. There was a photograph of a grandfather clock belonging to Henry Ware Eliot, Eliot's hotel papers, a note from UNESCO asking him to fill in a questionnaire on the divergences of meaning manifest in the contemporary use of the word 'democracy', which she also found amusing, a photo of Eliot unveiling a plaque, a poem that began 'In the beginning was the Word/ Superfetation of roev', 'Mr Eliot's Sunday Morning Service' (the number of polysyllabic concoctions was a result of Eliot's habitual burrowing in the thesaurus), some truly terrible poems under the heading 'A Note on War Poetry', but nothing about Milton, nothing about the auditory imagination, nothing, in short, about 'The Music of Poetry'.

The paper must be in the other box, which had to be more illuminating; it could hardly not be. What if it wasn't? Her hands trembled as she replaced the elastic bands. 'You're getting ahead of yourself, Elizabeth,' she said. 'Just open it.'

The second box was better. The first paper was an essay entitled: 'Sir John Davies' in which Eliot stated, *'Davies is not troubled by the reception of form without matter . . .'* A few pages on he was writing of the 'Our Father' and how the effort to understand it with intellect defeats its purpose. He was writing of Johnson, of sound and sense, of how Tourneur's loathing of humanity exceeds its objective correlative, is a 'horror beyond words', how Kyd's *Spanish Tragedy* proved to be 'intractable material' for *Hamlet*, and then, most excitingly of all, of a state of affairs that *'induced in myself a depression of spirits so different from any other experience of fifty years as to be a new emotion'* in a draft for an article that would appear in the *Criterion* in 1939 – right between the first and second *Quartets*.

Her heart beat more freely now. Even without the paper on Milton she would have something to work with. She saw herself once more on a long road with a clear destination, getting nearer and nearer. 'I'll read through everything briefly and see what I want to look at in more detail,' she said. 'Maybe by the end I'll have more idea about where I'm heading. I'm working largely in the dark but that's not such a bad thing. Lots of new things come from working this way; no bright light is ever discovered in broad daylight.' She was surprised to find, however, that the aching in her chest didn't subside and it was all she could do to stay in her seat.

The sun rose over the square and swaggered in the azure above the dome, licked the carpet into life and edged the tables and chairs and those sitting at them in whiteness. She found herself glancing at the two gentlemen. Time Past and Time Present, she thought; or should that be Time Past and Time Future? As one read a page he passed it to his companion, who received it without a sound. They were like a little machine, lifting papers, replacing them, reaching for the next. The old man's brow glistened, the younger was pale and earnest. They were no doubt looking for something of great academic import, she thought, and it was so reassuring to see another two souls toiling on a day like this. And yet something about the reverence, almost tenderness, with which the young man presented the papers to the elderly, the care with which he helped him lay the papers on the grey foam rest and placed lead weights on the pages, made her uncomfortable, as if the action referred back to her in some way, though she couldn't think how.

By mid-morning she was further along than she had hoped. At twenty to twelve she finally came across the essay on Milton she had seen in the British Library. Eliot was picking up Milton's 'interlunar cave' of *Samson Agonistes* in the 'vacant interstellar spaces' of the *Quartets*. Milton's use of the word did not simply suggest that the cave was empty but that the moon's presence intensified the night's darkness and the daylight's desertion:

> *The sun to me is dark*
> *And silent as the moon,*
> *When she deserts the night*
> *Hid in her vacant interlunar cave.*

And the moon was silent, she thought. To the man who couldn't see, the last hope lay in hearing. Now she noticed something else too: light was lost but sound was the thing that was missed; the sun's darkness was equated to the moon's silence. How strange, she thought, that she had never seen this before. And without Eliot's resurrection of the lines she never would have. Poetry was unique in that way: it brought its own past into the present, was the strangeness in recognition Eliot identified in the *Quartets*: 'known, forgotten, half recalled/ Both one and many'. Well, here Eliot had not only resurrected Milton but transfigured himself as well.

The sun was brighter then and the glare a white heat on the back of her neck. Across the room the old man's head began to droop. At half past twelve it was so hot she moved her chair to the end of the table. At forty-five minutes past the young man helped the older to his feet, handing a cane to him that lay on the floor, said something to the archivist and they went out. Perhaps she should stop too. She collected her cardigan, left the boxes open and told the archivist she would be back after lunch.

She bought sandwiches from the covered market and sat outside the round sandstone room among students lying on their sides or their stomachs on the lawn or lounging in the stone seats built into the walls. The flagstones were scalding so she opted for the grass and there was a pulsing beneath her body she wasn't sure belonged to herself or the soil. Professor Stone didn't 'do' summer. The season drew up darker currents in her like moisture, whereas winter incubated them. Detachment was infinitely harder to achieve in the heat because bodies were so much more troubling: breasts itched, noses shone, hair became lank, eyes dull; the ongoing offensive against perspiration stepped up a level. She unstuck her legs one from another and a bead of sweat slipped startlingly down her back. Her feet squelched in their stockings but she didn't feel able to take off her shoes; if she was thirty years younger, perhaps. She was hot in her cardigan but couldn't remove it for fear of perspiration stains on her blouse.

She adjusted her glasses and unwrapped the sandwiches, remembering the lunches she used to prepare in her student days. She had prided herself on being self-sufficient, didn't eat in Hall once, though it was not so much for financial reasons as social ones. She passed her fellow students in quads and on staircases for three years without knowing their names, except the twelve of her tutorial group. She supposed she could have tried to befriend a few of the girls – Jessie, the Irish girl with hands like spider's legs, horny nails, skin like alabaster and gently hunched back; or Hannah, the dowdy New Yorker, sloping bosom, dirty nails, fags, bed-hair – if she had known how to chit-chat. In fact, though, she could only muster words to analyse and dissect. Conversation was enervating and left her heart racing, her body damp with sweat. She didn't think the bookish girls would have taken to her anyway because she was one of them only up to a point: the skirts and jumpers, flat shoes, glasses, oily skin and virginal hair, they were all right. It was the eyes that let her down, so dark as to be depthless. In any case she could not afford to be distracted from the magnitude of the task in hand, that of impressing Professor Hunt. It was easier to eschew human beings than interact with them. The gaze of people was a force field she couldn't bear long without the sensation that she was suffocating. The gaze of young men in particular produced an agitation that translated itself into a gelid glare and strident walk; now young men didn't see her at all; at fifty-three she had ceased to exist.

She frowned a little, stretching her legs in front of her in imitation of two girls to her left but as soon as she had the girls glanced at her and she drew her legs in again. When she looked back they had turned away. How did people know what to do with their bodies? she wondered.

How did they know how to behave when in one another's company? It appeared to be a simple enough art, but you could never master it successfully if you had not at the precise moment in life when nature primed you to do so; after that, however hard you practised, your lack of proficiency would always show. She lifted her chin as if to sun herself but the sun made her eyes water. '*The sun to me is dark, and silent as the moon*'; it was strange how intense sunshine could feel like darkness but that was what she felt now: blindness, and a weight on her head that made her dizzy. She removed her glasses and put her hand over her eyes. As you say, there is no need to meet. And why did she think of that now?

She finished her sandwiches and was about to get up when her eyes were drawn to a movement on the far side of the square in the shade of the church wall. A boy had rounded the corner and pulled a girl against him. His back was to the wall. Professor Stone had always watched couples at the edges of her vision, the women as much as the men, who were more effusive and hence more interesting. What she had been left with over the years was a jigsaw: a man's hand, a woman's head, an arm, a leg. Seeing a man slip his hand into a woman's lap she averted her eyes, her heart battering for minutes on end, on the point of erupting, the smallest of movements excruciatingly difficult, only to find when she turned back that he was doing nothing but reaching for a sweet. She would emerge from these bouts of surveillance sticky, sick, breathless, while the couple, oblivious, wandered away. Afterwards she felt that they had somehow benefited from her attention unbeknown to themselves, that she had given something precious that had not been reciprocated; it was always a couple's disappearance rather than their demonstrations of love that left the greatest sickness behind it.

She watched as the boy in the shadow of the church wall

caught the nape of the girl's neck and turned her head in order to kiss her more deeply. She watched the girl press her hands against his trousers. Professor Stone smiled and closed her eyes but her heart beat strangely. When she looked back their jaws were moving rhythmically. She was reminded of a mother bird feeding its young: there was the same blankness, the same absence of emotion, which was paradoxical, because it was probable the participants felt a great deal. She supposed. She didn't really know. She scanned the square casually for appearance's sake before looking back. There was such ease between them. Their hands had dropped to each other's hips now, the kissing become more languid and sensual. The professor's own lips had parted a little. Perhaps it's love, she thought. It was always like this: the same quietness, the same lack of pretence. She pulled up a little grass. They are young, she thought, to be in love.

She didn't look again for a couple of minutes. The girl was pulling the boy by the hand while he hung back playfully. The aching in the professor's chest had suddenly become piercing. 'Don't leave,' she whispered. 'Let me see you.' The boy appeared to have heard her because he waited a moment before launching himself off the wall and following the girl. As he caught her, the girl screamed piercingly – brilliantly, the professor thought; she was sure she could never produce such a pure dart of sound, so wild and inhuman, a peal of the gods! – contracting all the terror and joy in the universe into one marvellous point. That sound tore the day to shreds; the pieces fluttered, they spiralled, furled left and right, settled like snow on the grass, on her skirt, her shoes and tights, and as if she was attached to the sound she stood, brushing something invisible from her lap and began walking to the gate.

The cry went on existing as she crossed the square, in spite as well as because of her – she didn't know, but her actions seemed curiously belated, or was that in advance of the event? She didn't seem to be fully present any more but floating. She stumbled, could hear only her heart. Was this detachment? she wondered. Or was it the sun? She felt peculiar, as if she was watching herself from a distance, conscious only of a stillness, a heat at her centre that encompassed the aching in her chest and revealed the day to be a façade, staggering in its meaninglessness – all except the boy and the girl in the shade of the church wall. She glanced back towards the church as she entered the lodge but the lovers had disappeared and she felt the loss in her chest, where the cry, too, seemed to have imprinted itself.

She had thought she would finish the second box of papers that afternoon but did not. She thought she would scan *Four Quartets* again but didn't do that either. The silence of the archives was too pressing, the panelled walls too close; the rustle of paper, tick of the clock and tap of the archivist's keyboard were suddenly all unbearably distracting. She was glad when five o'clock came and she could hand the boxes back to the archivist and consign herself to the welling symphony of the afternoon.

The Second Day

Professor Stone was lying on her side compressed as if by an unearthly weight, a sound making her heart beat hard. She turned in her sleep and threw off the blankets but went on dreaming. When she woke she was in her bedroom in the house by the sea, and lay beneath the eaves, listening in darkness. Then she heard it again.

Somewhere a woman is crying.

She pulls the blankets over her head and puts her fingers in her ears. She rocks, but she can still hear it. She pushes the blankets back and gets up. The landing is bright with moonlight. She goes along it till she comes to a door. The noise grows as she enters, and now she can hear the sea too, washing the rocks below the window.

She goes to the bed and feels her way along it. She has reached the pillow before she realises it is empty. Then she begins to sink through a viscous substance, even as she stands there, which parts beneath her and closes above her head. She has made a mistake: it is disturbing precisely because the nature of it cannot be identified.

Though the bed is empty the crying continues. It seems to be coming from the window. She goes to it and looks down. Below in the oily black water dark heads are bobbing. The seals have come to the bay again and are talking to one another. She watches for minutes or maybe for hours. Then the seals swim away and she is alone and there is no sound but the sea, saying 'now', saying 'again', saying 'always' over and over.

*

Professor Stone came up out of sleep suddenly, as if out of water, sending droplets of consciousness in all directions. She sat on the side of the bed, passing her hand over her head, waiting for her heart to stop thundering. The pain in her chest that she had noticed since she had been in the city was already pronounced.

She did not look at the view as she drank tea, though it was, if possible, even more beautiful than the day before, the distances a film of gossamer, the poplars shimmering columns above a river of heat. She did not marvel at the age of the stairs as she descended. 'Lovely morning,' a gardener said, as she crossed the quad. But she had not noticed the morning, which was breezy, with a sky of blue silk; she was preoccupied simply with walking, which seemed to be a difficult business right now.

At the door of the lodge she waited while a group of students in gowns and mortarboards clattered past, then went in and enquired what time dinner was served. 'Six,' the porter told her. She signed her name on the chit and was about to leave when the porter said: 'There's a note for you.'

'Oh,' she said. 'I didn't think anyone knew I was here.'

She peered at the envelope. '*Professor E. Stone,*' it read. The *es* were half-moons. Her heart beat once, very hard.

Elizabeth,
  I take it you're now ensconced in college and hard at it. If the work isn't too all consuming I should be in my room this evening after seven . . .
  Best,
  Edward

She folded the paper. The porter was watching. She tapped the envelope and laughed, strode out of the lodge, caught her cardigan on the door, came back, released herself, remembered she would not need to dine in Hall after all, crossed her name off the list, handed the board back to the porter and went out. She began walking briskly up the street, her chin high. She nodded to a man wheeling a bicycle. The morning, she now noted, was very fine indeed.

There is a light, a certain hour of the day, when activities recede into stillness and a quality in the air changes. In summer it is from seven to eight, in winter four to five. In the city of books the change is so gradual and so slight as to be almost magical, the shifting sensed rather than noticed. The light doesn't blaze out only to swiftly decline, as it does in hot places. It doesn't break across the sky in colourful violence, as it does near the point where the lighthouse flashes; it lessens, it hesitates, it imperceptibly mutates.

After the sunlit hours in the garden, after the bustle of the high street, a warm front, a dusk front moves in. It seems to come from the river. It slips through arches, alley-ways, gardens and quads, circles a chapel and passes a church, eddies the steps of a circular room with a roof bluer than the sky; you look up from your desk and it's there, it's happening, it's all around you. Some small sigh of restlessness drawing things away, at the back of the evening, as the day reaches out to the night.

You get up and return your books to the stack, making sure the pink slips are visible and your name can be read, you collect your pencils and papers, which for a time were at home here at this desk the sun picked out, sweep them into your bag and leave the desk that was yours for a day, and the evening is beckoning, gusts shuttling along cobbled streets interlacing themselves with smells from college kitchens, bells calling to evensong, and something pulling, drawing hand over fist through air suffused with pigments of light – light changing even as you watch but cannot see; you move down a low-ceilinged staircase, circumscribe each time-sloughed step, down, down, down; and beyond each window bay the evening is there, waiting.

It may be filled with gusts of light summer rain; it may be blank, muted, laden with the day's heat; it may be ghostly, snow pending, or raging, jewelled sun and equinoctial wind chaffing a sky smarting and scoured past blue. It may be all these things but the moment suspended is always the same: you walk into a courtyard, you pass a statue, and it's here, it's happening, it's all around you. You walk under an arch and down stone steps into a square and now there are people and bicycles and a faint hum of traffic and bells tolling near and far, far beyond other things, insistent yet half slipping, as the evening itself. And down by the river where the water snakes dark between tall poplar trees, the dusk slips lower, creeps towards the front of the stone buildings, sun-warmed, rain-pitted, wind-crumbled buildings, standard bearers looking out to sea, or so they always seemed to her, guardians of the roses; where lights blink on now here and there, solitary bastions in the gathering dusk.

It was at such an hour poised between day and night that Professor Stone left the archive where she had been working and walked through the city of books to the college of her former tutor. The evening was the definitive time of day in the city of books, 'the violet hour', Eliot called it – Eliot, who loved all things that lay between two others; the hour when you could if you were lucky glimpse the real city behind the façade. The night-time city was not as sure of itself as its daytime counterpart; it could not sustain the show put on for tourists and TV crews, the yearly round of parents and undergraduates; each evening the city took itself up again, tracing its wounds and its stories, ran its fingers over the rosary of what had been, then as morning arrived gave itself up again to the big top of the day.

She loved this hour more than all others but this particular evening paid it no attention. She had been unable to concentrate all day. The note Edward Hunt had sent, in characteristic fashion, told her very little: was he pleased to be seeing her again or simply discharging a duty for old time's sake? Had she made a mistake trying to get back in touch with someone she had known in another life? She had finally grown so tired of thinking about the note that she had thrown it away, and now the hour had arrived, and as is often the case when we desire and fear the arrival of something in equal measure, she was in a state of querulous, even daring indifference; each expectation and apprehension, quenched and re-arisen a dozen times, had formed a static in her head so that the evening, which was grey and beautiful, hushed by the sounds of cars and buses, soothed by the river flowing coldly beneath the bridge with a dark smell of algae, set alight by the chilled birdsong pattering among trees and bushes of college gardens, was lost upon her.

She was walking briskly, head erect, as if on her way to some professional engagement, but she was also a little dishevelled, her hair thin and tufted, collar askew, tights creased at her ankles, a shoelace trailing. She hadn't allowed herself time to see how she looked, partly so she couldn't imagine how changed Edward Hunt would find her and partly because looking at her own reflection – always an occasion for woe – was, since the cancer, something she didn't do at all if she could help it.

She turned into a cobbled street and bells from a tower, square and rough-hewn, began to chime. It was the chapel she thought had been to the left of her room when she came to the interview; the room where she had sat and done battle with 'The Sparrow Hawk' was just over those rooftops – and suddenly for an instant she was there again, seventeen, at the tiny desk, memorising the words of famous men. She reflected how impossible this would have seemed then, that she herself should be an author, a professor of English poetry; she tried to grasp it but could not. It was rather demoralising, since if she didn't grasp it now then when would she?

She passed railings where a small orchard bordered a narrow path. Just a little further on was the chained gate where she had stood and watched his window during the first year. She did not turn down the path now but continued along the street and entered the lodge.

The interior was larger than she remembered; there were spotlights in the ceiling, the counter with sliding panel had been replaced by a floor-to-ceiling glass partition, the brass bell by intercom – and was that CCTV? She was just passing through the door to the quad when she heard a voice say, 'Miss Elizabeth!' and turned to see a white-haired, rosy-cheeked porter beaming at her.

'Albert –'

'Miss Elizabeth, I thought it was you – after all these years.'

'You remember me—'

'Of course I do; you haven't changed a bit. Except you've done something to your hair . . . It's a bit shorter.' He rocked a little on his heels.

'How are you, Albert?'

'Can't complain, a few aches and pains, but mustn't grumble.'

'I can't believe you're still here. You were close to retiring when I was an undergraduate.'

His shoulders shook. 'Oh, they don't get rid of me that easily – and what brings you back?'

'I'm doing some research in King's College archives.'

'Oh, yes . . .'

'Some papers by T. S. Eliot.'

'Very nice; and where are you nowadays?'

'London. UCL.'

'Teaching, is it?'

'Yes, and a few other things. I'm writing my second book, actually.'

'I always knew you'd be one of the ones that stayed with the books,' he said happily. 'There's those that go off into the world and those that stay on; you're a stayer. On your way to meet Professor Hunt, is it?'

She flushed a little and laughed. 'Yes.'

'Ah, won't keep you, then.'

She said brightly: 'Not at all. It's wonderful to see you, Albert.'

'When you going back?'

'Not for another two weeks.'

'I'll see you again, then, will I?'

'I hope so.'

'Lovely. Well, I'll let you get on. Couldn't let you go without saying hello.'

'I'm glad you did.'

She was about to go when he said: 'You been keeping all right, Miss Elizabeth? You look a bit on the thin side.'

'Oh, just busy, Albert,' she said. 'You know what it's like.'

'Oh, aye. Never stop, I don't, always on the go.' He nodded to a television behind the counter on which a game of football was being played, then held up a finger and disappeared behind the counter. When he returned he was holding a photo. 'My granddaughter.'

'Really?' She adjusted her spectacles.

'Ten months. Never gives any of us a minute's peace.' He grinned. 'Me and her are best mates.'

She shook her head. 'Gosh, that really is – that really is something . . .'

'Isn't it?' He beamed. 'You better get on, Miss Elizabeth – or should I call you Professor Stone now?'

'Oh, no, Elizabeth is fine.'

'Well – we'll catch up again.'

'We will.'

She hurried, checking her watch, but she wasn't late. It was strange to see people one had known a long time ago: they were always unchanged and changed completely, and somewhere within that contradiction lay the state of ourselves, she supposed. She didn't know whether to be pleased or disconcerted by the fact that she had apparently changed so little.

She entered the tunnel. When she came out the sun was sinking behind her and the path along the lawn lost in shadow. There was the horse-chestnut tree, boisterous in the evening breeze, there was the building, there was the window. 'Well,' she said. She came to the steps. 'Here we are,' she said. She went up them.

She passed into the darkness of the corridor beyond. It smelt as she remembered and her stomach lurched. She hadn't known the building smelt of anything at all till she smelt it again – but, yes, there it was, unmistakable: polish, wood and silence. And here was the corridor of glass.

The glass was now reinforced, the frame teak, and the old metal door had been replaced, but the rose garden beyond it was as she remembered: still unreal, still ghostly, though she thought there might have been a greater symphony of colour years ago, a more boisterous tangling of bushes and bowers, the lawns more severe, the hedges not so gentle. Were things always less sensational than one remembered? she wondered. She passed into the darkness beyond. There were the stairs, his nameplate, the handle, the door.

She stood there for a moment, her eyes closed, weighed down by something unspeakably heavy, and it occurred to her it was not too late even now to go away. She could send a letter saying she had been unavoidably detained; she could not reply at all and let him think she had never arrived. She opened her eyes and knocked at the door.

It had all seemed so different in London in the glow of her recovery, then discovery; the future a shining road along which to walk. But now she was awash in the future and it was just like the present, the road no longer shining but ordinary grey tarmac, more winding than she had imagined, its destination still very much unattained.

She was recalled from her thoughts by the fact that the door remained shut. She immediately looked at her watch, although she had looked at it not five minutes before, but these days it was a competent quartz; the second hand was moving with clipped and impeccable precision. He had said six and six it was.

Twenty minutes later she got up from the stone stairs and retraced her steps along the quad. Wind was picking up in the river meadows. The horse-chestnut boughs appeared to be levitating. She caught a scent of roses and walked more quickly. She wasn't thinking; there were only jabberings masquerading as thoughts. She didn't feel as if she was walking either; the movement felt more like floating. She wondered how one could feel discomfort and derealisation simultaneously, and it occurred to her that perhaps discomfort was derealisation, a pain that could not be got close to; a novel idea she was not disposed at this moment to analyse. She would leave a note in the lodge saying she had been but not to worry, he was a busy man, could not be expected to remember. And she was busy too, she said to herself; and it didn't matter, not in the slightest. She felt tired suddenly. It would be good to get back to her room.

She was rounding the corner of the tunnel when she collided with a grey-haired figure in jeans and jumper whose arms were full of papers. 'Oh,' she said. 'I'm sorry.'

She bent to retrieve the papers but the man did not. He stood looking at her. Then he said: 'Hello.'

She stared, coloured, straightened.

'Hello.'

'That's a fine welcome.'

'I'm sorry; how are you?'

'I was all right. Now I seem to be in rather a mess.'

'Let me help—'

'I think if might be better if you didn't.'

Nevertheless she took half of the papers and they began to walk back the way she had come.

Boots: black, scuffed, laces knotted three times. Jumper: too large, small hole near the cuff. Scent: something like rain, something like hair, tobacco. Hair: grey but still rising in ridiculous tufts. Voice: if possible even gruffer. Hands: blotched, swollen, reddened. It was with a feeling bordering on euphoria that she realised he had hardly changed at all. Had she? A great deal probably. Then she remembered she had caught him in an attempt to evade her and said: 'Here I am, following you, I'm sorry . . .'

He said, not quite looking at her: 'Yes, for once you're early.'

She stopped walking. 'It's twenty-five past six.'

'Yes, and I said seven.'

'Seven?'

'Elizabeth, for an intelligent woman it's amazing how often you manage to get the time wrong.' He began walking again. 'Not much has changed, has it?'

She followed after a moment, her face hot, glad that he was not looking at her – and then they were by the steps and he was, and she saw that his eyes were glinting with the look of disapproval she had loved; that he was half smiling, and that his face, too, was much as it always had been, if a little wearier, a little softer at the edges.

She raised her chin imperiously. 'Shall I come back? I can see you've got work there.'

But he said: 'I think after thirty years I can forgive you for being half an hour early.'

The room was pleased with itself in the lamplight. A cold smell of honeysuckle and fermenting roses drifted through the window. Beyond it lonely spirit forms of poplars shivered. The Bach was still there but not the New Order, the masks but not the Fender. Photographs, kettle, mugs, toaster were all present and correct – and could this still be the same rug? Apparently it could. The room, like its owner, appeared to be arrested in some other dimension; except there were more books than before, if possible, lining the windowsills two rows deep, occupying the space under the table and a new bookcase by the door. She said: 'I see you've got rid of the sofa.'

'The springs nearly did one lad an injury.' He stowed the papers he was carrying by his chair. 'I would have kept it.'

He went to the sink, filled the kettle and flipped it on. 'So, thirty-three years. This is an honour.'

She laughed. 'Well, as I said in my letter it's because of the papers I discovered in King's College.' She sniffed in a business-like way. 'And how are you?'

He nodded, apparently looking for something. 'Good, yeah.'

'I wasn't even sure you would still be teaching.'

'Oh, they haven't put me out to pasture just yet.'

'I didn't mean that; I just thought you might have, I don't know, got tired of it . . .'

'Well, I'm not much good at anything else.'

He raised an eyebrow but the smile was joyless and she was shocked by his tone. And there was something else, as he tapped a packet of cigarettes and lit up, that she didn't recognise: the look of disapproving pleasure he had turned on her a moment ago had vanished; now he appeared to be looking through her to something else. He said: 'You've lost weight.'

'Not intentionally.'

'And your hair's different.'

Her hand went to the scar, then she remembered. 'I cut it.'

'It was better before.'

The kettle clicked off.

She stared at him shaking instant coffee into mugs, pouring on water. 'So what's been happening?' she heard herself say brightly. 'All these years.'

'Well, too much to fit into five minutes.'

'Yes . . .'

She looked around again.

'This, that, the other, a few women, a few different departments, the usual academic crap, the grand meta-circus of nothing.' He turned to her. 'But you know all about that now, don't you? You're part of it.'

He stirred the coffee – unnecessarily vigorously, she thought – poured in milk and shoved the fridge door shut with his foot. 'How many years have you been teaching?'

'Seventeen. Thank you.' She peered into the depths of her coffee.

'You were at UCL last time I checked.'

'Yes, still there.'

'Matthew Cullum looking after you?'

'Yes. He's a wonderful head. The department's come on in leaps and bounds under him.'

From his armchair she heard him take one of his gulps. She tried to follow suit but the steam seared her face and she had to set it down again. They were silent for over a minute and she said: 'You know, I can come back another time; I'll be here for two weeks . . .'

'It's OK.'

It didn't seem like it. Her initial estimate had been wrong: everything had changed, just not the surface. It was astonishingly difficult to think of something to say, and the harder she thought the more outlandish the suggestions her mind supplied. She took a sip of coffee. It was reassuringly bad. On another occasion she would have shouted for joy, but her heart was beating hard and the aching in her chest that had been with her since she arrived in the city was now staggeringly painful. She said: 'I see Albert's still here. Shouldn't he be retired now?'

'Oh, he's as much of an institution as the college is. They couldn't get rid of him if they wanted to.'

'Yes,' she said. 'I suppose the job is what keeps him going.'

'Oh, no. He's happily married. He's just had his first grandchild and never gets tired of telling everyone.'

She said, 'So what have you been doing?' then remembered she had asked him before.

'Well, teaching. America for ten years.'

'Yes,' she said, then wished she hadn't because she couldn't think of a good reason why she would know this unless she had been monitoring him.

'Did you read my book on Marston?'

She had.

Had he read her book on the Restoration stage?

He had not.

There was another lengthy silence.

She was about to get up when he inhaled, as if waking, and said: 'So, your new project, tell me about that.'

She held on to the cup tightly. She said: 'I'm interested in the way the music of a poem affects a reader's appreciation, whether as Eliot said, "genuine poetry can communicate before it is understood".'

'Go on.'

'What are the ways in which we "understand" poetry? What does "communicate" mean anyway? Does a poem sometimes communicate and at other times not? If poetry does communicate below the levels of conscious feeling, how is Eliot able to provide us with such a detailed account of its operations?' She could feel her neck becoming hot; red patches would be appearing. It was ridiculous, she thought, that he should provoke exactly the same response as he had when she was an undergraduate.

'In the Hyland Bequest there are heaps of papers from the late thirties and forties that Eliot was writing coterminously with the *Quartets*. They'll be an invaluable insight into his working methods at the time, as well as his ideas about the "auditory imagination".'

It suddenly occurred to her that she could not be absolutely sure of this; the papers might be useful, they might not; she would probably be able to write the thesis either way. She wondered why she hadn't seen that till this moment. What was she doing here, then?

'In one of the essays, "The Music of Poetry", he writes that the poet is occupied with the frontiers of consciousness beyond which words fail, though meaning still exists. I wanted to look at sound as an autonomous force that could uncover deeper forces, the buried life of a poem . . .'

'Interesting.'

It was amazing, she thought, how he could take a word and shred things with it.

'There are lots of buried things in Eliot,' she said, a little hotly.

'Sure, but you'll have to be careful how you go about phrasing this stuff. It's like arguing for the existence of God.'

'I'm aware of that.'

And then, in spite of his lack of enthusiasm, in spite of discovering only a moment ago that she was not doing things for the reason she'd thought she was, she said: 'But however it turns out, this project feels different from anything I've done before. It feels – alive.' She laughed quickly. 'I'm not making much sense, but I've been struggling with Milton for eight years and it was all so . . .'

'Dead?' The boot had begun to swing in earnest.

'Yes, actually. In spite of everything, I still didn't feel I'd written what I could have.'

'Indeed.'

And suddenly he was there again, had returned from wherever he had been for the past forty minutes and rejoined her where they had left off thirty years ago.

She said quietly: 'It feels different.'

'It's ambitious. I don't mean for you, for anyone. I imagine that sound is, by its nature, a very difficult thing to talk about. But I think you can do it.'

'Thank you.'

'In fact, I'm sure you can.'

She folded her hands, which were trembling.

The light had faded outside the windows; the hour of transition had come and gone, the city once more itself and the world one of reflections. He said: 'They'll be locking up soon.'

'Yes.' She stood up.

'It's good to see you. We'll meet up again before you go back. When is it? The end of the month?'

'But I thought—'

'I've got a lot on but I still want to read this.'

'Aren't you busy?'

'Yes, I just said. Check your pigeon-hole later this week.'

The city was in darkness; gargoyles were lurid beneath orange streetlights, the sky a muddy haze above black spires. It had gone well, she thought. He had said he would read her thesis. Though he had been peculiar, his manner unplaceable. And he didn't like her hair.

Had he wanted to see her? Had he not wanted to at the start but had by the end? Had he wanted to at the beginning and not at the end? No, he'd wanted to see her at the end because he had said, 'It's good to see you,' but that meant he hadn't to begin with. 'Stop it, Elizabeth,' she said.

She had forgotten the taste of the night, how sounds washed around you. Her ears were ringing. The wind caught her as she crossed the square and she felt a flash, pure light; half pain, half euphoria. The world was new and it was old, she had forgotten and she remembered. She was waking.

The Third Day

Professor Stone sat up straight and opened her eyes wider. The heat really was quite debilitating. On the trail of a hot wave came a cold one but the cold one was illusory. She had never known the city like this. There were sure to be some fainting fits in the exam schools today, she thought, though it was bad enough here in the archives. She wiped her forehead with her handkerchief. Welcome to the twenty-first century, she thought, then wondered whether the city would survive it.

Her two companions were in their usual places, the elder flushed, looking at the moment as if he wasn't long for the world himself. Down in the square, surfaces shimmered; shapes were draped in a gauze of indeterminacy. Tourists were sitting in the shade of the dome, drinking from bottles of water. Those walking looked as if they were sleepwalking or moving along the seabed. She was suddenly reminded of something Eliot had written somewhere, that most people were 'only very little alive'. Eliot was obsessed with buried lives, unlived lives, the life of the living dead. But then he himself might know a thing or two about that.

T. S. Eliot had shocked the world in 1957 when at sixty-nine he married his secretary, a woman thirty-seven years his junior. There was a picture of the two of them at a theatre in Chicago in 1959; she was looking at it now, squinting through a swathe of sunlight at her desk in the archives. Valerie was wearing a cream satin evening gown with low-cut décolletage, draping herself across T. S. E.'s arm while he consulted the programme. He himself looked every inch the proud new husband: bow-tie, Brylcreemed hair, peering around like the cat who'd got the cream. Apparently they had been going for drinks after work together for years, he had sent her roses, all under the eyes of the Faber crew. A buried life indeed.

Eliot had been married before (a marriage unconsummated by all accounts) to the vivacious, neurasthenic Vivienne, whom he had met in Oxford during the spring of 1915. They were married in London on 26 June 1915. It was a decision that drove him to the edge of breakdown and his wife, after a lifetime of illness, into a mental asylum. But his impulsive decision to marry, despite how it appeared to many, seemed to Professor Stone not the action of one who was bold, but one who plunged into any action because he knew himself to be at risk of taking none at all; what was at stake was making something happen, however that might turn out. After all, this was hardly Lord Byron; this was the creator of that arch procrastinator J. Alfred Prufrock, he of the 'hundred indecisions', 'visions and revisions', of the compulsive 'Do I dare?' and 'Do I dare?' She saw Eliot's first marriage as a reckless attempt to 'force the moment to its crisis'. And crisis was what he had got; the ballast of his marriage formed *The Waste Land*.

Four Quartets looked in a different direction, towards the possibility of redemption, though written at a time of great personal and national darkness. The first quartet, 'Burnt Norton', in which the seeds of the entire work lay, had been inspired by a visit Eliot paid with Emily Hale during 1934 to a manor located in Gloucestershire. Hale was a friend from Eliot's youth whom he corresponded with most of his life. If what Professor Stone suspected was true, Eliot had made a renunciation or, more in keeping with the *Quartets*' ghost of something 'eternally present' but 'unredeemable', failed to act. Could that failure have been to do with Emily Hale? she wondered. According to some sources,

Hale had believed she and Eliot would marry. Or was the preoccupation with inaction a reflection of the one action he did take – the marriage to Vivienne – and lived to regret? Either way, and perhaps from a young age, ensconced as he was in what appeared to have been a stifling maternal environment, 'the world of speculation' came to exert a powerful influence upon the poet's imagination.

She herself believed there was much to be said for speculation as opposed to action. Keats had a point when he said that unheard melodies were sweeter than those that were heard, for 'piping to the spirit ditties of no tone' they didn't pander to the 'sensual ear' but played to the soul and were hence incorruptible. Much could be experienced in the world of speculation – why, anything at all. Her own life might be considered by some to be a life unlived, but though there was no denying it was a small life, a life spent in rooms, removed from the cut and thrust of human exchange, here was the wonder: she was sure she had lived a life fuller than most sitting at her desk. What her life lacked in spectacle she had more than made up for in substance, and substance was the thing, she often reminded herself; depth. Of course, that didn't mean it was easy being an explorer of invisible shores, embarking once again upon the white sheet of the page.

In contrast to Keats's praise of 'unheard music', however, 'what might have been' became something of an obsession for Eliot. Thus the cold finality of 'All time is unredeemable'. Here she and Eliot parted company because although it was understandable to consider alternative vistas – sometimes unavoidable (there had been images, imaginary scenes that had been coming back to her ever since she'd arrived in this city) – it didn't do to dwell on them. Eliot, on the other hand, seemed determined to go over and over and over alternative lives. The question was: what did this mean for the rhythms of the poem? She believed that the musical qualities of poetry could assert themselves through a poet rather than purely be tools of his, and she believed this was what happened in the *Quartets*; that though their subject was music Eliot had worked instinctively, deploying the musical elements of verse in an intuitive rather than mechanical way. This must mean, then, that there was some extraneous force, an intelligence, at work, if not independently of the author, then being channelled by him in some way.

She removed her glasses and covered her eyes, which were hurting, and then she heard something. She looked down and saw her pencil careering towards the edge of the table, brought her hand down too late, bent to retrieve it from the carpet, then stopped halfway and hung there. After a moment she raised herself and sat very still. Her head had hurt badly just then, on the left-hand side.

She held it in her palm, breathing lightly and evenly. 'It's all right,' she said to herself. 'I'm probably dehydrated. I'll go and have a drink.' But before she could, an exhaustion so profound assailed her that her head sank on to her arms and the heat of the day and a sensation of speed and a great darkness swallowed her up; the archives, desk and papers disappeared and instead she was standing in a hallway.

She has been in this hall before: she recognises the barometer, the hallstand, with its mirror of carved leaves, and beneath it the black boots. Beyond the open front door is a cobbled alley in which the tops of buildings lean over their bottoms, and through the other door a tiny front room with beamed ceiling, sofa, bookcases and enormous table piled with papers and books. She looks down. She is wearing a sundress and sandals. Her hair is in pigtails. She must be no more than eight.

A slap of salty wet wind takes her breath and she turns to the door. And now she sees that the view is no longer the alley of Tudor buildings but a bright seafront: she is standing in the hallway of the house by the sea, and it is how it used to be on early summer mornings when the whole lurching mass of gulls, sea and sky are borne up in great gusts of sunshine and salt and the waves are crashing like cymbals.

She goes towards the door and there are steps leading down to the pavement where she and her mother sit and put on sandals to go to the beach and when they come back up sit to empty their shoes of sand – and now here is her mother coming downstairs, and the stairs are those of the house by the sea: wide, bare oak, going up and up and up. A floral scarf is tied around her mother's head. She is wearing a necklace made of wooden beads. She looks carefully at her mother and feels a rush of nausea. She wonders what sort of day it will be.

Then a man comes into the hall and she sees that it is Professor Hunt. It seems perfectly natural for him to be there, that she should know him; here he is like a friend of the family except that she and her mother do not have friends, and they are not much of a family; she sometimes feels she and her mother are not related at all and are really strangers. The professor and her mother move around her. He is manoeuvring a hamper, tripping a little as he seems wont to do. Measly shins poke from his shorts; sinewy arms and turtle-neck protrude from his T-shirt. He doesn't have shoulders to speak of. But her mother, coming back from the kitchen, has limbs that are strong and brown, large smooth shoulder blades, her neck long and graceful.

She is suddenly glad she is a child and doesn't have to think about having a body. Yet even as she thinks this she becomes aware of it in all its chubby, grubby, eight-year-old glory. As she looks down at it now it appears to her to be distended. She turns her head, but she can still see her arms out of the corner of her eye, her stomach, knees, toes, the end of her nose. The thought of going down to the sea is instantly too much; the thought of the hot sand, of taking off her dress, wading into the water – the more her mother and the professor bustle, the more she realises she cannot do it; the greater their excitement the stiller she becomes. If only she was a stone or a lamppost or a fence! But even the breeze is stirring her, lifting tiny hairs, provoking little rushes and shivers of blood.

The professor looks up and comes over to her. He pushes her fringe back and smiles at her. That is all but she is suddenly filled with towering hope. He goes back to his packing as if nothing has happened – but it has: she will be able to do it now, go to the sea after all; she will go into the sun, over the hot sand, right to the edge of the water. She will wade in, let it take her, swallow her up. She will stay with them all afternoon. But first she must fetch something.

'Where are you going?' her mother calls, as she runs to the stairs. She has the look she wears when she is washing Elizabeth's hair or tying her shoelaces.

'I've forgotten something.'

'Quick, then.'

Her mother turns back to her packing, but the professor watches as she runs up the first flight, along the first landing and up the second.

There are more stairs again after that because the house has three storeys and her room is at the top. As she reaches the third floor she can hear her breath. She bursts into the room and looks around. A shell lies on the windowsill, flat on one side and glossy on the other, mounded like flesh. Underneath, where it is flat, pink lips curl inwards, against which if you press your ear you can hear the surf. She grabs it, is about to leave, when she catches sight of herself in a large oval mirror.

'Hurry, Elizabeth,' her mother calls.

'I'm coming,' she shouts back, but she can't hear her voice. She tries to shift again but her feet won't budge. She is encased in something hard, has become a small statue, albeit with pigtails, sundress and sandals.

There are sounds downstairs like furniture being moved. 'Wait!' she cries, but makes no sound. Within stony ribs her heart beats frantically. She hears a car in the street and tries desperately to move her feet. She hears voices and the sounds of feet on the area steps. 'Stop,' she calls. 'Wait for me!' inaudibly – and this time her heart beats so hard it shatters whatever it is that is enclosing her and she is able to run to the window. Down below her mother and the professor are getting into a black car. She runs out of the room and along the landing.

There is a roaring that terrifies her, though she knows it is coming, and she remembers at this point she has had this dream before. The roaring goes on as she runs down flight after flight, her sandals clattering, body heavy, as if she is still to some extent encased in an invisible cast. She reaches the hallway and it is empty, the front door open, the black car disappearing around the curve of the road.

Then the seafront is fading, she is standing in the other hallway; darker, older, herself – fifty-one? Fifty-two? What do years matter when so many have passed? She is grown.

It is raining outside – she can hear it hissing on the roofs, smell the sulphur of newly wet soil, see the darkening cobbles – but on her lips she can still taste the sea and her hair is wiry with salt.

She looks down. In her hand, like an object smuggled from another world, is the shell. It is smaller, or she is bigger. When she puts it to her ear she can still hear the surf pound. She doesn't want it now: what good is a seashell when she could have had the sea?

The professor woke roughly, sun lapping the base of her neck, wiped her mouth and sat up. The archive was empty. It must be lunchtime. Her head felt thick.

The pain in her head seemed to have disappeared but her left hand was stiff. There was a mark in the palm as if something had been pressing it.

Burning

Of all the terrors of this life, and some were considerable, that posed by the act of bodily congress was for Professor Stone undoubtedly the greatest. 'Who invented this torment?' Eliot wrote in 'Little Gidding', and answered: 'Love. Love is the unfamiliar Name/ Behind the hands that wove the intolerable shirt of flame.' He was talking of Christ's love but might just as well have been talking of romantic love; till he had met Valerie, his sex life by all accounts bordered on intolerable. Elizabeth Stone counted herself luckier. She had never been threatened by the spectre of sex directly except once.

In fact the very thought had been enough to deter her from closer inspection; the whole business of bodies, of attaching oneself to another, of opening or being opened, entering or being entered, seemed to her a deplorable and deeply disturbing business, to be embarked upon only under the greatest duress; the irony being that a great deal of poetry concerned itself with precisely that, veiled of course in metaphor, in beauty, in irony and wit; despite his general aversion to the subject, Eliot had written some surprisingly ribald lesser-known lyrics. Love and its attendant throes was a favourite subject for poets, though Professor Stone was privately convinced that the comparisons to universes, poles, Heaven and Hell were empty conceits, that when people talked of a broken heart they were being fanciful.

She supposed poets were so enamoured of love because it purported to offer elevation from the temporal – though it seemed terrible to her that the portal should be through such a laughable vessel; the human body – her own in particular – struck her as a sorry conduit for any sort of rapture. When she had seen the male reproductive organ in school, whose various stages of activity the biology teacher had done an admirable job of explaining to thirty giggling students, the discomfort she experienced bordered on catatonia; the look in the eye of the thing, its downright ridiculousness; its craning, plant-like mindlessness was a dead weight in her heart for weeks after – and for that moment she was redundant, invisible, washed up on a shore of infinite blankness and consumed by an incinerating heat.

Her senses were used to mortification. At the vicarage there were no preservatives, perfumes or cosmetics. Her foster-mother Rene used vinegar as disinfectant, salt to loosen stains. Food was rationed, soap cut into strips, hot water restricted to inches. But Elizabeth didn't need to be discouraged from exploring her body: she was already appalled by its functions, its secretions, the oil of her skin, the acridity of earwax, the strange aromas of body and of hair. She covered her skin all year through, never walked barefoot, sat on grass or unplaited her hair. She skirted objects, didn't look at people, timed how long she could concentrate, sit still, stay awake, go without food.

Only once did the despised vessel give any hint that it had a will of its own. Told to step in for a classmate in a school play and caught up in the moment, a tissue of endorphins and stage paint, she flung herself against a wall, raising her arms above her head. The gesture was unscripted, her co-star – a hell-raising tyrant – was quite put off his stride, her peers bewildered, but the teacher cried, 'Wonderful, Elizabeth!' and she promptly woke up. People looked at her askance after that, boys in particular: she had violated a preordained belief they held about girls like herself and was now that worst of things, 'an unknown quantity', to be greeted with looks of infinite distrust. If only they had known it had been as bewildering to her as everyone else and that she had no intention of ever letting it happen again.

There were no other public displays but in private she was often beside herself with an emotion she couldn't identify. She punched typewriter keys, tore skin at the sides of her nails, bit down till she tasted blood. When she was ten Rene had marched her to the bathroom to wash her hair. Her skull had collided with the basin; the woman's large fingers had caught the fine hairs at the base of her neck; she had seethed at the kneading, the pounding, the squeezing. Afterwards her vision had pulsed, she could not get her breath. She had run down to the foot of the orchard where she retched as if she would void herself of some unutterable substance and had come back to the house after dark. She could not remember any other outbursts, though there was a scar on her arm whose provenance she was unsure of, and another on her thigh. Perhaps it was why she was afraid when the mood swings had begun in her fifty-second year.

As for sex she was only too glad the whole sordid to-do had passed her by. In institutional life she had found a welcome enclave from the faster currents of life, and in time became an institution herself, 'Elizabeth' to colleagues, 'The Stone' to her students; sometimes affectionately, some-times not. Once, stapling fliers for a Geoffrey Hill lecture to the faculty notice board, she heard one of them refer to her as the 'Virgin Queen' to general amusement. Sometimes, in order to allay an objectless anxiety, she asked herself what a virgin was. A virgin, in its most basic sense, was simply one who had not been joined to another; who had not been entered; broached; breached. A virgin was a fortress then, a thing of purity, even if that purity was rather unusual, rather laughable, rather – sad.

To put things into words calmed her. Despite the

precision of definitions, however, despite the fact that there was nothing shameful about it, even though some people chose to remain as she was (which, of course, she had too), on occasion she had found herself pretending, to people she was sure she would never meet again, that she was married; and once, at a counter in Boots, many years ago now, that she was even with child. And the glow that had infused her. The weight that had lifted from her head, her shoulders and knees. The lightness she felt as she floated along behind the helpful assistant to the relevant aisle. It was astonishing what a little make-believe could do. She didn't analyse her action too closely, put it down to natural creativity, an ability to fabricate to an almost unlimited degree alternative vistas for purely hypothetical purposes. But how it freed her. How it let her soar. Permitted her to inhabit, if only for a moment, an entirely different sphere, after which she could return a hundred times more easily to the one in which she found herself.

There hadn't been any boyfriends, though one or two men had been interested, especially when she had passed the bloom of youth. She seemed to settle into her fate then; cardigans and gelid stare suited her more. The suitors were either much older – Frank, the fifty-something-year-old 'actor' she had met at an embroidery class whose stomach had preceded him, hair was an artistically cultivated grey tangle, skin sprinkled with psoriasis and nose a beak – or unbearable: Gabriel, the balding archaeology student at King's whose body odour imbued the air around him with the smell of wild garlic, wore fedoras and Bogart-style mackintoshes, serenaded her on a classical guitar with long yellow fingernails and brought her unruly bouquets of buddleia that wilted in jam jars and filled her tiny lodgings with the smell of cat pee. Such attentions made her feel worse than none at all and she promptly set about making herself more invisible than before.

She had always hoped secretly that something would happen unexpectedly, a stranger would appear, because however distasteful the workings of bodies were, however grotesque the act of intercourse, it was without doubt easier to go through life accompanied, for social, financial, even medical reasons (it had been proven that people who lived alone died younger). Besides, if she did meet someone who didn't object to spending his life with her, they needn't get down to that dreadful stuff: there were plenty of other diversions – what was wrong with travelling, walking, talking, cooking a meal, cultural trips?

She spent twenty years knowing it probably wouldn't happen but the five per cent that said otherwise kept her sitting and looking and acting as if it might. When she reached the age of thirty-five she decided that if she could convince herself nothing would happen she could spare herself untold nervous energy and actually be in a position where it would be more likely to do just that. But she was still acting with an agenda. And, in any case, it was hard to shake off the habits of a lifetime.

There had never been a man in the house by the sea; her mother hadn't known any, to her knowledge, or, at least, none besides the milkman and shopkeepers. She had never enquired about her father, and later, when she knew how babies came about, it seemed to her impossible that she had ever had one. Her foster-parents merely served to compound the mystery of sex. They had not produced a child, whether through choice or inability she didn't know. The vicar seemed to her like a woman: his skin and hair were softer than a baby's, his nails rounded and well-kept, and Rene – unshaven, broad-shouldered, moustached and heavy-handed – if anything, like a man. She found herself gazing at men, at their stubble, which grew so bestially, at their hair, so different from her own, even when it was long, though she couldn't say how exactly, at their jaws, their muscles, their swagger, surliness then sudden grins; she found herself fascinated by the liquid yodel of their raucous voices, the lazy eyes that could turn upon her so suddenly to terrifying effect.

As a teenager she was both fascinated by sex and horrified by it. It was hardly surprising that words held the greatest eroticism for her, though not the words found in books written for the purpose of titillating ('entered her' – what was she? a lift?). In any case it was unwise to read anything too stimulating because the outlets for the resulting tension, which was merely muscular and shouldn't be viewed as anything more profound, were limited. Usually a brisk walk dispersed it, or a hot bath. If all else failed a translation of Gower could be counted upon to do the trick. There were times, though, when only one thing could be done, and she consoled herself that, according to a survey in a magazine she had read sitting in a dentist's waiting room, 70 per cent of women and 95 per cent of men engaged in the practice on an alarmingly regular basis. For Professor Stone it was a purgation; a necessary evil that freed her mind wonderfully to devote itself once again to more important things. When called upon to perform the activity she did so briskly, with pursed lips and small frown. She was, as it happened, settling down to the distasteful business the evening after her sweltering day in the archives of King's College, the evening after her troubling dream about her mother and the professor of poetry, the afternoon her head had hurt once, badly, on the left-hand side, settled in the bathtub in the small bathroom, her watch on the side (ten minutes, sometimes twelve, it rarely took longer), when she heard something.

It was about seven o'clock, certainly no earlier, though perhaps a little later because the dining hall was already open and groups of students in subfusc were trooping across the quad. Someone was groaning. It sounded like a

130

girl. In fact, she was grunting; the sound was truncated and spasmodic, as if she was in labour or straining to pass a stool.

The rest of the world abruptly fell silent. Heat enveloped the professor and she became very still. The sounds continued, helpless, abstracted, supplicatory. She could not hear the boy; of course, it might be a girl, one never knew these days. The first time she had heard such sounds was from the girl who had lived next door to her in her first year at university. She sat against the wall, tuned higher and higher, but though the lovers snapped she did not; she was shaking by the time they had finished, weaker than if she had run a marathon. She emerged the next day possessed with a knowledge too terrible for words; the world was a new place. The realisation that this was what people did was staggering.

It was strange that overhearing sex should be so much more disturbing than seeing it because, of course, she knew the mechanics, the ins and outs. Over the coming years there had been other opportunities to witness the aural arts of love. She wasn't sure why the chronicling of each detail was better than ignorance but she listened to the creaks, the coughs, the laughter, the thumping, squeaking, muttered 'Oh, God' or, if the participants were enthusiastic, to screams and lust-filled roars; she listened to the pause, the murmur, the running tap, the flush of a cistern, the return of everyday voices. The worst thing was when she thought they had reached the dénouement only to find that the plateau was transitory and the thing still had some way to go. The sensation she experienced while listening was not pleasure but extraordinary pain. Nevertheless she listened as if her life depended upon it.

Afterwards she went back to her work with eyes very bright, imbued with a heat that remained long after the most violent encounters had grown cold; and as she wrote or read, boiled an egg or brushed her teeth, stood in the supermarket, waited for a bus or caught a train, she asked herself again as if it were a thorny philosophical question there was some pleasure in mulling over, such as, What is truth? or, Is textual meaning contained in the person speaking or hearing? – just what it meant that such a thing had never happened to her; why no one had seen fit to embark upon this experience with her. Usually she fell back upon definitions again, reducing the equation to its simplest terms: it was only that two people became one; only that she could not be because being one frightened her.

Water cooled on the professor's skin as the sounds above continued with more vigour. She sat up slowly and bent forwards so that her head was resting on her knees. She drew her legs into her body. The aching in her chest that usually accompanied such bouts of surveillance had become so pronounced this evening that breathing was difficult. She thought: Perhaps it's because I'm back here in this city. Perhaps it's because I'm old. She hadn't admitted before how difficult it had been to return here. And she had never admitted that she felt old.

The evening deepened, the sounds continued, but the professor was no longer thinking of the girl upstairs. She was thinking of another evening, another girl, and whether the memory was doubly pungent for being so long buried or whether it was the shock of seeing herself as she would a stranger; clearly, as if for the first time. Professor Stone groaned.

A girl with glasses and thin limbs is standing at a window, balancing, it seems, about to topple forwards. She has watched the round of parties and gatherings from this spot for weeks now: students clutching bottles, students clutching high heels, students clutching each other. It is her first term in the city of books and no one seems to be taking studying seriously except her, and now, six weeks in, she has become invisible as she supposes was inevitable; people bump into her, look through her; if she speaks in a tutorial they look around with astonishment as if a voice has materialised out of thin air. But tonight is the last night of term and everyone is invited to a party in the bar – ghosts included – and so although she knows no one she has bought a dress, something she has never done in her life before and probably never will again, and is toying with the idea of becoming visible, if only for a few hours.

The grass below the window is insanely smooth, chilling in its perfection and terrifying in its indifference to the bursts of laughter that ricochet around the sandstone walls like gunshots and make her heart beat fast. She wishes she could be grass. There is a pain in her chest and she waits there at the window until the pain makes it unbearable to stand there any longer, her centre of gravity tips forwards, and she goes to the sink.

She shaves her legs and armpits, and dresses (purple with puffed sleeves, from British Home Stores). She sprays her hair and applies eye shadow she bought that day as well as she can, never having worn it before, holding her glasses in front of one eye then the other. She looks at herself, sits on the bed and waits for another ten minutes, pinching the skin on the back of her left hand. Then she gets up and goes out.

She is in the grip of a sort of mania as she crosses the quad; a delirium, an ecstasy of terror. As she descends the cellar steps to the bar, she cannot even hear properly, bounces off the wall, stumbles down the last step. Amid jostling shoulders, smoke and thumping music she threads her way to the bar, presuming this is what one does, and leans on her elbow. This is also what one does: she has seen it in films; she half expects the barman to slide a drink to her. Instead she is ignored for several minutes, then discovers there are free drinks on a table. She takes a plastic beaker and stands against the wall to sip the watery cider. A line of sweat runs down her left sleeve and drops from her fingertips to the floor; she brings her arm up and holds the beaker with both hands.

The effort has already been superhuman but now it occurs to her that the ordeal is only just beginning because she has yet to speak to anyone and that is what everyone else appears to be doing – or they are dancing; dancing is out of the question. She scans the shining sea of faces and shoulders, the air kisses, bobbing breasts, tries to think amid the clamour, to single out a non-threatening target with which to interact.

After three or four minutes she decides that she will hold out ten minutes more, for the sake of the dress as much as anything (it cannot actually be seen in the dark), when there is a voice at her shoulder and a person is saying: 'H-hi, my name's K-K-Keith.' The boy has an absurdly symmetrical face, is licking full lips. 'I l-l-like your dress.'

'Thank you.'

'I-I've seen you around. W-what are you studying?'

'English.'

'I-I'm studying l-l-law.'

'Oh.'

'I-I like your dress . . .'

He asks her to dance; later it occurs to her that she could have said no. He leads her through the crowd to a small, jostling space between flashing lights and she promptly becomes a block of concrete. He points his elbows and turns his torso from side to side. She has never seen anything more ridiculous. Her heart is murdering her; her face aches as if she is crying, but she is not crying: she is smiling, or trying to. There are hoots and shouts from the rest of the room, thrashes, whoops, the gleam of hungry eyes and hot faces, but the pair dance decorously, their faces averted from one another, and for longer than she thinks she can bear.

Afterwards he brings her to his room. They briefly discuss English and law, the merits of the college over the faculty library and their respective schools. Then he says, 'I-I think you're very b-b-b-beautiful,' and sits on the bed beside her. 'C-can c-can c-can I k-k-k-kiss you?' She thinks she is going to faint with discomfort, but she doesn't want to offend him, and cannot think of anything to say that will not.

When he pulls away he is swallowing, breathing heavily, his eyes half closed. He grabs her arm. 'Don't leave.' His stutter has vanished, the hand is surprisingly firm.

She says: 'I have to go.' Then she says: 'I don't want to.' But her voice is breathy and lost in her throat.

He is feverish, appears to be seeing something beyond her; there are beads of sweat on his head. 'Stay still, you don't have to do anything.' And then he is trembling, pressing himself on to her, fumbling with his flies. He presses her back on the bed and makes a noise as if someone is shaking him very fast, and when she risks a look he is assaulting himself furiously with his right hand. She shuts her eyes.

When it is over he fetches a T-shirt and says breathlessly: 'G-G-God, that was intense.' He wipes himself and hands it to her, smiling now, once again full of goodwill. It is a moment before she takes it, and then raises herself, the sprayed hair listing to starboard, to wipe the stain from the dress.

She returns to her room by back passages and for the rest of the night sits on her bed staring at nothing. Over the next two terms she sees him occasionally across the quad. He begins dating a girl who lives on her staircase and seems happier than she was with his performance. When they bump into one another his eyes pass over her. The bar is not ventured into again, books take up every spare minute, the phenomena of sex a chapter not to be reread.

Dusk was deepening in the bathroom, the sounds above escalating fast. The professor listened till the final act, then closed her eyes. She sat curled, her arms around her knees for a few moments longer before stepping out of the bath, and when she did, her movements were slow, as if a battery had run down. She wrapped a towel around herself and went to the door.

The room beyond was in darkness. Laughter and voices drifted up from the gravel paths, a distant clamour from the hall; if she wanted dinner she would have to hurry. She stayed where she was. She could have been sleeping because her eyes were closed and her breathing was regular, except she was upright, and her knuckles, gripping the doorframe, were perfectly white.

Whoso List to Hunt

He is talking about Sir Thomas Wyatt. Bells are tolling. Gusts are lifting the horse-chestnut branches into a grey sky.

Edward Hunt's room is as she remembers, perhaps marginally neater, a result, she guesses, of it being the end of term rather than the beginning, as it was when he interviewed her. They are sitting on the embattled sofa, a few odd chairs and the threadbare rug, the chosen apostles, arrayed at his feet, breathing air heavy with tobacco and the mealy smell of books. She glanced at him once as she entered. So: there he was; she remembered now. Then she found a place in the corner between the sofa and the window and didn't look up.

They are veterans now, second-years. She has waited for this moment and finally it has come, but it is not as she imagined it would be. The college is as it was – the porter; the quad; the glass corridor; the garden of roses – but the professor of poetry is not the same. He is waggling his boots, flicking through his book in heated flurries, surveying them with all the tenderness of a wolf. What is more, he doesn't appear to have noticed her. Has he heard about her exam result? About how her right hand didn't recover for weeks? She could drink only sugar and hot water? She had forgotten what day it was, where she lived, her name? If he knows nothing else, he must have heard about her mark – all the tutors have – and at the thought of this, pleasure washes over her with sickening relief. The wave is followed, however, by a dart of fear: from such a victor what feats will he expect? This very hour she must reassure him that she won't let him down, he was right to choose her; she must raise her hand and say something that will stagger him with its brilliance. She must somehow find words, but he is saying, in a dark voice: '. . . and words, in a society where the monarch is God, are a dangerous commodity.'

Then he begins to read and she remembers something else now: the way he holds a book, breathes more deeply as he reads, and how other things fall silent:

> 'Whoso list to hunt, I know where is an hind,
> But for me, helas, I may no more.
> The vain travail hath wearied me so sore,
> I am of them that farthest cometh behind . . .'

He rests the cigarette over the ashtray, the tip quivering (she had forgotten that his hands shake: Why is that? she wonders). 'So,' he says. 'What do we think of that?'

The fact is she thinks a lot; she could give an entire lecture on this single sonnet. She has thought of little else for a week and the page in front of her is a medley of black, red and blue ink, a tissue of asides. But now she has seen him again everything is different – and, it seems, looking around, she is not the only one who is struggling for words. Her fellow students have been stunned into silence by this man who looks more like one of them than a tutor, refuses to be called anything but 'Edward', smokes cigarettes back to back, swears like a sailor, wears bovver boots and clothes with holes in them, and looks as though he could detonate at any minute. As the silence continues he slaps the arm of the chair, growls, 'Come on! I'm not here for the fun of it.' And now it is hopeless: no one can speak. So he scans, hunting his first victim.

She ducks her head, heart battering, but she thinks she is safe: the armchair is partly obscuring her, though he may be able to see the top of her head. What happened to her plan to impress him? Her comments, the page crammed full of them, just waiting to be said?

'Marcus.'

Her shoulders sag with relief and she opens her eyes.

Marcus coughs, his knee bouncing up and down. 'Erm – it's quite claustrophobic, isn't it?'

'I don't know. You tell me.'

'Erm, well, yeah . . . it is . . .'

He taps the cigarette exasperatedly. 'OK. We have a sense of enclosure, poetically, politically, personally. What else? Kirsty.'

'There's a danger in pursuing the thing you want because it's taken by someone else,' the girl says.

'Good.' He takes another puff. 'And who is this someone else?'

'King Henry the Eighth?'

'Right. Anything else?' He inhales and holds the breath, leaking little clouds of smoke from his dark nostrils.

'It's a love poem,' someone says.

'OK . . .'

'An unrequited-love poem,' Hannah says. 'But we're not sure if that's because the hart won't or can't reciprocate. Though I think that would probably mean certain death anyway.'

'OK.' His voice is deeper: he is easier now. 'Is it a sonnet?'

'Yes.'

'How do we know?'

'Fourteen lines, iambic pentameter, divided between an octave and a sestet. Petrarchan,' Hannah says coolly.

'Good. Now we're getting to the heart of it. And what exactly has Wyatt borrowed from Petrarch?'

She could have answered every question so far, but she could answer this one particularly well. This, if she were timing things perfectly, would be her moment. She would begin by saying that Petrarch's '*Una candida cerva*' is an exalted neo-Platonic symbol, and the golden horn of Diana, goddess of chastity, enhances the purity of the beloved, but that Wyatt introduces sexual bawdry and cynicism into his sonnet so that the visionary nature of Petrarch's '*una candida cerva*' is completely written out. She would say that the words Petrarch (a potential claimant for 'Caesar' and crowned in Rome as the king of wits) places in the mouth of his deer: '*nessun me tocchi*', are reappropriated and revalorised by Wyatt as '*noli me tangere*', thus returning the phrase to its original form and reducing Petrarch's phrase to imitative secondariness, disqualifying Petrarch from occupying the position of Caesar either in relation to the deer or the tradition of the sonnet and thus transforming Wyatt's own position as a 'follower' for ever. If she was timing things perfectly this is what she would say now. A wave of searing blood sweeps up her neck and into her hair. Now, her heart roars. Do it. Do it! But her arm won't raise itself and neither will her head. She feels his eyes pass over her and after a moment she hears him say: 'David.'

She is falling. But there is no need to panic, she tells herself. The way she will do this, the way she will play it is to wait for him to come to her; then she will astonish him. Yes – that's better; but she will not be the one to volunteer information, she won't show off. She will let him come to her. Though she must admit she is surprised he hasn't noticed her already.

David is saying: '. . . and the fact that Caesar inscribes his ownership on the deer's neck seems particularly ominous in light of Henry the Eighth's wives' fates.'

'Indeed.'

He liked that – she can tell by the deepness of his voice. 'Remember the sense of menace wasn't simply an aesthetic effect,' he is saying. 'The poem wasn't circulated privately in manuscript for nothing.'

Her heart is hurting. She fixes her attention on the rug at her feet. There seem to be fleur-de-lis there, though why they should be cavorting in trees she doesn't know.

'Everything is encoded,' Kirsty says, 'though the letters are "plain".'

Now that was a good point. She would have thought of it, she is sure. She tries to think quickly but for a few minutes her mind is blank. When she returns he is saying: 'You can't flee from the king any more than the hart can. He'll find you.'

She should speak after all; she shouldn't wait for him to find her. It won't seem like showing off now; in fact, if she doesn't speak soon she will be conspicuous by her silence.

Jessie says: 'It's inverting the traditional religious connotations of Jesus's words, "Don't touch me because I am not yet risen." Here Caesar is the king and the hind is Anne Boleyn.'

'Excellent,' he says, and instead of blushing Jessie whitens with pleasure. And now she knows she must speak because everyone else has answered.

He is saying: 'Yes, "Caesar's I am" is a particularly vivid illustration of the word-made-flesh motif, and one that simultaneously recalls not only Jesus's words to Mary Magdalene, "Do not touch me for I have not yet risen", but his earlier instruction to his disciples to "Render unto Caesar's what is Caesar's", nicely confusing state and religious loyalties; a reminder, if Wyatt's readers needed it, that the Court, which held the power of life or death, was now also the centre of religious influence – had just become so in fact. That's why the dating of this sonnet is so significant – indeed, the reason why this sonnet could only have been written before a certain time . . .'

The date, she thinks, the date . . . And even as her heart begins to palpitate, his eyes find her. It is as if he has smelt her fear: the black eyes glint in satisfaction – she remembers now their particular penchant for her distress; their unique ability to make her feel she doesn't possess clothes or even skin but only internal organs. 'Elizabeth,' he says, his pleasure evident. 'Can you enlighten us?'

She stares at her page in all its biroed, arrowed, annotated glory, as if by staring at it hard enough she can conjure something that is not there and never was; there is no date, she is sure of it – 'Whoso List to Hunt' one of the many sonnets by Wyatt that cannot be dated exactly; but she should know the significance of that too apparently. What makes it all worse is that she suddenly sees, now he is looking at her, that he knows everything, hasn't forgotten her, has heard about the exam result; his eyes have a fire, a familiarity that wasn't there when he spoke to the others. She sees she is still his discovery, that he has waited to teach her, and now he is waiting for her to illuminate them all – that he has made her wait, as she believed she was making him, for this very moment. Her heart is beating so slowly she feels as if she is moving to and fro. She hears herself say: 'When it was written . . . does it say? I don't think it does – does it? I mean – I know it was published in 1557, that was when Richard Tottel published the collected anthology, but I'm not sure when Wyatt wrote this particular sonnet . . . I'm not sure of the significance of the date in this particular case . . .'

'Oh.' He makes no attempt to disguise the disappointment. She is dimly aware that he says: 'Can anyone help Elizabeth out?'

There is a willing volunteer. 'Henry the Eighth accused Wyatt of committing adultery with Anne Boleyn and imprisoned him in the Tower in 1536 and Anne was beheaded the same year, so Wyatt couldn't have written the sonnet after 1536 because the "hind" would have been dead. In fact she was married to Henry in 1533, so it's likely to have been written before that,' Kirsty says smugly.

'Indeed. Does that make sense, Elizabeth?'

She nods, her face scarlet.

'Was there something else you wanted to say?'

She cannot hear herself for her heart but she presses on anyway: 'Yes, there's an interesting juxtaposition between, ah – wildness and ownership: the hart wears a collar, is Caesar's but also wild.'

The thinness of the remark is immediately obvious.

'Indeed,' he says politely and it is worse than if he had brought her up outright. Silence closes over her.

He begins to talk about the Henrician court, its cruelty, its favouritism, its mercurial politics. She writes, along with the others, turning pages, pretending to check, nodding for appearance's sake, writing gibberish.

When it is time to leave, she gets up. 'Essays in my pigeon-hole by five o'clock Friday,' he says. 'No excuses. Oh, and avoid the Penguin edition at all costs. Unfortunately it's the only edition Dingwell's have. Why are they so fucking crap?'

Then the door is closing and they are walking down the corridor, past the shattered rose garden, down stone steps, beneath moody October skies and the plunging branches of the horse-chestnut tree.

She tries to rationalise what has happened: she made a mistake. It is not a disaster. She left it too late, that's all; she should have answered earlier. The answer she did give wasn't a bad answer, just not the sort you would expect of a girl with the highest marks in the university. He will simply know he was wrong about her. That is all. He is probably not even as disappointed as she is.

They pass through the lodge. Albert calls: 'See you next week, Miss Elizabeth.' She smiles and waves to him but can't speak because her face is set in some kind of mask.

They go up the street, the boys aping their new professor, cocky now that the inquisition is past, taking tortured drags from invisible cigarettes, mussing their hair, growling in gruffest Mancunian. One grimaces, farts and makes a comment about textual heretics.

She lets them go on and, when they are far enough away, sets her knuckles against a wall and drags them till they are wet.

Words and Music

She should have gouged the left hand: it is difficult to hold a pen; she should have thought. Think, she tells herself. Think.

She is sitting in the Upper Room beneath the eyes of the gods, three days after the fateful first tutorial with Edward Hunt. There is only one thing to do now: write an astonishing essay. Of course, she had always intended to write an astonishing essay but her recent humiliation makes it vital. She likes Wyatt, which is a start. She likes the sound of him, the blockish incantation, the clandestine courtly words that ring ominously, like footsteps in dark passageways. But after three days she has written no more than a paragraph. The paragraph goes like this:

In 'Whoso List to Hunt', as in the Epistolary Satires, the desire of the speaker to be where he, in the Stoic style of self-possession, declares himself to be (Kent and Christendom), remains in doubt, just as the moment of ineffable joy and presence when Christ said to Mary, 'Do not touch me,' becomes a fleeting moment of irredeemable loss, reaching towards some presence which always evades grasp, a confused and painful recognition of cold immutability. The hunt never ends and never begins because neither it nor the speaker has anywhere to go.

She grips the pen more tightly but no more will come. Can the hart of desire, finally within reach, be escaping at the very moment she stands on the brink of attaining it? Was it for nothing she forged ahead inch by inch all last year? She would give anything to go back to that year now, yet when she was there she wanted to be here. Is this how time works, she wonders, tantalising with promises of the future, then making us wish we were back in the past?

She finally manages to write twenty-two more paragraphs, submits the essay – a garbled little piece of theory – and buries herself in Middle English. A week later she gets it back:

Good essay, Elizabeth, especially for a first attempt in entirely unfamiliar territory. There is much here to savour and admire: especially sensitive and persuasive readings of 'Eyes That Last I Saw in Tears' and the 'Penitential Psalms' for instance. But I do think your argument might be strengthened (and occasionally qualified) by more intense concentration on the physical production/transmission of the texts you discuss.

There is also the question of style: if you want to say something, Elizabeth, say it. You have become lost under mountains of theory.

If you can solve this, very little work needs to be done in order to turn this into a healthy resource for Schools.

The comments aren't that bad. But the mark – the mark is C plus.

She sets to work on the next essay in a dream, digging herself into the gruesome world of Inns of Court satire and Elizabethan Grotesque. If she closes her eyes she can see Edward Hunt's lips saying these words: 'virulent', 'spurious', 'scurrilous'; see how much he loves them. He didn't ask her any questions this time and she didn't proffer any answers.

She has been making notes for a week now. The bundles have been getting bigger. By day she tries to rein them together, a spider's web of interlinking strings and marks. By night she wakes floundering in an ocean of paper. The dynamic has changed: she is afraid of words now and they have sensed her fear and grown stronger. When she finally makes a start at five in the morning in the college library it is because writing anything at all, no matter how poor, will be better than existing another second not doing so.

The form of the language in Elizabethan satire [she writes] *mirrors the nausea and disgust of what it conveys. The satirist's production of a word-self, continually growing in size and potency, coincides with the progressive elimination of a real self, his multi-vocal pyrotechnics simultaneously implying verbal abundance and empty loquacity: 'res' and 'verba' joined Janus-faced back to back. The narrator wishes to rid himself of his task if he knew how, but his words are brutally cut short, shot 'full in the throat' or 'stick fast in mire and are clean tired'* . . .

Halfway through she falls into a waking dream in which hordes of words armed with toothpicks lift up her finger-nails. When they begin on her eyelids she cries out and wakes to find someone shaking her. Hannah and Jessie are staring at her. 'You were talking,' Jessie says.

'Sorry,' she mumbles.

'How long have you been here?'

'All night.'

'You need to sleep,' Hannah tells her.

'I'm fine. I just want to get this done . . .'

The next day a note arrives in her pigeon-hole: '*Come to my room at 4. Edward.*'

She waits at the bottom of the stone steps. The day is grey and blustering. A voice says, 'Are you cold?' and she turns to see him coming along the corridor wearing the stone-washed denim jacket and a shapeless jumper, of which he seems to have an endless array. 'Go on in,' he says, and bounds past her up the stairs. 'I'm just going for a slash.'

She sits on the knobbly sofa, her feet amid the fleur-de-lis, flanked by Johann Sebastian Bach and Ian Curtis, ambassadors of sober fortitude and godless despair respectively, and wonders which would be the more prudent stance to adopt. She knows she is here for only two reasons: he is either angry or he is disappointed. Neither of which she can do anything about.

The door slams, he crosses the room and drops into the armchair. 'So,' he says. 'How are you?'

'Fine.'

'Are you?'

'Yes.'

'That's not what I hear.'

'Oh.' She smiles at him briefly. 'Well, I am.'

'Again not what I hear.'

She frowns and looks at her knees.

'What's this about staying up all night in the library?'

'I didn't.'

'I know that you did.'

'It doesn't matter . . .'

'It does.'

His face is twitching with something. 'Why do you say everything doesn't matter? I wouldn't be talking to you if it didn't matter, would I?' He is trying to light his cigarette. 'I've got a million and one other things I could be doing.' He chucks the lighter away and looks up. 'What on earth have you done to your hand?'

She flushes and covers her knuckles. 'Nothing.'

He glares at her. 'Something else that doesn't matter, I suppose.'

He watches her with blackest intent for a moment, then gets up and puts the kettle on. Beyond the window rosebushes rustle. The dusk is coming but clouds are still rolling over the river meadows, branches levitating; the sensation she has is one of infinite and gnawing unease. He pours hot water, hands her a mug, goes to his seat and takes an amazingly loud slurp of coffee. If she wasn't feeling so desperate she would find it hard not to laugh. She raises her own mug, takes a sip and almost spits it back out. Besides being scalding – despite being scalding – it is the worst coffee she has ever tasted but the discomfort is a welcome distraction. She wraps her hands around the mug more tightly.

'You haven't been back two weeks and already you're in some sort of state. You did amazingly in Mods, you've got nothing to prove, so what's bothering you?'

'I'm not bothered.'

'Let's make a deal: I won't lie to you if you don't lie to me.'

'I'm not lying!' She looks at him.

His voice takes on a tone of darkness. 'You forget that I can read you.'

She can feel tears pricking and grips the mug more tightly. 'I just wanted to write a good essay . . .'

'And you did. I know you didn't get the mark you wanted but I want you to do better. I know you can do better and I'm going to see that you do. The fact is that essay made me angry. I felt like putting you over my knee and giving you a good hiding.' He laughs at her face. 'It's a joke, Elizabeth, but I'm serious about the essay; it was a travesty – drowning in theory. Did you understand what you'd written? I certainly didn't. It was just words; sounded good, meant nothing.

'But what I really thought was, where's Elizabeth? What happened to the girl I met at the interview? You said you felt the sonnet, d'you remember? You said you didn't think Shakespeare was in love – a heinous thing to say – and I loved it. But this thing you handed in was like a car manual. Elizabeth, whatever writing is it should begin with feeling. That's what poetry challenges us to do, Elizabeth: feel things. You got caught up in words. Go back to the music.'

He looks out of the window. 'I still haven't and probably

never will read anything like your interview essays. There was an immediacy, a spontaneity that I've never seen before . . .' He smiles. 'Not that we see any of that in the everyday Elizabeth.'

There is a soft tinkling sound and boiling liquid is seeping through her skirt, the cup in two pieces, the handle still attached to her thumb.

He jumps up. 'Are you OK? Did you hurt yourself?'

She doesn't know, is as surprised as he is and in a great deal of pain. He tears handfuls of tissues and thrusts them at her, then passes the box, saying: 'Yes, yes, use them up.'

He watches her blot her skirt, holding it away from herself, her face burning, and says: 'I always seem to be rescuing you in some way. At the interview you fainted, if I remember. My God – was that a smile I just saw?'

It is. A smile is blossoming painfully, obscenely, though there is nothing really to smile about, and she keeps her head bowed and goes on dabbing because she discovers to her horror that if she isn't careful she will cry.

He says, 'Do you know how much better you look when you laugh?' then sighs as if it is a hopeless case. 'You don't like yourself very much, do you, Miss Stone? What I'd like to know is when you began feeling like that.'

She goes on dabbing at the skirt fiercely. He regards her for a minute, then takes the wet tissues from her and she places her hands over the wet patch.

He says: 'Anyway this working's got to stop, OK? I'm worried about you. There's a community of people here but no one ever sees you.' He ruffles his hair. 'I want you to know you can come and talk to me if you're worried about anything. I want to be your friend, not just your tutor.'

She realises she is staring at him and tries to lower her eyes; his own are very dark and very bright. The moment passes. His leg jerks into action, he clears his throat. 'And now I have to turf you out. Take the rest of the day off. Go and do something you enjoy – preferably involving human beings. And try to stop injuring yourself.' It is as she goes down the corridor he delivers the deathblow. 'And don't worry,' he calls. 'I'm sure the next essay will be a masterpiece!'

The Fourth Day: Morning

A masterpiece. Could one tell what one was writing before it was finished, Professor Stone wondered, or did you only know once you had written the very last word? She was meeting Edward Hunt again this evening and must report her progress with 'The Poetics of Sound' but so far was no further along. She glanced at a puffy scar that lay across the knuckles of her right hand. He had said: 'You got caught up in words. Go back to the music.' Well, music was the problem now. It had all seemed so easy standing in the foyer of the British Library, but now she was beginning to think Edward Hunt might be right: writing about the music of poetry was akin to speaking the divine name: forbidden, impossible, a contradiction in terms.

She removed her glasses and rubbed her eyes. She hadn't slept well. The couple upstairs hadn't renewed their lovemaking but she had found herself dreaming the dream she had dreamed when she was ill last winter, the dream of the kitchen and the table and the stranger. This time the kitchen was deserted and she was alone at the table. She heard footsteps in the corridor but the door did not open and she woke aching with grief and lay awake thinking of those words of his about masterpieces the afternoon she spilled the coffee, before throwing off the bedclothes and taking up the *Quartets* again, but was no further along when light came. A breeze touched her arms now and she was glad of it. Thinking would be infinitely easier if only this heat would let up, she thought; everything seemed to be slowing, her brain, her eyes, her blood – and was it her imagination or did the left side of her head feel tight? She sat up straighter. She wouldn't think about that.

Across the room the elderly gentleman was undoing the top buttons of his shirt. His fingers trembled a little. The shirt was the old type with no collar and she could see the folds of his neck, white like a baby's, and now beneath it the shape of his vest. In the centre of the younger man's shirt was a dark oval of perspiration. Mad dogs, Englishmen and academics, she thought, because that was what they were, she was sure of it; and it was so heartening just now to see two like-minded souls treading the same high and lonely road as herself because years, whole lives, could go into researching a single poem, a single book – and it was possible occasionally to wonder if some of those had been wasted ones. This was what Elizabeth Stone had heard about people whose lives were over through age or illness or simple bad luck: that the thing they most wished to have again wasn't wealth or health or even love but time; time made everything possible and so was the one impossible, one unredeemable gift. That was why she was overjoyed, at this point in her life, to know she hadn't wasted it – though every so often there were inevitably moments when one wondered if one had made the best possible use of every moment. Perhaps, for example, she should have devoted herself to Spenser rather than Milton; if that was true there were ten years wasted right there. Perhaps she should have looked into Eliot sooner. And so, set against these uncertainties, it was immensely reassuring to see these two figures here at nine every morning outside the panelled door waiting for the pretty young archivist to come tripping along with the keys, in her sandals and sundress; to see them sitting across from her all day, seeking the grail, scanning one page, moving on to the next.

The archivist was busy in the small office adjoining the archives and she felt free to watch the two men unobserved.

She had heard them speak German and in their mouths the language seemed ancient and venerable, rough-hewn and pure, like a mountain spring rushing through ferns and moss and flinty rock. She thought again that they were beautiful; she didn't usually fall back on such banal adjectives but just now couldn't think of a better one. The light was making an aureole of the old man's hair; the younger's cheeks were milky in the heat and blue veins rose from the backs of his hands. They were definitely on some sort of mission, she decided. She had a moment of fancy in which she imagined they were angels sent to earth to bring something back; perhaps they had brought something to earth, she thought, like the magic objects children attempted to transfer between worlds in handkerchiefs. Angels were supposed to have lifetimes, weren't they, and, like humans, progress towards transcendence or damnation? Perhaps they had been sent to earth as a penance, the chief of police relegated to checking parking tickets. Or perhaps they had come to save someone. In any case she had no doubt that their work was of the utmost importance, else why would such a frail and elderly man be sitting day after day in this sweltering room? Why would this young man – no more than a boy – stoop over his papers with a seriousness that bordered on the devout? Yes, they reassured her beyond measure. And then, as she turned back to her work, they disturbed her, and she didn't understand why.

She sighed, propped her head on her hand and gazed at the paper in front of her. The marks she had made above the lines merged and separated again. Suppose, she thought, there is a pattern to existence – nature was not random, mathematics had proved that – an imprint in all things that self-replicated, a formula that repeats itself *ad infinitum* and to which all things conform – a song, a blueprint. Suppose there lay within each thing its own vibrational signature; how could one tune into it? Music was a great facilitator. She had heard that brain-damaged people regained some use of their mental powers when exposed to certain types; not herself, of course. She gazed again at the scansion marks. They reminded her of something. As she looked at them now, through half-closed lashes, they were like breakers rolling in from the sea, but that wasn't it. What, then? Some sort of code. Morse, perhaps. She had read that people became more proficient at receiving Morse code when it was taught as a language that was heard instead of read, and that to reflect the sounds practitioners begin to vocalise a dot as 'dit' and a dash as 'dah'. Dit, dah, damyata. Shantih, shantih, shantih.

The church in the square struck the quarter and her stomach lurched. Oh, God, she thought. Oh, God, just let me write something. Then she looked up and the old man was blinking and tugging at his collar. She rose to her feet, then saw that he was holding a piece of paper up shakily, standing. He was persuaded to sit by the young man and they began to talk in excited voices. The professor sat, too, her heart beating hard. So they had found what they had been looking for. The missing piece. Who knew how many years had led up to this moment?

The old man was rising, gathering his jacket and dropping the cane, which the younger retrieved for him. A cool gust rushed in as they opened the door, went through, and it shut with the familiar clatter. The archivist came out of the antechamber and turned to Professor Stone. 'I think they found something,' the professor said.

'Oh, I am pleased,' said the young woman. 'They've been searching for leads on the old man's sister for weeks.'

She looked at the young woman. She said: 'I'm sorry?'

'They were researching papers bequeathed to the archive by the old man's sister,' said the archivist. 'They lost touch when they were young; they weren't sure she was still alive.'

The professor blinked. 'His sister?'

'Oh, I do hope they find her. There isn't much time, the old man being so elderly himself . . .'

Professor Stone was silent for a moment. 'You mean,' she said a little severely, 'the gentlemen are not academics?'

'Oh, no,' said the archivist. 'No, it was for family reasons they requested access to the papers.'

Professor Stone frowned. Then she craned her neck to the side in a curious movement, as if it was stiff. She said: 'I see.'

The archivist excused herself and went back to her work but the professor stood a moment longer before sitting down. And when she did she was surprised to find that a heaviness so sudden and so total gripped her that it was some minutes before she could bring herself to lift the pencil. She had written no more than a few words when a rustling made her look up.

A crane fly was bumbling towards her across the desk, rising then dipping, its legs trailing against the papers. The professor dropped the pencil and sat back. She had always harboured an irrational fear of long-legged insects. As it grew nearer she moved the chair back. Then she jumped up and waved a piece of paper frantically but the insect only rose angrily before settling on the papers that were right in front of her. She shooed, but this time, though it rose and hovered drunkenly, it sank back almost immediately, and after a moment its legs sagged a little.

She stared at it, breathing hard, her glasses dangling from their chain. She had heard that the creatures only lived a day; this one looked as if it was going to die right there in front of her. She shooed it again but though the draught from the paper buffeted its body it didn't move.

She closed her eyes and swore softly. There was nothing for it: she would have to move all her papers and the box files. She seized the papers either side of the insect, flinching as she did, her heart beating wildly because at any minute it might fly up into her face, into her hair, and relocated to the end of the desk, but she had hardly read more than two or three sentences when she realised she needed the papers the insect was resting on. Well, it was too bad, she would just have to make do with what she had; she wasn't going near the thing again – it had already disrupted her quite enough. Nevertheless from time to time she found herself glancing back at the insect.

The sun was hot on it. 'Well, if you're going to die you've chosen a stupid place for it,' she said. 'Why not a nice shady corner – why not under a leaf? Anywhere but my desk, for goodness' sake.' She worked aimlessly for another fifteen minutes. When she looked back the insect was trying to rise, its legs slipping from under it like a bad skater. 'Oh, just die,' she muttered. 'Please just die.' She read a while longer. When she looked again it wasn't moving at all, though she thought one of its legs had sagged a little.

It was half an hour before she looked again. This time the insect was quite still, poised crookedly, one leg bent under it. Had it been like that before? she thought. She didn't think so. She returned twice more to the poem and twice more glanced up again, then sighed deeply and closed her eyes. It was no good, she would have to move it. She would do it now and be done with it. She would put it outside. It could die there if it wanted to.

Her hand shook so much when she touched the sheet it was resting on that she jostled it and the insect bumbled away blindly across the desk and she jumped back. She tried again, but it blundered into the pine partition at the back of the desk and attempted to climb it, legs scrabbling. She stared in disbelief. Now it was not resting on any paper at all and in order to move it she would have to slide a sheet under its legs. She seized one of the Xeroxed pages of *Four Quartets*, on which she had scored iambs and spondees and anapests, and holding it at arm's length advanced like a knight on a dragon.

She slid the paper towards the crane fly but only succeeded in pushing it forwards. She dropped the paper, turned and wrung her hands violently. It was some moments before she could turn around. When she did she seized the sheet and slid it towards the insect hard. It rose crazily and she saw its furious eyes and its long nose and strange face, and dropped the paper, her heart beating so hard that it slowed and she felt sick. She gave a small gasp, almost a cry, and in one movement swept the insect to the edge of the desk with one hand, caught it with the other and ran to the window where she dropped it – meant to drop it – outside but, failing to raise her arms high enough, deposited it on the sill, then turned gasping, and dragged her hands over her body again and again as if she would flay it. It was some minutes before she could look around.

When she did she saw that the crane fly was exactly where she had left it. 'There!' she cried. 'There's the window.' As if hearing her it rose shakily, hovering for a moment, like a rickety magic carpet, but succeeded only in colliding with the sill. She watched it try to rally again but this time it couldn't and had to resort to stroking the sill with the tip of its foreleg.

She was crying and didn't know it. I should have moved it earlier, she thought. It will die here now and it's my fault: I left it too long in the sun. But she couldn't bring herself to pick the insect up again.

She returned to her seat and replaced her glasses with a trembling hand and took up her pencil, but she couldn't find her thread, and it was not long after that that she closed the box files and went out of the room without looking back at the windowsill.

The Fourth Day: Afternoon

The archive felt empty that afternoon. Professor Stone asked if the gentlemen would be returning and was told they would not. She didn't know why this piece of news should affect her so badly but it did. In fact, it was hard to stay in her seat. Once, she glanced at the windowsill but couldn't make out the crane fly.

There were now six hours till she met Edward Hunt and if she didn't make her discovery soon she would not be able to work. All the symptoms were present: inability to concentrate, sweating palms, lurching stomach – most uncharacteristic and most worrying. She had been unable to eat any lunch and had sat looking at her hands on a bench in the square. She suddenly remembered she had felt just the way she did now once before. But that time she was not sitting at a desk on a summer afternoon but on a parapet in winter, at midnight.

Several hours after midnight to be precise, and not really a parapet, more of a balustrade, but Elizabeth Stone is sitting on it, and it is winter, and beneath her feet there is fifty feet of air, and beneath that five small fir trees in terracotta pots, and beneath those paving stones bordering a quad. This ledge is where the pigeons sit in the day. When she is writing in her room they are her constant companions; she is used to their incessant cooing, the manic blink of a round red eye. There are no pigeons now; they are all tucked up in their nests like good, sensible birds because it is cold – surprisingly cold; so cold she should be shivering but she is as still as a stone.

Moonlight rests like a skin on fir trees, benches, dining hall and chapel. A plane drones in the vaulted dark above. There is no wind and the sound carries, warping in the frosty air. It seems to suggest there is nothing unusual in what she is doing, in the slab beneath her legs, the blackness beneath the soles of her shoes.

On the desk through the open window in a pool of lamplight lie the dismembered remains of an essay. It is her second essay for Edward Hunt and it is three days late. She received a note in her pigeon-hole this morning, which said: 'Where's my bloody essay?' The note was terrifying; nevertheless she still hasn't been able to finish it.

The problem is two-fold: it isn't just that she is confronted with texts that refuse to be written about, it's Edward Hunt himself. Professor Hunt expects the world, expects her to rise from the ashes of her defeat and present him with a masterpiece. She has been in this room for three days and three nights; she has wept and fasted and prayed, but so far nothing has risen except three suns, and they have all set again. She has waited for the stone to be rolled away but no angels have come; and now she would rather slip away into this blackness than submit an essay that is only worth another C because worse, infinitely worse, than the threat of another failure is the expectation that she will produce gold. Well, she has been spinning for days but there is only straw.

She knows about essays now, the groundwork, the angle, the development point by point, but that is all theory; each essay for him is a unique and unrivalled horror, in which colour-coding and word-maps, thought-trees and brainstorms, plans A, B and C fail to help. What is more, this time he has assigned them texts that neither need nor acknowledge a reader, defy attention, exegesis, are self-enclosed, self-projecting, self-abusing – whip themselves up into an onanistic lather over nothing; texts that declare: 'He that thinks more badly of me than myself, I scorne him fore he cannot' – all typical of the crazy, contrary, topsy-turvy world of Elizabethan Grotesque, but not helpful to the feverish undergraduate who wishes to excel.

And so, faced with an impossible task, she has taken Edward Hunt at his word – didn't he encourage her to say what she was feeling? She has said she has given up, suggested that the texts should be taken as a template for a type of literature on which no critical purchase can be gained; that the writer and reader's interchange removes the act of interpretation from a plane of shared discourse to another plane altogether, that when verbal meaning is transferred to a non-verbal realm that realm is more akin to music and so cannot be spoken about. It is a cheap trick and one he will see through immediately.

It has come as something of a surprise to her that she does not want to live any more – at least, not in a world in which she has disappointed Edward Hunt. She has never enjoyed life particularly but it is still rather shocking. Before she came to the city of books, though unhappy, she never considered suicide. Now there isn't even any uncertainty. The only thing holding her back is the thought that there is a chance – a very small chance, granted, but a chance nonetheless – that she may kill herself for nothing: that the essay may actually be tolerable, worth a B, perhaps.

The sky is reddening now in the east, the violet-orange of the night giving way to real colour. It won't be long before someone comes into the quad. If she is going to jump she must do it soon. She asks herself again the all-important question: is the essay on the desk behind her a disaster? She tries to read the words as one who has never read them but cannot; she has eaten and breathed and dreamed them for more than a week now, and when she wakes she has mouthed them.

Suddenly it occurs to her that she can put off the decision to slip from this ledge: she can wait to see what mark he gives her and then come back to it; then there will be no hesitation; she can consign herself to oblivion wholeheartedly – perhaps she can even find a more private, failsafe way to die. She only came out here in the first place because she couldn't find anything to tie around the light-fitting and there are no baths on her floor. Why didn't she think of this before? She is not thinking clearly.

The moment she realises she can postpone death her body slumps forward and her arms begin to shake. She must be careful, must get herself back over the balustrade before she gives in to relief. She tries to shift her weight backwards but her arms are now so weak that she cannot lift herself. Her heart moves up to her throat. She closes her eyes and tries to take deep breaths but this only makes her faint. She opens them and shifts backwards very gently; she shifts herself again, and again, then suddenly topples on to the balcony in a heap.

After a while she gets to her knees. She cannot remember her body ever feeling so heavy or slow. She crawls back through the window, scraping her leg badly, and latches it. Then she lies on the floor by the radiator with her eyes closed. She goes to the desk, puts on her glasses, staples the essay together and puts on her coat.

She walks to the lodge through frosty quads, walks slowly because the ground is jarring, her knees bend more than they should, and in the lodge slips the envelope containing her essay into the pigeon-hole. It will reach him by mid-morning. 'I gave up,' she writes on the front.

That moment passed and now here was another, infinitely more important, though she could not have imagined it then. The whole of her career rested on this moment; the whole of her life; there was not much else to it. If she didn't pull her ideas about music and poetry together now she never would. The reader – the reader she had always been writing for – would ask her this evening what she had discovered, and she would not be able to answer.

The sun was low now over the earth and the city solidifying like molten metal, while the sky, which was dark blue, seemed to be weeping the way that a wound does. The city was nearing the in-between time of day again and Professor Stone saw that the evening would be especially beautiful because the heat had bruised the day, broken it, and its perfume would linger late into the night. The evening would be beautiful, and if she could just find something to say she could go out and be part of it.

'I'll read from a different part of the poem,' she said to herself. 'Sometimes that works. I'll do that and then I'll leave it.' The thought of leaving the poem without having found her thesis was one of the most frightening thoughts of her life, but she had been putting off this moment since she had had her grand idea; perhaps she had always secretly known that it would be impossible. She flicked on in the poem and began to read from the second movement of 'Little Gidding':

> In the uncertain hour before the morning
> Near the ending of interminable night
> At the recurrent end of the unending
> After the dark dove with the flickering tongue . . .

She suddenly saw something she had missed before: Eliot was letting near rhymes slip in medially, sometimes terminally, 'Compelling the recognition they preceded,' she murmured. The lines were a parody of poetry; Eliot was teasing the reader. She remembered something he had written: 'Neither arrest nor movement,' Eliot had said. '"Neither movement from nor towards, ascent nor decline . . . And do not call it fixity. We can never arrive,"' she said

quietly, and on this hottest of days she suddenly felt cold.
'There is no end, because arriving would render time
redeemed. And hence unredeemable.' Unredeemable, because
already redeemed. Could that really be it? She turned back
to 'Burnt Norton', feeling her way as one dowses for water,
despite the pencil, which was trembling unhelpfully:

```
    /    /  _   _   /  /
Time present and time past
 _   /  _   _   /  _ _   /  /  _
Are both perhaps present in time future
 _   /   /  _  /  _ _   /  /
And time future present in time past . . .

   /    /  _   /   /  _
Time past and time future
 _    /   /   _   _   _  /  /
What might have been and what has been
 /  _   /  /   _  _  /  _   /  _
Point to one end, which is always present.
```

(ll. 44–46)

The words said that time was unredeemable, but the
sound of 'time past' was contained within 'time future';
rhythmically 'time future' was analogous to 'time past'
and 'Time present'; what 'might have been' was the inverse
– and equal – of 'what has been'. 'And they all point to
one end,' she said. She should have expected it. The paradoxical truth of the Gospels, the way up the way down,
the way forward the way back. There had to be two
rhythms; there had to be equipoise. That was the hidden
music, unheard until it was noticed; that was what enabled
the poem to be 'still' and 'still moving'.

'Eliot using "present" in two different ways,' she scribbled,
'doubly disorienting – yet ultimately illuminating. Because
the duplication of rhythm, sound, allows meanings to merge,

present time to also be in presence as that which is before us. Brain assimilates all "presents" into one.' She was going to write more but instead removed her glasses and placed her hand over her eyes. 'Thank you,' she said, to no one in particular. She had it.

BOOK III

'We had the experience but missed the meaning.'

*

'Dry Salvages'
Four Quartets, 1941

Happiness

When nineteen-year-old Elizabeth Stone submits her second essay to Edward Hunt she doesn't know it will change the course of the future. Grey mist is rising from the river meadows as she walks back from the lodge. Sitting on the floor of her room she watches the sun emerge from it. And when the light is everywhere and the pigeons have returned to the ledge and there are footsteps and voices below and bells calling to breakfast and prayers and the sound of buses and cars in the high street, she crawls into bed and sleeps the sleep of the dead.

That week the city of books undergoes a strange transformation. Vast numbers of seagulls alight on ledges and battlements and towers, filling the dry city air with the ghosts of seaweed and surf. The main reading room of the library is closed because of a burst water pipe that tears the wall as if it were no more than a curtain; snow comes down like feathers; a bell breaks in the church in the square – an event that has not happened for at least three hundred years – and a new one fitted that rings oddly among its aged compatriots. But all these things go unnoticed by Elizabeth; she studies in the Round Room instead of the Upper Room, trudges through the snow; doesn't see the gulls, smell the surf or hear the bell.

At the end of the week Edward Hunt asks her to stay behind after the tutorial. There is sleet in the air. She hears the horse-chestnut rushing in darkness beyond the window from her perch on the last but one step of the stairs as she waits for the others to leave. The rose garden is in turmoil tonight, the grey air above the red-brick walls weeping and buffeted, dark feathers of yew chasing invisible phantoms of night. He opens the door, shouts, 'OK!' and she gets up and goes in.

He makes coffee, hands her the biscuit tin, sits with a thump in his armchair. She doesn't think she has ever seen him so agitated as he is this evening. His leg is swinging, he is tapping his cigarette packet, ruffling his hair. 'Have you managed to get some sleep?' he says. It doesn't look as if he has.

'Yes,' she says.

'Good.'

She decides to forestall criticism, or at least lessen the blow, and says: 'I'm sorry about the essay.'

The boot swings higher. 'I hope you didn't miss lectures to do it.'

'No.'

He raises his eyebrows, the mouth twitches.

'A couple.'

She goes to take another sip of coffee and then gives up. Politeness no longer matters. It is obviously as bad as she feared.

He inhales and looks out of the window. 'Why do you think this essay is bad?' He scratches his head, taps ash, scratches his head again.

She knows what he's doing: he's seeing if she's even aware of her shortcomings; if she isn't it will bode ill indeed. 'There's no argument,' she says. 'There's no consideration of any particular school of thought. There's no structure; there's not much of anything, really.'

He takes another puff, worries his hair, then, with a great bounce, leans over, retrieves her essay from the top of a pile beside his chair and wings it to her.

'Aren't you going to look?'

'I'd rather not.'

'We can't go any further till you do.'

Her shoulders drop. She turns to the last page.

I could go on . . . endlessly . . . with observations, but not criticism. Simply the best essay by an undergraduate I have ever read.

A smile wobbles on to his face, vanishes, explodes and then vanishes again. It's interesting to watch. 'What do you think now?'

She sits very still and a great heat is all around her.

He snorts and pushes up his hair. 'I read the last bit at six-thirty this morning. It takes a lot to make me pleased then. I kept shouting: "This is good!"' The boot is bouncing higher than would seem possible, joined as it is to a human kneecap.

Still she says nothing, though she is breathing deeply and fast.

'Well?'

She swallows and shakes her head.

'What?' He taps the cigarette. 'What don't you understand? Elizabeth, critics can't write the way you do. It's spontaneous, original, alive.'

'I didn't think—'

'What didn't you think?'

'I don't know.' Because she is not really thinking in the normal sense of the word any more, only gently vibrating, so she cannot be expected to know what she was thinking or what she knows. She has no idea how long they have been sitting there. She supposes this is happiness but it's not as she imagined it would be: it's more like sadness; it's a burgeoning, a breaking apart; if this is happiness then she is only just bearing it.

Then he says: 'I think we should meet.' As if it was necessary, with things as they are, as they stood, in light of the situation.

Another period of time passes before she hears someone who sounds like herself say: 'Oh . . .'

And the person who sounds like Professor Hunt say: 'What do you think?'

And the person who sounds like herself replies: 'OK.'

He makes a grunting noise that could be 'Right.'

Then he rises, and they stand for a minute as if they would shake hands. And there is some incredulity that they have just arranged this thing they were able to arrange all along. There is amazement at this power they possess.

He says: 'Next week.'

'Yes.'

'I'll drop you a line.'

'OK.'

She looks at him very briefly, then goes out of the room, past the blasted garden into the surging night, and wonders how long the interval is between flash point and death in cases of spontaneous combustion. Turning out of the lodge she startles an elderly don. She goes up the street running, orange light splashing her hair and her bag and the essay, her face upturned, rain and tears wetting it.

The Still Point of the Turning World

She met him tonight. There was rain on the glass and rain in the heights and she couldn't see out, just herself and the room, running with water and brimming with light. She was weightless, wait-weary, hearing clocks strike, flare and die out; and bells that always told her in clarion motion the timing of things have quite changed their tune, are weighing their anchor; moments are lingering longer than ever, and strokes never sounded so long or so slowed.

They are meeting at eight. It is raining outside and there isn't a world, just a room and a page, a hive and a cell; each quester, each light. All day she has been following words with her finger, hearing clocks strike, till at last now she is rising, putting away papers, returning books to the stack, climbing steps that curve around a wall and passing a man in a pool of white light.

They will meet at eight. It will be raining out there and the room will be brimming and bowing with light. She will look out and wait for the strokes that refuse to be struck and go out of the room up steps that curve round a stone like a bowl, up from a womb and look out, at the night filled with rain and the rain filled with light.

The professor of poetry and his pupil walk away from the Round Room towards a road leading off the square. It is eight o'clock in the city of books; a Thursday, Hilary Term, February 1980. The girl stopped in the doorway of the building before she went down, to see him wait. He didn't see her. She held the moment, didn't spend it. She held it, and saw him, and then she went down.

So it goes, see the moment passes, will pass, has passed, is passing again. The wind took it then or maybe the rain did, swept it high over the square and the town and the crossing, the bridge and the river, the gardens and plain. See time starts, will start, is starting once more. A lamp shudders, a bolt groans, somewhere something cracks. One foot then the other, the rhythm commences, and we begin, too, for with time we are back.

She doesn't look at him at all now; they don't say much more than 'Hello'; she knows he is wet and that he is smiling. She thinks: This is happening. Then nothing else.

The things she notices are shoes, the steps mismatched and overlapping, ambling oddly side by side. Shoes that never negotiated cobbles together before, appearing and vanishing beneath legs swinging left and then right.

He says, 'What a night,' and something else she doesn't catch, and is walking close as if to shield her, but he doesn't need to because there is heat all around them and a very great light.

They turn at a corner where the winds meet and go through a door beneath the sign of a horse and groom clanking on a chain. The room is heaving and bright and they are stunned for a moment, their faces wet. At the bar he says, 'What do you want?' sees her confusion and smiles. 'Take your time,' he says.

She tries to remember what women drink, realises she doesn't know and says loudly, to save anyone having to ask her a second time: 'A pint of beer. Please.'

But the ordeal isn't over. 'Which one?' the barwoman says.

She flushes, selects any and roots for her purse. He closes her hand over the money and smiles at the woman. 'And a Coke, please.'

They find a small table. She is worried she should have ordered a Coke too. She is worried they will run into someone from the tutorial group though they are not doing anything wrong; she doesn't know what they *are* doing, that is the problem. Is this some sort of unofficial tutorial? She has her books and her latest essay with her in case.

She decides to make a start on the pint – she surely should have ordered a half? – while she is ahead, and with the first mouthful makes an unfortunate discovery: she doesn't like beer. He laughs loudly and says: 'Leave it. We'll get you something else.'

But she says fiercely, 'I like it,' and takes an even bigger gulp.

He looks around the room, inhaling, easing into his first cigarette. 'I used to come here as an undergraduate,' he says. 'There was a don who had a Great Dane. I was terrified of it.'

'You came here as well – I mean, to university?'

'Yes.'

'Which college were you at?'

'Newbury.'

'Did you study English?'

'And classics.'

She takes up the pint again. She mustn't let herself be distracted from drinking; this is one task at least that she can discharge creditably. When she looks up again, he is gazing at her in evident enjoyment. He bends forwards and whispers: 'Have you ever been in a pub before?'

She considers a moment, then shakes her head.

He laughs loudly. 'My God, Elizabeth, where've you been? Locked up in some ivory tower?'

She wipes her mouth. 'With my foster-parents.'

'Foster-parents?'

'Yes.'

'I didn't know that.'

She looks across the crowd. 'My mother died when I was small.'

'I'm sorry.'

'It's all right.'

'Have you got any other family?'

She shakes her head.

'Do you get on with these foster-parents?'

'They're all right. I haven't seen them since I've been here, actually.'

'What – you stayed up in the holidays?'

She nods and grins at him.

'What are you going to do when you finish?'

'I don't know – do another degree, get a job.'

He picks up his Coke, shifting his cigarette to his other hand. He looks concerned but he says: 'Well, you've got a gift so when you finish here the world is your oyster. You can do whatever you like.'

She takes another mighty slug, then places the glass on the beer mat and discovers it is necessary to perform the movement carefully. She doesn't know if the feeling that the ligaments in the back of her neck have been cut is owing to the beer or something else but is daunted by the fact that there is still a good third to go.

'What do you want to do?'

'Write something.'

'I'm sure you will. There's an obsessional feel to your writing, an urgency, as if you're exorcising something – it's great, that's what makes it alive.'

But she shakes her head. 'You don't know what it's like,' she says, 'writing those essays.'

'I wouldn't bank on it. I used to be a lot like you, you know. It's the terror of failure that makes you so good.

Someone who found it easier wouldn't write as well. You summon it, dredge it, from some unplumbable depth.'

But he doesn't know what she means, about writing for him; that kind of terror.

He is looking fondly at the cigarette. 'You will write something.'

He looks around the room and his face falls a little, and she says: 'You don't like being here, do you – I mean in this place?'

'How d'you know?'

She shrugs. 'Where would you rather be?'

'Oh, nowhere in particular. I really don't think there's anywhere I'd feel more at home. Before this I worked in cities up north. I suppose I'm as at home in academia as I'll ever be – and there are good things about this place. I get to do pretty much whatever I like now the college are used to me – and, of course, every so often someone comes along who makes the job worth doing.' And he looks at her.

Outside something crashes against the wall. The chain jangles frantically in the wind. She flushes and turns back to her pint and he says: 'For someone who's never had a drink before that went down a treat.'

She covers her mouth and he turns to blow out smoke. When he turns back, he says: 'Have I told you how much better you look when you smile?' Then he frowns. 'And why d'you keep looking at your watch? Is there somewhere you've got to be?'

'No,' she says.

'Then why are you counting off the seconds?'

'Because I'm – happy.'

'Happy?'

'Yes.'

He laughs, then the smile slips away and he blinks and taps the cigarette. 'Good. Well, I like talking to you, too, so we're even.' He draws his head back a little and says, apparently brushing something from his knee: 'And we can meet again. Would you like that?'

She says: 'I have to go to the toilet.'

He laughs. 'OK, but you can answer the question first, can't you?'

'Yes.'

'Is that a yes you can answer the question or a yes you want to meet up?'

'Yes. I'd like to. Meet up.'

He watches her go through the crowd, first one way then the other, hot and bothered in her tank top, spectacles steamy, and says, as she passes a second time: 'That way, I think.'

In the toilets she stands in a cubicle and leans against the wall. She comes out, goes to the washbasins and stands in front of the mirror but doesn't look up. When she does raise her eyes, the pupils are black and enormous. They take in the pig-pale lashes, the spectacles, the fringe, kinky from the rain, then close again. It is some minutes more before she goes out.

When she returns he says: 'By the way, do you know who you want to study for your special author next year?'

'Milton.'

'Oh, wonderful. You'll enjoy Milton. I've got a great edition of *Paradise Lost* you can borrow. What have you read?'

'All of it.'

'What – all of Milton?'

'I think so.'

He shakes his head. 'And what did you like best?'

'I'm not sure. I liked *Samson Agonistes*.'

'Indeed . . .'

'*Samson Agonistes* is in the Eliot poem you sent me – "O dark, dark, dark, they all go into the dark", except that Eliot uses "interstellar" instead of "interlunar".'

'Really.'

She frowns suddenly. 'You know those quartets?'

'*Four Quartets*?'

'Yes.'

'What about them?'

'I thought I had heard them before.'

'Had you?'

'I don't think so. That's what I was trying to tell you in the letter. Though I made a mess of it.' She looks down. 'I was trying to impress you.' Outside something crashes again and they hear the wind squeal and fall upon itself.

He says quietly: 'Have you ever considered that I might want to impress you?'

They stand under a light at the corner of the street in the centre of the city; she gives him her new essay and he puts it inside his jacket. The rain is coming down in flurries, the heavens are taking leave of their senses, but everything is still. She supposes they must still be inhabiting the world in some way or people would bump into them, but though she can see what the wind is doing she cannot hear it, and she cannot feel the rain, and feels only a ring of fire all around them. She is sure they must be giving off some pulse, some force field – people must see a light emanating from them – but no one stops, no one exclaims.

*

Thirty-three years later Elizabeth Stone makes her way from the archives where she has been working to the place where she will meet her old tutor Edward Hunt.

It is seven o'clock, a Friday, the end of Trinity Term, and the promise of holidays and freedom is in the air. The evening is vibrating with heat, the sky no more than a haze and the great library sailing through its meridian like a galleon. It has never looked so splendid as it does now, with every windowpane flashing light and every stone turned to amber. Just now, the spires clustering around the square remind her of promontories reaching out to sea. The sky still holds the light of the day and its heat, as the sea does in summer. It is strange, she thinks again, that this city has always seemed to her like Chaucer's 'litel spot of erthe', 'that with the see Enbraced is' – because the sea is many miles away; in fact, in the whole of the British Isles it might be harder to find a place further removed from it. Perhaps it is because the land is so flat here, she thinks, the sky so large and filled with light. Or perhaps it is because the buildings are pitted and smoothed and abraded as if by water. Some even bear what appear to be tidelines part way up the walls. And then there is the rawness of this city, its starkness, the impression it gives of immensity, that nothing can change it, that its walls and turrets and squares are as immovable as an iron cliff's frowning front.

She passes the Round Room beneath the blue dome, the gate where she and Professor Hunt met years before – on an evening that could not have been more different from this, but nevertheless here, at this very spot. This spot here, she thinks, as she looks up at the steps, and now as she passes, that spot there.

There are finalists everywhere, their arms around one another, singing, drinking from bottles, waving balloons and banners, wearing capes, masks, party hats, boas, their gowns slipping, shirts open, ties around heads, shoes in hands, many of the men bare-chested. As she turns down a narrow street leading off the square she is swallowed by a group of them and feels obscurely happy, as if their carousing is a celebration of her own private triumph and the years that have led to it; the contribution her thesis will make to the world and the new field of enquiry it will open up.

When she arrives at the Horse and Groom a few minutes later it, too, is heaving with black and white bodies waving glasses and bottles aloft. He is standing in the road so that she doesn't miss him, wearing his indefatigable denim jacket despite the heat, looking rather boyish, his hair even more tufted than usual, smiling at the mayhem. There is no room inside so they sit beneath flowerboxes at a slotted picnic table. 'Good day?' he asks, and she tells him it has been, 'Though it didn't begin very promisingly,' she says. 'And you?'

'Yes.' He smiles. 'A good day.'

He is mellower tonight, more observant, less harried than she has seen him. From where they are sitting they have a view down a broad street leading into the centre of the city, up a long leafy road heading north lined with colleges and official buildings, and past the great library, the square to the south. Behind them, twisting away in a golden stupor, is a narrow street at the bottom of which, if you follow a high sandstone wall, you arrive at the river; the plain; and a road that leads out of the city to the west. They are at the centre of the city and the heat has pooled here; there is a pink dustiness to the street, the pavement too hot to touch with bare feet, the tarmac sticky. They are at the centre of the city, but it feels to Professor Stone as if they are at the centre of the world and a circle that has been traced around them – many circles, and each circle has as its centre this point, which is still, in spite of the jostling bodies and hubbub. The evening is burgeoning in the last light and the rowdiness of the crowd serves only to further set it apart, as a discrete entity engaged in some private reverie, slipping all the deeper because it goes unnoticed.

He says: 'There hasn't been this sort of weather for years.'

'Yes,' she says. 'It was quite unbearable in the archives today. I was thinking about the poor finalists in exam schools.'

He gestures to where a boy is spraying a group of girls wearing underwear over their subfusc with champagne. 'Well, these ones are all right.'

She smiles wryly and says: 'I remember it well.'

His eyes glint mischievously. 'I can't imagine you drunk.'

'No . . .'

'How did you celebrate?'

'A Victoria sandwich from Marks & Spencer, I think.'

He laughs loudly, then coughs. A new development, she thinks, a little twist of age.

She says, 'I ate it in the river meadows, reading up for the MA,' and then wishes she had not, because it brings up the uncomfortable matter of her last year in the city of books, the last term she was taught by Edward Hunt.

But perhaps she has been concerned unduly because there is no sign that he has heard; no sign except, perhaps, for a downward glance as he taps the ash from his cigarette before looking round expansively. He says: 'So how is it coming?'

She has waited long for this moment and sits a little straighter in an effort to contain her pleasure. 'I've got something to show you.' She places two pieces of tracing paper covered with pencil marks on the picnic table, one on top of the other.

He frowns, peers closer, then holds one down by the edge. His hands are red and more swollen than she remembers. He is holding the cigarette away from the tracing paper in his other hand and it trembles. The tremor, she is gratified to note, has always been there.

'What am I looking at?'

'The rhythmical templates of *Four Quartets*.' In spite of herself she is flushing a little. 'Eliot, in parts of the *Quartets*, really is trying, for the first time in English poetry, I think, to make verse a purely musical vehicle.'

He inhales and raises his eyebrows.

'It's like a mystical induction.' Her eyes are bright behind the glasses. She is rushing. Stop, she tells herself. Stop. But she continues: 'Or perhaps I should say a "musical" one, and from here, from this starting point, I hope to talk about other poems, other poets . . . possibly prose . . .'

She gathers the tracing paper, ready to talk about other things, because it doesn't do to dwell on one's success – though this success has been a long time coming, a lifetime, actually, and she feels it wouldn't do much harm to bask in this moment just a little longer.

It seems he agrees with her because his eyes are shining. 'I knew you'd do it.'

She shrugs and puts the papers into her bag, brushes something from her skirt and straightens it, smiling pleasantly, as if nothing much has happened, and glances around. But her body has been transformed into molten matter; she has been dismembered and dispersed – the sensation is exquisite; for one moment she no longer has to hold the disparate and painful pieces of herself together but can let them drift on the tides of the evening, knowing nothing can be lost, and yet, even as the first waves of gold ebb gently away and for a moment leave her cold, she wonders if it has been quite worth all the effort, all the years; a very small part of her cannot help wondering if this success, in its inordinate and unexpected and incalculable wonder, can ever, really, balance all of that.

Late rays of sun are sinking behind the roofs of the great library. Cars pass into the high street and up the long, leafy road to the north with a reverberation that warps and rustles the matter surrounding it with ever-echoing, ever-receding sighs. She inhales briskly and says, 'Do you remember the last time we came here?'

'No,' he says. 'Did we?'

The medley of warmth and brightness vanishes. 'Yes, the first time we met up. The wind was so strong the sign was knocking against the wall all night.'

'Oh, yes. Sorry. It was a terrible night, wasn't it?'

The world is once more liquid light. 'I'd never been into a pub before.'

'You drank a whole pint of beer faster than I drank my Coke.'

Her mouth twitches. 'Actually I'd never had beer before either.'

He says: 'I presume you've acquainted yourself with the awful stuff by now.'

She smiles, but she isn't thinking about what he has said, then suddenly decides she has to say something, and just as suddenly she knows that this is what she came to the city to do, though she hasn't known it till this moment. She sits up, opens her mouth – and a boy who has had his back to them loses his footing on the kerb and stumbles into their table.

His eyes are glassy. 'Sorry,' he says, and promptly veers into another. His friends bear him away to the kerb where he sits down with a bump.

Their drinks are spilled, or what is left of them. Edward Hunt flicks drops from his hand, smiling. 'We can go somewhere else if you want,' he says. 'The trouble is, everywhere will be the same tonight.'

'No, no,' she says, 'it's fine.' And then she says, 'Edward . . .' and his name intrudes so strangely into the clamorous air that for a minute she cannot continue, until she realises the pause itself is exaggerating whatever must come next. She laughs and straightens her beer mat. Then she swallows.

She says: 'I never meant to leave things as they were. I didn't intend them to end – like that. I wanted you to know.'

He is studying his Coke, a small frown playing on his face, but he is smiling as well, and after a moment he says: 'It's all right, Elizabeth. I know.'

'Good,' she says. 'Good . . .' She laughs again, and then

because the relief is so powerful she closes her eyes for a moment, touching her temple.

'Headache?'

'No.' She takes her hand away, smiling brightly. 'Just tired, in a good way.'

'You're working too hard.'

'Well, I suppose I have to,' she says. 'I can't be up and down to London all the time—' And then she stops talking and becomes still, wondering what is wrong with her this evening and if she is fated to say one wrong thing after another.

But again, after a moment, he saves her, and says quietly: 'Then we'll have to make the most of it while you're here, won't we?'

'Yes,' she says. 'And thank you – thank you for making time to see me.'

He smiles tightly at that. Again it seems that his face will cloud; but after a moment his leg begins to swing and he says, frowning and tapping the cigarette: 'There's a concert before you go back, a string quartet. I wondered if you wanted to go.'

She stares at him. Is this some kind of joke? He couldn't have suggested anything worse. How can he even suggest such a thing after what happened the last time?

But his voice has taken on the tone of darkness that she loves and he is saying: 'Don't worry, it's Haydn, not Beethoven. I wouldn't do that to you again. Of course,' he looks at her mischievously, 'if you'd rather not risk it . . .'

She smiles. 'Why not? That would be pleasant, break the work up.'

'That's what I thought.'

'Let me know how much the tickets are.'

'We'll talk about that.'

Unimaginable Zero Summer

Professor Stone is lying in bed. There is laughter in the dark beneath her window, scrabbling and muffled thuds. From the river meadows she can hear the blare of party hooters. There is a crash below and the cranky sound of ceramic rolling across concrete. Finalists trying to climb the Virginia creeper. The gardener won't be pleased.

Something heavy falls on to the lawn. The laughter becomes silent and helpless. There are gasps, breathless voices, a whoop; the sound of stumbling feet. The revellers retreat to the other side of the quad. They pass through the archway, their steps sandy on the flagstones. She hears trees swaying in the darkness, the last bus in the high street sigh and depart, a small bird twitter in nearby shrubbery.

She wants to sleep. There is much to do now she has found her way with the poem. Tomorrow she must go to the archives first thing. But the pain in her chest won't let her drift off and there are sights and sounds and smells that have been coming back to her for days now, in this bed beneath the eaves, or waiting on the kerb in the main street to cross the road, or walking to the shop to buy milk, or standing by the railings where the big roses grow, looking out over the river meadows that possess a surplus, an excess she cannot extrapolate: she is standing in darkness watching a figure move inside a lighted window; she is standing in a rose garden and the edges of things are lost in whiteness; she is walking up a street that seems to slope upwards.

She asks herself what happened and the answer is

'nothing'. But these are the moments others cluster around, moments in which it strikes her now she may really have been, as T. S. Eliot would say, 'alive'.

In his last quartet Eliot wrote of an 'unimaginable/Zero summer'. If someone had asked Professor Stone about the summer she was taught by Edward Hunt she might have described it similarly. The six weeks were set apart, a shimmering mirage of heat, light and stone, and now each day a hundred tiny things – the heat on the playing fields, the prisms of cloud in the morning, the sound of her shoes in the cloisters – remind her of it. Afterwards she talked of that summer in only the most general terms. She would say that she had done things she hadn't since she was a child: swung her arms as she walked, balanced on kerbstones, trailed her hands over surfaces, lain down in grass and watched the movements of clouds. She might have said that she and the professor had communicated by a series of asides and rejoinders, but not that she kept the notes for years, delighting in the pens and the papers, the postcards and envelopes, the fold here, blotch there, half-moon *e*s, ant-like *g*s, ambitious *y*s; the trademark ellipses, tantalising, arch, faintly coquettish, trailing into nothing, into thin air . . .

You have managed, I am sure you realise, to create three masterpieces instead of one. I await the next essay with excitement and some trepidation; meanwhile I remain awed, if somewhat bewildered as to what to suggest next . . .

Outdoor adaptation of The Duchess of Malfi *at St Catherine's on the 9th. Want to go?*

She may have said she borrowed several of his books, but not that the real reason she did so was to inhale the musky smell of tobacco, that she treasured the waxy flakes of lilac ash that fluttered out from between the pages and disintegrated upon touch; she would not have said that the purpose of reading these volumes was not to digest the printed words but the ones written in the margins and that her highest excitement was occasionally adding a small rejoinder of her own: '*Sterne figures the Fall as a fall into language, but Locke's chapter on association of ideas didn't appear until the fourth edition of the* Essay *(1695) so could not play a formative part in the author's piece-meal scheme of things . . .*'

She wouldn't have said he lent her music. Music without words, cassettes in plastic cases, Bach, Beethoven, Chopin, Mozart, with indications as to which passages offered the greatest rewards to the attentive listener. The cassettes, unlike the books, remained firmly closed. She read reviews instead; that summer she spent as much time revising airs, adagios, rhapsodies and sonatas as dissonance, sprung rhythm, imagery and paradox. Sometimes music was playing in his room when she arrived and on those occasions she did not stay long. She didn't think he ever guessed, not even after what happened at the concert, her true feelings about the matter.

Sometimes they went walking, to the river mostly, taking the path between the chapel and the orchard, breezes stirring the luminous horse-chestnut flowers and taking her breath more completely than a hundred November gales. One afternoon, when the clouds built up to astonishing heights, they walked to the meadows to the north of the town – she forgets what they are called now. Once or twice, coming back to his room through streets tepid with twilight, blanched with warmth, and fettered with smells of dinner from college kitchens – going the back way into college through a small door in the garden wall sprouting weeds and wildflowers – they heard three cycles of bells ebbing and answering one another, as if remembering something only to forget.

She would not have mentioned the walks, or the music. She may have said they found it necessary to meet to discuss work: Milton, the poet as playwright, the perils of authorship, the art of Defoe, but not say that sometimes for hours afterwards she had stood by a wrought-iron gate looking on to the back of his building; that it was cool by the gate, breezes stirring the yew trees, night flowers opening; that there were many in the half-dark which gave up their scent.

They never entered the rose garden, though it was in its prime, the flowers chaotic, clustering, spilling in glorious and drunken disarray; the door was locked and so was the gate. 'I must get the key,' he said. 'Remind me.' But she didn't.

She would not say that when she came back to her room, dusk thickening in the warmth of the eaves, below her the sounds of feet and voices, silvery clink of tableware – sometimes the chapel piano – her body was warm but she shivered, that she woke hours later and the day was curdled with light and heat, and gardeners were talking, water sprinkling, bicycle wheels ticking; she would not say that days did not really begin or nights end but both took place within something larger.

If her mind asked why she slept little but wasn't tired, could concentrate on nothing at all, felt full though she hadn't eaten, present yet insubstantial, taut, as if tethered to the earth yet existing in unfathomable heights above, she told herself she couldn't be sure other people did not experience similar things. If it enquired further, threw up things harder to explain – why Edward Hunt passed the end of her cardigan belt around his finger one day, and leaning forwards said, as if thinking aloud, 'I wish I had something like this;' why he replaced her pencil in its case lying next to him in a tutorial, closing the lid as if he wasn't putting her pencil away in case she forgot it but sealing her soul for eternal safe-keeping; why his face was transformed whenever he saw her, in the supermarket, in the street, in the square, the covered market, the lodge; why he always saw her first, why neither could stop smiling, while people parted, bells rang, showers came, cyclists rang impatiently or moved around them like smaller planets – she would reply that he was fond of her, she was his discovery; of course he was proud of her; of course he was pleased.

If her mind enquired even further, asked why when he was absent she wished time would speed up and when he was present that it would stop altogether, why after she left him there were hours of helpless weeping and a pain in her chest that made breathing difficult, she directed it to other things, reminded herself that there were many things in life that could not be explained; an afternoon towards the end of term for example, when he presented her with an envelope that contained a ticket to a string quartet's concert. She was quiet for such a long time that he bent down, peering around the curtain of hair, and said: 'Where've you gone?'

She fought valiantly and at last said: 'I'm very happy.'

'No,' he said. 'You're unhappy; now how have I managed that?'

Music of the Spheres

For as long as she could remember Professor Stone had lived with a pain in her chest. The pain came and went with varying intensity, could be sharp or dull, a sensation of tearing, or gnawing, or aching. She could be without it for months on end only for it to slyly reinstate itself when she wasn't looking. She went to see a doctor about it the winter she moved to London from the city of books. She was too young to have heart problems but he arranged for tests anyway. The results being negative, he sent her away with the advice to rest, lighten up, and join some sort of group; she hadn't had to resort to such extreme measures, however, because as she became busier the pain subsided a little.

The pain in her chest had been present when she was a child, and the few memories she had of it were heavy, as if shrouded with a veil that she must push through and which clung to her. The first was walking back from town one afternoon along the seafront with her mother, when she saw a child of her own age fall and graze her knees. The mother swept her up and, talking softly, took the child to a bench, where she continued to cradle her. For a while Elizabeth was nowhere and everything was still. She could not hear the traffic or passers-by or the gulls or the surf but, watching the child, felt in her own body an unearthly heat where the woman touched it, where her hand cradled its head, its legs – this charge. Presently she carried on walking, the pain in her chest, her mother unaware she wasn't alongside.

The second time she remembered the pain distinctly was a rainy winter afternoon, climbing rocks by the shore, possessed with a surly heat, climbing away from her mother, intending to fall and punish her, she couldn't remember for what, when she slipped, quite unintentionally, into a pool of surprising depth and astonishing coldness with a gulp like a stone. Her mother waded in and lifted her out and ran home with her, almost as wet as herself by the time they arrived at the house. All the time her mother ran a bath, soaped, flannelled and dried her, shrugged her hot clammy limbs into dry clothes, blasted her hair with the drier and set her in front of a fire with a mug of cocoa, the angry heat remained, her body continued to be stiff and awkward, her teeth chattered in tacit accusation – until she suddenly noticed that her mother's teeth were chattering too, and her face was white, her own hair dripping on to her shoulders. She looked at what she had done; the heat liquefied, became the familiar toothache in her chest that this time she couldn't shake off for days.

The pain in Elizabeth's chest was tied up with one thing in particular, though the memories of it had now merged into one: a box in the front room of the house by the sea, on a shelf in an alcove at the side of the fireplace; a large box, the colour of the sky, that played music. In the evening the rooms of the house on the cliff pressed close, and silence and stillness became portentous, made palpable by the rushing of the sea beyond the window, which was neither silent nor still, and her mother disliked both. So she read aloud, played with the child, took her to the beach, to the cliffs, to the town, and when the child had gone to bed she played music. She would pour herself a drink, go to the box on the shelf and lift the lid.

Beside the box, filling that shelf and the next, was a collection of larger and smaller shiny black spheres. The spheres were the only things in the house that were expressly her mother's. If they were scratched they could skip or screech or repeat; if they were dropped they could shatter; dust could damage them and so could heat. If they were played at the wrong speed they could sound drugged and low, or shrill and wound-up.

The child was not allowed to touch the spheres but she had seen them close up, banded by thousands of fine concentric circles, described in the vinyl like rings of a planet. It was the circles that made the sound, her mother said; she was not allowed to touch but occasionally, on wet afternoons or days when her mother sat wrapped in a blanket, too ill to read or play or go out, she had seen her remove one of the spheres from its port-holed paper sleeve, hold it gently in her red hands, her palms at right angles to the edges, settle the sphere on a turntable inside the blue box, lift a metal arm attached to a needle, press a switch and set them in motion. There was an anxious moment when the sphere dropped suddenly – had her mother done something wrong? But the machine knew what to do and presently a second arm, thicker and more business-like, jerked across and lowered itself gingerly. It held a needle that pinpointed the matter – a tiny resolute sting. As the sphere spun, music began playing.

The music didn't have words: it was full of strings and sawings, groans and meanderings. The child stood on a chair and peered into the box to see where it came from. She watched the arm travel up and down on the black water, the needle moving steadily towards the centre, then, at the very last moment, jumping sideways, as if it itself had been stung, before lowering itself in a subdued and stilted manner to the side, as if uncomfortable, embarrassed by what it had done. While they were spinning, the circles engraved on the spheres resembled dark water traversed at great speed. At the centre of each a paper bull's-eye – blue or red, purple or yellow – pirouetted like a skater. You could tell the sphere was moving because as it spun the label rippled a little at the edges; you could tell it was moving because the light catching it made a ragged white path, like the moon did on the sea when it came to the bay to let people know there was something above them. But though the label trembled, if you half closed your eyes it appeared to be stationary; and though the path flickered as if it was living – and perhaps it was for that moment that something passed through it – it never moved from its position; it remained still.

There was something unnatural about the thing, no apparent relation between the spinning circle and the sound that filled the air. One was tangible, the other was not; one visible, the other existed nowhere; or everywhere. The child's eyes ate up each movement: the needle bent to its task like some proboscis intent upon nutrition; the sphere itself, which appeared to warp and rise from itself as if from some terrible heat. She was more amazed by the spheres than the box; that, to some extent, with its contraptions, levers and arms, looked as if it could make something happen. The spheres were flat and inert, incapable of producing anything at all until the needle touched them – though they must contain something, something ingrained, engraved imperceptibly, which suddenly erupted into life.

She had watched her mother's eyes grow dark as she listened to the music. She had watched her disappear although she was sitting in front of her, be put to sleep here and wake somewhere else. And now something really was happening. So this was music; this was what it did. She was frightened the first time she heard the music and frightened every time after that. She became very pale and very still. She would ask if they could go out. She would fetch a book. The music stirred her; it made her chest ache. Sometimes the pain was so great that she turned her attention to the spinning circle itself, as if by studying the physical means of this phenomenon she could counter its alarming effect. Perhaps one day her mother noticed her quietness while it was playing; perhaps she saw her sitting stone still. Most of the time she didn't play the music until Elizabeth was in bed. When she did it was preceded by a day of pronounced quietness on her part, more than usual watchfulness on the part of the child, and a stillness and silence that could not be dissipated. Their most powerful ally against the silence was poetry. Poetry could bale the silence out for a while, reconfigure it into pattern, offset it with rhythms of its own.

Music was different from books. When her mother read books, they rode the words; the words could only do things they permitted them to do. Moreover, each of them existed within their own kingdom of words, made the words their own, though the words were identical. But the music did with them what it wanted, was unbridled and, instead of bequeathing to each their own private sphere, joined them indissolubly together. It was impossible to remain alone: she found herself slipping, sliding into her mother. The music didn't stretch in a line or fill pages that could be turned one by one. She couldn't say: 'There we were,' or 'Here we are now'. It was a canopy, a mesh that enfolded Heaven and Earth. If the words they read in books created worlds, music changed the very fabric those worlds were made of; warped, weft, merged them. If words separated, allowed her to conquer and objectify and divide, music made everything one. The child didn't want to be one; being one frightened her.

The first time the music woke her she sat up in bed and it was filling the house. It seemed to her that that was precisely what the music was doing: infiltrating the walls like water in a sandcastle, seeping through the floors, rising step by step up the stairs; bulging, bursting, submerging the next; snaking along the landing, curling with shocking suddenness around the legs of her bed, as if the sea she ran from in dreams was now filling the house. As it rose, she tried to make herself hard against it, seal up the cracks, make herself a stone or a pole or a bench, something that would float – or sink – but not be broached, not be breached, not be entered. And she could not.

She tried to go back to sleep but her chest was aching. The pain was one with the music. The pain waxed and waned with each breath. She stumbled downstairs crying; she would tell her mother, she would make it stop, but when she reached the front room she heard another sound, a sound that could not be heard from the top of the house: the sound of a woman weeping. She had never heard her mother cry before; for a moment she even wondered if it was her mother. And then she knew that it was.

The weeping went on longer than she had ever cried; she couldn't think what could have caused it, couldn't imagine what was that bad. It must be the music, she decided – but if it was so horrible, why did her mother listen to it? She tried to think what she should do but the pain in her chest made thoughts break up mid-sentence in her head. She wanted to open the door but could not make her hand turn the handle. She wanted to run away but thought she should go into the room. If I was brave I would go in, she thought. But she wasn't brave, she couldn't bear it, and she stayed where she was. At last she sat on the bottom step of the stairs and consigned herself to it, to going up and down, moment by moment. The weeping stopped shortly before dawn, just before the music itself did. Before her mother could open the front-room door, she crept back to bed.

The next day her mother was grey and her eyes red but other than that seemed no different. She didn't ask her mother why she had been crying or if she had done it before, but every night after that she lay listening. If she heard nothing she would go along the landing to her mother's room and check she was in her bed. If she heard music she knew that her mother had not come to bed. Sometimes she went downstairs and sat on the bottom step. Sometimes she heard crying. Sometimes she was not brave enough to go down, and curled beneath the blankets, unable to sleep for the pain in her chest. If she did drop into sleep it was from a great height and she woke up only to fall again, and the music went on filling the house. The next day she would wake trailing something behind her, a dream, a scent, part of the music, and know she had failed her mother and the music had won. Sometimes she didn't hear the music at all but in the morning knew it had been there because the house seemed to be distended as if by osmosis; the walls were warped, carpets wrinkled, her mother was pale, perhaps shivering, her hair lank, sometimes wrapped in a blanket, as if she, too, had been drenched and washed up, cast ashore on one of the armchairs in the living room.

Elizabeth remembered only one night she heard the music clearly and it was the summer her mother disappeared. She heard it in her sleep and sat up immediately, as if she had been waiting for it, or it for her; as if it had all happened before, and she suddenly remembered. There was a large moon beyond the window and its white seemed to be blistering. The sea was sighing, offering its familiar platitudes, but tonight she didn't listen. When she arrived in the hall the front room was empty and the door ajar. She knew her mother was not in the house and there was no point in calling her. Inside the music box the circle was still spinning, the light from the moon flashing upon it, making a white path on the black water. The sphere suddenly seemed to her evil, circling over and over, the jagged path on its black water portending disaster. She backed away and huddled on the first step of the stairs, pressing her fingers to her ears, bearing with the pain in her chest, and waited.

She didn't know how long she had been there but she

knew she had fallen asleep more than once when she heard footsteps outside the front door and a moment later her mother came in and shut the door softly. Her face was like chalk, her eyes wide and dark and her hair windswept. She passed Elizabeth, went into the front room and turned off the music, then came towards the stairs and jumped as she saw her. The wild look went out of her face and it softened; she sat down on the stairs beside her and put a hand on her head.

She could feel the cold from her mother's clothes and smell the salt in them and knew she had been down to the sea. She couldn't speak for a long time and when she did it was a whisper. 'Where were you?' she said.

'It's such a lovely night I went down to the beach,' her mother said. 'I'm sorry; I would have asked if you wanted to come with me but I thought you were sleeping.'

'I was,' she said. 'But the music . . .'

Her mother took her hands, which were small and hot and clammy, in her own, which were large and cold and mottled with wind or with water. The child turned her head away and would not look at her mother and her mother was quiet for a while. Then she said: 'Let me show you.'

She wrapped her in a coat and took her in her arms and went out and shut the door softly behind them and they stepped into that brilliant night beneath the swollen moon that was swelling the sea and making a path on the water, past the night flowers that grew on the cliff, and the child smelt the sea and the flowers and the wild and savoury scent of the night and forgot about the music and the house.

Above them great stars were hanging, and around each was a small aureole, as if the star was vibrating slightly, was here and there, was still and was not. Brightness pressed all around the child and with it certainty, each thing crystalline, exposed like a negative, and she thought: It will be all right.

They walked along the shore, leaving one set of prints, the woman talking in her low voice about all sorts of things but really saying the same thing over and over; saying that nothing had ended and nothing was lost, a message the sea took up and repeated, and as she listened the pain in the child's chest went away and she forgot about the black sphere in the box and the jagged path of white light and looked up to see other spheres spinning in blackness; another path, made by the moon on the water, and the sea saying, 'again', saying, 'now', saying, 'always', over and over and over again.

The Seventh Day: Afternoon

Elizabeth Stone stood at the sink in the little bathroom trying to fix her hair. There wasn't much to fix but her fingers were clumsy, creative endeavours being usually left to her brain, and she was tired. She had been tired all day, in spite of the promise of the concert that evening, or perhaps because of it; felt she was trailing something behind her, a dream or the line of a song; something she couldn't remember or quite forget.

She could hear voices in the quad below and bicycle wheels bobbing over cobbles. The heat even at this hour was surprising, though the sky had clouded and the air was so still that sounds sheered away sooner than they should, like a tennis ball cut dead with a racquet. Between each of the sounds there was a static and beneath the static a palpable silence.

She gave up with her hair, flexed her wrist, which was stiff, and stepped back. Powder, lipstick, red dress; not that sort of red – a demure damson, but still red; not that sort of dress but nevertheless silk; not an elegant dress even, but still a dress. Was it a terrible mistake? She had spent all day among busy Sunday shoppers trying to find something appropriate (since when had so many people shopped on Sunday?) and the assistant had assured her that the dress was appropriate for a small concert, and not 'dressy' in the least. But now, seeing her back, arms and calves laid bare in their humble flaccidity, seeing her stomach peep shyly beneath the material that the assistant had assured her, being bias cut, would be flattering, she wasn't so sure.

She inspected her face – well, you had to put a little makeup on with a dress like this, but the colours felt strange and gaudy. The eye shadow was the biggest mistake. She had bought it that afternoon but hadn't thought to buy makeup remover and now the only way to get it off was soap and water; not really an option when she should be leaving, should actually have left. She picked up her blue mackintosh and went to the door; the weather didn't render it necessary but the dress did.

As she descended the little black stairs she remembered once again that other evening, that other concert. But there was no reason why this evening should turn out like that, she reminded herself. No reason at all.

*

She is nineteen, Elizabeth Stone tells herself, there are lots of things she hasn't done yet, there is no need to be ashamed that she has never attended a concert. In fact, though, this is not the reason she is beside herself. The real reason is something Edward Hunt will never guess if she can help it: that for as long as she can remember she has detested music. Even if she did confess her secret he wouldn't believe her; after all, who hates music? No one, especially one who professes to appreciate poetry, whose pitch and rhythm reverberate in the gyre of the ear. Music and poetry are made of nearly identical elements – they are soundscapes, require silence to realise and appreciate, deploy harmony, refrain, pitch, tone, contrapuntanality. So she has pretended to like music – at times she has pretended to love it – and she has done so brilliantly; she is sure he has had no idea when she is talking about a famous andante that she has never actually heard it, when eulogising about a rapid-fire conclusion between piano and orchestra, quicksilver and firmly pointed accents, that she read the words in the

Classical Review. But this afternoon she will have to pretend better than she has ever done because she will be sitting beside him, listening to a live string quartet for at least an hour. And yet, despite the enormity of the challenge, she is buoyant, and it is a testament to this buoyancy that it has lasted all week, despite what she knows the weekend holds. And she can do it. She is sure. She can feign absorption, perhaps even delight.

It is a Sunday, the end of Trinity, and she is walking down a narrow cobbled alley flanked by black and white timber-fronted houses. She stops before a low black door, a door that appears to have been sunk into the matter of the house like a brand – or perhaps the house has grown around it because the lintel and doorstep spill like bark around a band in a tree – checks the number, and knocks. So this is it. She has tried often to imagine where the professor lives – and it is here, in the very heart of the city, five minutes from the square and the library where she spends all her days. There is thumping on what sounds like stairs, then the door is opening and he is saying: 'Come in, come in . . .'

His hair looks as if it has had a run-in with a brush because it is lying flatly and somewhat morosely on his head; his face is shining as though he has scrubbed it with a hot flannel, and he is wearing a shirt and a jacket; the jacket appears to have been through a washing-machine and the shirt is unironed, but still, it is something of a transformation. 'I'll just get my keys,' he is saying.

The hall is dark and smells of books. There is a barometer and a hallstand and a mirror frame carved with leaves. Through a door to the right, an oak table is covered with books and notepads and papers and magazines; there is a room, too, but it is the table that grabs one's attention, filling the room like something from *Alice's Adventures in Wonderland*. The room has a low, beamed ceiling; the walls are lined with shelves and bookcases, and these, too, are filled to bursting. In the corner, stairs lead upwards. She waits by a sofa. Light falls from a deep-set lattice window looking on to the street and, despite the smallness of the window, it is piercing in the room's dimness. Through another, even smaller window, she can see a backyard: socks on a washing line, thick and white; and on the windowsill a row of potted plants in the familiar state of demise. Her gaze returns to the enormous table, and a red cover with golden lettering catches her eye.

She can see only part of a picture but what she sees makes her start. She peers closer, then loosens the book from the pile of others. A woman with long, shining hair is sitting on a white horse, a knight in chainmail gazing up at her. Her breath catches. He comes back in and she flushes.

'I'm sorry,' she says, replacing the book.

'That's an old one,' he says.

'Where did you get it?'

'I've got pretty much every book under the sun,' he says. 'I don't remember where I got that one.' He pats his pockets. 'Ready?'

She badly wants to open the book but he is impatient to be off, excited as a schoolboy. She has never seen him like this, and she gets up, nodding. But then he says, 'Oh, I've got something for you,' and he goes to a bookcase and pulls out a black, wrinkled book with the words *Paradise Lost* chiselled into its blackness and hands it to her saying: 'It's old, take care of it.'

She stares at the book, says: 'Thank you.'

He locks the door and they go down the street talking about Milton, she clutching the book he has lent her and telling him her ideas about *Samson Agonistes*, about the pillars in the temple, about notes and building materials, sonic dissonance and verbal disarray – all sorts of far-fetched and clever and earnest young notions – and he nodding, his eyes black and shining.

They are happy; that is how they would appear to a passer-by. They themselves are not aware of anything, however, except perhaps a velocity, an ease of movement, a vague hilarity; although one doesn't know if the other feels this, and in fact at this moment it is hard to say which is one and which is the other anyway. They turn into a street where a white building with pillars and a round window is set back from the road, and he tells her that this is the Music Room. They go through double doors beneath a small porch and a smell of wood and of age washes around them – of time itself it seems to Elizabeth Stone, yellowed and curling; centuries of blinking and baton-tapping, fingernails and polish, resin and cat gut. There are wooden stands and a wooden stage, empty except for four chairs and music stands, and wooden seats curving around in a semi-circle that is already full of people; the quartet must be popular. 'I've heard them twice now,' he says. 'They blew me away the first time with their rendition of Haydn's "Farewell".'

They sit near the top, and as soon as they are seated she realises she doesn't know what to do with her body and won't know for the next hour and fifteen minutes. She doesn't know why it should be so different sitting here from sitting in a pub or in a park or in his room; perhaps it is being in the company of these smart strangers, who are also mostly sitting in pairs; perhaps it is the decorous shuffling, the polite murmur of anticipation; or perhaps it is simply that they are sitting side by side for the first time and, contrary to what she had expected, it is much more alarming than sitting opposite one another.

Afternoon sun is pouring through the round window above their heads and, coupled with the high white ceiling and stark walls, it lends the room a feeling of a chapel, of humble consecration. The sunlight shines on his freshly combed hair, which even now is beginning to spring up. It glints in the motes suspended around them, illuminates the grain in the benches beneath them and transforms the skin of their hands into vast deserts. The sunlight seems to be one with the silence, which is more liquid than sound, and she suddenly sees that it is the silence, veiled only slightly by the murmuring and shuffling, that is the source of her unease; that the room is built to foster silence and nurture it.

He beams. 'All right?'

She nods vigorously.

'I think it's going to be good,' he says. 'I'm looking forward to the Beethoven in particular, the late quartets, you know.'

'When does it start?' she says lightly.

'Any minute now.'

'Oh, good.'

'Did you know Haydn built this place?'

'No.'

He tells her a little of the history of the Music Room but though she tries to listen she is aware only of the silence, which seems to be growing and rushing, like the sea, all around her. He breaks off as two men and two women dressed in black come on to the stage, bowing and taking their places, and the flotsam and jetsam of conversation and rummagings and shufflings breaks high over their heads as a wave of applause crashes down in a furore of white noise; she finds the heartiness embarrassing, the overwhelming unison, the way she is reined in, and relieved when she can clasp her hands in her lap.

There is a pause; the musicians settle the violins under their chins. Then they are off.

And she is gasping. This is Bach? It is an insult. It is an assault. It is inhuman! The frenzy, the enormity, the merci-lessness of it. She didn't have time. She has been swept away, thrown in a hundred directions at once, pressed back into her seat. She will have a heart attack, she will faint, she cannot believe he *knew* about this – they all knew, and subjected themselves to it voluntarily. The music is roaring, it is soaring, it is stopping quite still in the air; it is unbearable. She will tell him – but when she looks at Edward Hunt he is alight.

The Bach finishes as abruptly as it began and she is sitting back, her arms at her sides. 'Like it?' His face is shining. She nods dumbly, hoping he will mistake her speechlessness for awe; and it looks as if he has because he beams even more broadly and his leg begins bouncing. And now he is telling her – dear God – now he is telling her about the next.

The second piece begins with a single violin: tremulous, incandescent, then the chord, arcane, exquisite – almost humorous. It could not be more different from the first but, if possible, it is worse; she would not have believed it. All she can do – all she must do – is be still. She says this to herself. She says: How hard can this be? She invokes words, wrestles them down from the heavens, wrestles with the thing, spells it out in measured, reasonable sentences. Words will be her allies: brave, firm, orderly, possessing such different rhythms from the music. Surely the words will win out. But her constructions are in vain, the words have no chance at all: against the rearing field of water they are a matchstick flotilla, disbanded in an instant, in another tossed high like a mouse by a cat, reduced to fragments. The reason, she realises, is that the words last moments, the words are discontinuous, and the music is not; she must think of words constantly if she is to stay afloat; she must send out ship after ship. So she is racked, she is drawn out, attenuated by flutings, by sawings, meanderings so delicate they must surely be thoughts not sounds; by driftings slight as a feather. This way, that way the music takes her – and yet it is brutal. It fills her, stretches her out, and she aches with it, she heaves.

She will not be part of it. She balls her fists, wills her chest not to rise, her jaw not to ache – would will herself out of existence – but her body betrays her: her knees slip against one another, a muscle jumps, her breathing is ragged. They must let her out. She will tell him. But when she looks his mouth is open; he swallows and she sees this is all he can spare, that his body has been taken over. He has been put to sleep here and woken somewhere else. So: this is music. This is what it does.

At some point she feels she has been stripped, that her body and all its humble mechanisms have been exposed; its tiny parts, its little organs, its gurglings and flutterings and intimate pulsings, its secret passageways, all its defences have been put on show in public – or they have become part of the others' bodies. Yes. That is what has happened; and everyone in the room is one pulsing body, one monstrous, ebbing mass. And in the process, her body has also become his.

As it goes on she begins to understand something: it isn't the sounds themselves that horrify her but what they accomplish. The knowledge comes to her with the kind of understanding one scrabbles to arrive at in moments of crisis: the real problem is not the music but the person sitting beside her; or is it her, sitting beside him? Is it this, and the other bodies pressing in around them, and the strange creature that is growing between them? To be sitting side by side rather than opposite one another is strange enough, but to be sitting side by side and hearing these sounds is another thing altogether: it is the difference between walking and dancing, eating a meal with a person and sharing their fork. Is this what music does: merges things? And he has felt it, too, she is sure.

Movements are now a series of infinitely charged events which set off ripples that drench her in waves of heat. She is as still as a stone but feels she is slipping, sliding towards him. The seats are not level. Hers slopes to the left. She grips the edges, braces her feet but it makes no difference. Their bodies are pulsing together, their chests rising in unison. She will breathe differently. Their eyes are seeing together – seeing each other wherever they look. She won't look! She will look at the musicians, but he is watching them, too. Their hands. Lying so honestly side by side; so shameful, so fleshly, so blissful in their insidious collusion. She hides her hands; she can at least do that.

The music slows, it strokes, it whispers, intones, stretches itself out like hairs from her head. The hairs crackle. She is weeping, invisibly, her face a mask. His chest is rising and falling. She presses herself into the seat so forcefully she trembles. She squeezes her eyes shut. It goes on. The violin quavers, the cello groans, the strings wind endlessly, gloriously, unendurably – oh, it is cruel. It is intolerable! It is unendurable. Each part of her is wound more tightly; each nerve, muscle, bone clenches itself and teeters on a brink. It is a song, she tells herself. It will end. It makes no difference.

'Last one,' he says. His face is flushed. 'Beethoven now.'

She tries to smile but the muscles in her face tremble. She hopes he doesn't see that her eyelashes are wet. But this time he, too, seems glad to look back towards the front.

The last piece is strange, out of time altogether, and insinuates itself into consciousness, half nursery rhyme, half opus, half tragic, half ironic, and the minute she hears the opening bars she knows she is going to be ill. Something is being written around or above them, inscribed in the air above their heads; the rest of the world falls away like flats in a play and sweat is coming down beneath her hair. She is scattered, stretched across skies too vast to compute, spun to finest gossamer. The sensation is no longer of this moment alone, of this body – her body, his body – but many bodies and many moments; it is rooted deep and reaches back and she is absolutely shaken. It is all she can do to speak through the uproar, through the heaven and earth that are rearing and plunging, and the words that come to her are simple: let it end; it has come, now let it go. She says this. She prostrates herself, but the music is stronger. It intends to destroy her. It keeps touching, keeps touching her.

The miracle is that she goes on breathing. The music is inside her now. It is up to her chest; it is covering her heart. When her throat constricts she gets up. Chair-backs clatter as she goes along the row. She stumbles on the last step, runs through the foyer and is sick outside the door by a bush of laburnum. He appears minutes later and says: 'What happened? Are you all right?' She doesn't look back, is making her way along the steps. 'Elizabeth,' he shouts. 'Where are you going?' She doesn't turn round. He calls again and she hears his steps after her, but by then she is running, turning the corner, out of sight.

Low rumblings are breaking across the city. Large drops begin to fall. She runs on, dragging air into her lungs as if she has been drowning. The rain is lukewarm; it doesn't feel external to her but as though it is seeping from the pores in her skin. When she can't run any further she leans against a wall. A middle-aged woman in a mackintosh passes by clutching a yellow umbrella. The woman is crying. Elizabeth doesn't notice.

*

Hurrying in heels she wasn't accustomed to, infinitely glad of the blue mackintosh, Professor Stone couldn't help wondering again what Edward Hunt had done that afternoon. She knew she should have explained what was wrong. But she didn't know. She still did not. She had been to concerts since then – not many it was true. It hadn't been easy but after a few years she managed to sit through the more sedate ones. After that she went with colleagues and acquaintances, learned how to talk about music, even managed to form vague preferences. Now no one, she was pleased to say, would have any idea about her real feelings on the matter. This evening they were visiting the same Music Room they had thirty years before, but would hear Schubert's Piano Trio No. 1 in B flat major, a series of quiet aerial delights; not Bach at his most frenetic or Beethoven at his most unhinged. There was no reason, she told herself again, why this evening should bear any resemblance to the first.

The great library gates were chained as she passed through the square, the eyes of the Upper Room shut, the Round Room beneath the dome dark-windowed and magnificent in Sunday-afternoon somnolence. Dull rays of congested sunlight spilled their impartial gold on the brocade of the professor's heels, made her tights glitter, illuminated the crimson of the silk dress peeping wantonly from the mackintosh. The outfit appeared to her to be more ridiculous by the minute but she hurried as best she could, the dress rising in a most ungainly manner; so much for bias cut.

She was sticky as she turned into the cobbled street, her hair had fallen flat, and she was all of ten minutes late. She knocked on the door and waited, too distracted by her lateness to consider how incredible it was to be standing here at the very same door a lifetime later. When he opened it she couldn't read his expression. It seemed to contain astonishment, confusion and, unless she was mistaken, fear, in equal measure. She knew instantly that the dress was a terrible mistake, the heels, too. Everything.

He turned to collect his jacket. She apologised for being late. He said only, 'It's impressive,' and she wasn't sure how much humour and how much irritation were contained within it. He didn't look at her at all as they made their way down the alley, and she said, by way of explanation for the dress: 'I thought I had better make an effort . . .'

But he said only: 'I hadn't noticed what you were wearing.'

His expression was peculiar, shut up, glazed over like the sky. She concentrated on negotiating the cobbles, glancing at him once as they reached the main street. Could it simply be because she was late? she wondered. Well, there was only one thing to do now. She must go and listen to the music. She must sit quietly, then go home. She thought she could just about manage that.

'So, what did you think?'

'Good, very good.' Elizabeth pushes up her glasses. 'I particularly liked the way the violinist handled the Andante.'

In fact the Andante had tired her – but on the whole she is grateful because the concert has been a pleasant affair, quiet, stately, if a little predictable.

They are sitting at a wooden picnic table at the back of a tavern tucked away behind a jumble of roofs. Because it is Sunday the picnic tables beneath the umbrellas in the yard are filled with tourists rather than finalists and they can hear themselves talk.

'Yes, it wasn't bad.'

He is easier too now, one hand around his Coke, the other tapping a cigarette, looking into a sky in which bank upon bank of clouds are gathering, though the evening is still stifling, his strange mood earlier evaporated. He smiles periodically at a little girl who is running around in the episodic manner of very young children whose nervous systems seem to whirr into action for small periods of time, then short-circuit as if they have run out of information. When he isn't smiling at the little girl he is peering into his drink; when he isn't peering into his drink he is studying his cigarette; when he isn't studying his cigarette he is looking over her shoulder at a group of Americans; he is looking everywhere, in short, but at her, and has been all evening.

She tries to make him out and gives up again; she is tired; she reaches for her drink, and then from nowhere a bright light lances the left side of her head and the world goes black.

She sets her drink down clumsily, slopping it over the rim of her glass, but he doesn't see, is looking out across the courtyard. The pain disappears. She opens her eyes, the world is still there. She sits very still, breathing shallowly, and is then recalled by the sound of him laughing.

'Pardon?'

He turns back to her. 'You're not even listening.'

'I'm sorry. What did you say?'

He looks at her.

'I'm sorry,' she says. 'I didn't hear what you said.'

'In your own little world.' He shakes his head. 'Really, Elizabeth, it's a sort of disability.'

'My mind was just on something else for a minute.'

'It always is.' He sighs. 'I was talking about an idea for an article comparing Goethe and Schubert.'

'Oh.'

She takes a shaky sip of her drink, then sets it down again and touches her head.

'Concert too much for you?'

'No.'

He taps his glass and looks around. 'Anyway, as I was saying, it seems that Goethe had rather an influence on Schubert and I thought it would be interesting to look at the problems faced by anyone who writes in one language about the literature of another . . . Rather similar to what you're doing, isn't it?'

Then the pain opens its eye again and this time takes away her breath. She says, 'I'll be back,' and he stares after her as she goes into the pub.

She asks for a glass of tap water at the bar and takes a packet of painkillers from her bag. She knocks the pills back, places the glass on the bar, misses and bends to reach it but can't get up. Instead she crouches, her hands raised in front of her, like a child fending off something much bigger than itself, so much bigger there is no point in running or fighting or calling for help.

A woman asks her if she is all right. After a minute she helps her up. A man hands her her bag and asks if she would like him to call someone. She tells them that she is perfectly all right. She thanks them and goes back outside.

At the table she says: 'A headache. I was just getting a glass of water.'

But he isn't looking at her, he is looking at his drink. Then he turns to the high wall where small flowers are clinging to the stone, shaking a little in the breeze. He is smiling, a little wryly.

She says: 'Is something funny?'

'No, no . . .' But he is still smiling, and then he laughs. 'Actually, I thought you managed to get through tonight pretty well, considering.'

She says quietly: 'Yes, I did, didn't I?'

He smiles his new, strange smile, then frowns, as if something puzzles him. 'Do you know what the matter was all those years ago?'

She raises her eyebrows and blinks, contemplating the beer mat. After a moment she says: 'No. I can't remember.'

He exhales a smoke ring and watches it, raising his eyebrows. 'Just curious.'

The pills are working. They are marvellous things. Or

perhaps the pain has gone on its own, she thinks. Perhaps it would have gone anyway. Perhaps it isn't anything to be concerned about but something harmless. It has reappeared now, the second time in so many days, on the left-hand side. But perhaps it is not what she is afraid it is; perhaps it is something innocuous, scar tissue, regrowth, small adjustments the body makes in the wake of an intrusion. She has heard of things like that. Perhaps it is even a good sign, a sign of healing, like a finger that begins to itch when it is nearly well. But this is not itching; it is certainly not that. And why didn't Wright warn her about it? Well, it's pointless to worry; she'll see him when she gets back to London; she'll ask.

She says: 'I felt bad about leaving that afternoon.'

'Of course you did.'

She looks at him sharply, but there is no trace of insincerity in his voice and his eyebrows are raised inoffensively.

They are silent for a while. The little girl who has been running around begins to sing and they smile at her, not because either of them particularly feels like smiling but because not to do so would be to acknowledge the darker waters the conversation has drifted into. Then her father sweeps her up into the air, jostling her so that the laughter seems to be shaken out of her, like water from a fountain. Elizabeth Stone watches unseeing, thinking other things. She should let the thing about the concert go now but the pain in her head has made her combative – particularly now it has passed; pain he knew nothing about, then or now. And there is something else, which has rankled her all evening, ever since he opened the door, a feeling of being slighted, unreasonably judged in some way, and she is tired of being judged, so she says in a slightly louder voice, yet with a smile curling her lips: 'What did you think I'd done? Run off because I was bored?'

'Well,' he says, and he is smiling too. 'I didn't know what to think. You never do with you.'

Her jaw clenches, but she lets it go. 'What did you do? Did you go back in?'

'I followed you but by the time I got to the corner you'd disappeared. I think I went home.'

She traces the ring left by the glass with her finger. 'I felt guilty,' she says, 'after you'd paid for the ticket and arranged it all . . .'

'Did you?'

'Yes, I did.'

Then he laughs and says calmly, almost kindly: 'Elizabeth, really, what do you care about other people?'

She frowns, then she laughs. Then she says: 'I'm sorry?'

'Well.' He shrugs helplessly. 'You just don't seem to have any idea about the way things are done; you never have had; either that or you just don't give a damn. You breeze through life dropping things and picking them up again as the fancy takes you. I really think all you care about is your work.' He is still smiling. 'All these years I've wondered how you were, I waited to hear from you. Now you turn up out of the blue as if nothing happened, thinking we can just pick up where we left off, because that's what you want now. But it soon might not be. And where will we – where will I be?'

She feels as if she has been winded. She gasps, and then says: 'I must admit I think that's grossly unfair.'

'Well, you would, wouldn't you?'

She stares at him. 'Where did this come from?'

Then suddenly his smile disappears and he says: 'Where did you come from? Why did you suddenly appear out of nowhere? After a lifetime?'

She swallows and says: 'I told you. To look at the Eliot Papers.'

'Some mouldy old papers everyone knows aren't worth a fig. And have you found anything?'

She cannot believe what she is hearing. She says: 'I showed you.'

'That was your discovery, Elizabeth, nothing to do with the papers. The papers are neither here nor there and you know it. If they were they'd have been published. You could have come back any time; you could have come back ten, twenty years ago. Why now, Elizabeth? Why now?'

She blinks. 'I – I had a sabbatical. And – and despite what you think I really did want to see the Hyland Bequest.'

'That's a lie.'

'I beg your pardon?'

They look at each other.

She says: 'I have no idea what you're talking about.'

'Yes, you do.' He stubs out the cigarette. 'You always understand much more than you let yourself believe. And you are – and always have been – living a lie.'

People are looking now, and neither says any more for a minute. She would, but cannot think of anything and doesn't trust her voice not to shake. When she can speak she smiles, draws herself up and says brightly: 'Well, I think I had better head back. It must be gone nine.'

'It's not half past eight,' he growls.

'Yes,' she says, raising her eyebrows and smiling. 'But I've wasted another day, and I—'

'Wasted?' He turns to her.

She is tightening the belt of her mackintosh but stops. 'No,' she says. 'No.' She laughs quickly. 'That's not what I meant.' But he is turning his head to look around him. She says: 'I meant that I only have a little longer here, in the city—'

'I suppose this evening was a waste of time too?'

'No, Edward. It's always pleasant to spend time with you.'

'Pleasant?'

'Yes – no. Much more than that. I like it . . . very much. We're like old friends. I don't know why you would think that – I don't know why you would think that I meant that.'

But she had meant what she'd said a little, about the day being wasted. And now she wanted only to get back to her room and work; she wanted to finish the thing she had started years ago and present it to him; it was what she had always wanted, and now there was so little time left.

But he was saying: 'I don't think we are friends, Elizabeth. We're not even like friends. Friends don't disappear for thirty years and turn up pretending nothing happened. Friends are interested in one another. Friends tell the truth. But you are always pretending. Though you know as well as I do that something happened back then that can't be ignored, that can't just be swept under the carpet – that's here, now, between us, breathing down our necks.'

She stands and says pleasantly: 'Thank you for a lovely evening. It really has been most enjoyable.'

Then he stands too and says, 'How can you be so fucking detached?' and she stares at him as if he has shot her, too surprised to register pain yet.

He turns away with an air of disgust, and says: 'I don't think I do want to meet up again before you go back, Elizabeth. I'll get these.' And he picks up the glasses and goes back into the pub.

The Seventh Day: Evening

Professor Stone thought only of her thesis as she walked home, only of her discovery and the work that awaited her. A great deal had happened since that morning and she was glad to be returning to it now – returning with treasure, no less, for it was easy to forget her triumph in the archives in the light of recent developments. She had lost a day, but that could be rectified; she wouldn't sleep that night so she would work instead. If the headache reappeared she would simply take more tablets. No: she would take the tablets before it appeared. Tonight she needed to work without distraction; more particularly, she needed to work.

The city was withdrawing into itself again for its nightly vigil, the violet hour already upon it, but tonight the change could be noted even less than usual because the sky was no different from its daytime counterpart, except perhaps a little darker, a little denser, though something was undoubtedly afoot; the spires were no longer dreaming but poised, pricking a grey and gathering silence. She wobbled in the heels and was glad of the mackintosh; there is nothing worse than being dressed in a way one does not want to be all the while appearing as if one is. The outfit was a reminder that the evening had passed, and passed in a way she had not expected – so differently from how she had expected it to, in fact, that it was hard to believe it had passed at all and made her think that time itself might be nothing more than a grand chimera.

The blackbird and thrush were singing as she turned into the Deer Park, small flowers were closing, phlox releasing their scent. There were gnats in clouds – there were clouds; there hadn't been clouds for days. Night breezes were rushing in the tops of the pine trees, the choir singing vespers. The evening was beautiful as the day had not been, and it was disappearing, being caught away by the air into the night, and with it the substances of things in all their time-ordained specificity; because the singing could just as well be welcoming dawn as evening, the flowers opening to the sun as to the moon, and the sky, devoid of a sun – no more now than a tissue of memory blurring the greyness above lawn and trees – could as easily be heralding day as night. From a pile of cuttings and dead flower heads in a corner came the perfume of fermentation, rich with the heat of the afternoon, stronger as it mingled with the cold dark. She could smell privet and earth, more pungent at this hour than any other, where time had pooled and thickened. The only decisive indicator that night was arriving at all were bats' wings scissoring the dampness between the fir trees – though their shapes were little more than snippets of darkness itself and vanished into the element from which they emerged as soon as they were noticed. Professor Stone felt dispersed, her head scattered like chaff, but her body heavy as if she was walking along the seabed, and all around her the city was also at sea, as if bewildered by the currents of time before and time after.

She undressed to her petticoat, put the dress and shoes in a bag for the charity shop and swept the makeup into the pedal-bin. She scrubbed her face with soap and hot water, took four Nurofen and went to the window. She could hardly see the river now; the meadows were submerged beneath shadows and the playing field indistinguishable from the path, though the whites of the goal posts glowed dimly. The wind was rustling tall trees by the river, clouds rolling low on the horizon. She usually loved this time of day in summer when it was late but not yet dark and the weather changing – it lent such intimations of other worlds – but this evening her mind merely absorbed each aspect of the scene into a static of its own, though the moment seemed to have staged itself specially for her attention, with shifting light and curtains of cloud and a hollow rumble of wings upon darkness.

She went to the desk. There were two bundles of notes there: six months of work plus her findings in the archive. She had no idea what he had meant by saying the papers were useless; had he read them? He had assumed that, just because there weren't hundreds of scholars poring over them. Well, it was true the Hyland Bequest had revealed less than she had thought it would, 'The Music of Poetry' in particular: Eliot's ideas about the auditory imagination were not as radical as she had been led to believe; like many of his theories they tantalised but sheered clear of arriving, all the while giving the impression that they did. But he had no right to say that she had used the papers as an excuse to come back here. Anyway, if 'The Music of Poetry' was less illuminating than she had hoped, it simply left her more room to be creative; what would her own thesis be, after all, if Eliot had got there before her? As for the other things he had said, about detachment, about pretending, about living a lie, they were pure imaginings.

It was like the old days, she thought, as she typed up the title: desk, essay, lamp, the only difference now being that she was using a laptop instead of pen and paper. But she felt no excitement, only the aching in her chest that had been her more or less constant companion since her return to the city; only a restlessness that made her want to get up and pace about. She knew better than to pay any attention: first drafts were always the hardest, the time when the nebulous came down to brass tacks, the time when you saw if the thing would work. If she didn't get the basics right now it would be harder on the second draft, harder again on the third, by the fourth perhaps impossible. Speed and concentration were of the essence. Often her best work was done in one sitting. It was similar to an artist getting a likeness, she supposed: one got it quickly or not at all, the first strokes crucial, those to which one could return when there was a possibility of being derailed. Sometimes a first draft provided sentences that remained right to the end, sentences that possessed an urgency, a directness they would not have had if they had been more considered; it was the music he had spoken to her about all those years ago, the equivalent of a perfect line in drawing. Well, she would get them down, the essentials, tonight. It was the way she had tackled every big project. But now there was another incentive, a rumbling like chariot wheels and a rushing in the air beyond her window that told her she had only this night.

She began typing:

In 'The Music of Poetry' (1942) Eliot identified 'the sense of rhythm and the sense of structure' as those aspects of music which concern the poet most. The opening lines of 'Burnt Norton', first of his Quartets, alert us to the way in which the rhythm of a poem operates at the 'frontiers of consciousness beyond which words fail though meanings still exist' for although the words tell us that 'time is unredeemable', the spondee which signifies 'time past' is rhythmically contained in 'time future'.

Poetry assumes there are things in this world which cannot be understood by merely mental means, 'more distant than stars and nearer than the eye'. It does not pluck its judgement from the stars yet has 'astronomy'. The extraordinarily fertile cross-over in Four Quartets of words conveying physical sensation, sound and emotion ('footfalls', 'echoes', 'feel', 'move', 'tone', 'trilling', *'moving', 'movement', 'voice descanting', 'heaving groaner', 'ground swell') points to the body as the means by which the mind is brought into contact with the spiritual. The music of the poem must be sensed physically, a 'pulse . . . less strong and stronger', 'a sense of music . . . felt rather than heard', as Elizabeth Barrett Browning puts it in one source of 'Burnt Norton'. Henri Brémond, quoting Pere de Grandmaison, in* Prayer and Poetry, *a mystical treatise Eliot read before the composition of* Four Quartets, *noted that rapt absorption in music illustrates how in 'profane states of nature . . . we can . . . discern the . . . rough sketch of the mystical states of the soul' for, while listening, the 'effort to understand relaxes'. In contrast to semantic certitude such attention is analogous to metaphysical knowledge, experienced rather than intellectually assimilated, 'capable of registering, mimetically, deep shocks of recognition'.*

There had been moments in her own life, she thought, especially since her illness, when she had been unsure what was real and what was not; when, due to some trick of the clock or of the light, some coincidence of chemical or sense or motion, the boundaries between what was known and what was not had blurred into conjecture. She rubbed her eyes and poised her hands to begin typing again, then saw that the screen had become black. In the light of the lamp she could make out a face inside it, not immediately recognisable as her own. She could see eye sockets, hollowness of temples and cheeks, a broad shadow cast by the nose hovering in a cloudy substance that did not appear to be flesh. She hit the space bar; the words came back.

Eliot's interest at the time of writing the Quartets [she began typing] *was with 'excess' psychic material which refused to let itself be brought to light. He writes that Tourneur's loathing of humanity exceeds its objective correlative, is a 'horror beyond words'. Kyd's* Spanish Tragedy *proved to be 'intractable material' for* Hamlet, *and* Hamlet, *in turn, 'is full of some stuff that the writer could not drag to light, contemplate, manipulate into art, dominated by an emotion which is inexpressible, because it is in excess of the facts as they appear.'*

And what had Edward Hunt said? 'Detached'. He had said: 'Fucking detached'. What had he meant? Was she? If she was, it was rather ironic, detachment being the quality she most prided herself on having cultivated. But there was another sort of detachment, wasn't there, a useless sort? He had said: 'A kind of disability'. Could it be true, she thought, that she was one of those 'helplesse, pusillanimous & unweapon'd creatures', 'most unfit to do that which all mortals aspire to'? No. She was a respected academic, a person engaged in matters of some importance; no, it was not true. She made a meaningful contribution to the world, albeit a small one – who could do more? She was not being delusional about this; she was – if nothing else – a 'soldier above all the most exercised in knowledge of himself'.

She went back to typing, hitting the keys a little harder than necessary, then stopped again, because it suddenly seemed to her she had been defending herself against such claims all her life. He had said she understood perfectly. All right: just what was there to be understood? That thirty-three years ago she and Edward Hunt had gone to a concert. That during the course of that afternoon or maybe shortly afterwards something had changed between them. That was all. What came after were snippets. Waiting outside a lighted window, handing him a sheaf of papers, standing in a rose garden, walking along a street that seemed to slope upwards. Nothing happened if there were no words to describe it, did it? And there were no words to describe that summer. Nothing happened if there was nothing to note, and there was nothing to note; time itself seemed to have lost its way during the last weeks of that term. 'There is nothing to understand,' she said, 'because nothing happened.' Perhaps something happened for him, but not for me. Nothing. She asked herself if this was true, and she felt she could answer with impunity that it was. The problem, she supposed, was that any experience was essentially unknowable to another. He was simply being fanciful. It was understandable: he was getting older – perhaps he was nostalgic; perhaps he had regrets. Then she remembered saying that the day had been wasted and shut her eyes.

Presently, however, she inhaled, opened them and sat up straight. She raised her hands to type and her left arm wilted before her eyes; she tried to straighten it and could not. She tried to open her hand and it had contracted to a claw. She gazed at her hand, barely breathing. She gazed at the sunspots and ridges, the slips of skin at the sides of her nails, the small hairs that grew on the backs of her fingers, the ragged scar that spread across three of the knuckles and had been her companion now for thirty-three years, at the indentation in the second finger where pens and pencils had rested even longer than that, and could think of nothing.

When she flexed her hand again she was able to place it over the keyboard. 'Keep going for me tonight,' she said to her arm. 'Just tonight.' She didn't think any more about what had happened then or what it meant, and didn't ask anything more of her arm. She didn't feel she had the right. In a minute she flexed her hand again and, though it was stiff, she began to type, pressing lightly – so lightly, in fact, she had to go back and retype, which she could not do very well because she was shaking. '*Is it possible*,' she typed, '*that the experience Eliot underwent which provided the raw material of* Four Quartets "*exceeded the facts*"?'

She hadn't meant to stop again but found that she had. Was it true, she wondered, that some experiences could not be verbalised? Eliot was saying if one relied solely on words one might miss the experience because the experience could be extremely delicate, no more than a pulse 'less strong and stronger'. If that was true, at what level did knowledge of such experience reside?

And now despite the fact that time was pressing – pressing more than it had done in her whole life before – Professor Stone's hands dropped to her lap and she asked herself what really had happened thirty-three years ago, and what, if anything, could be said about it.

World Enough and Time

The day after Elizabeth Stone runs out of the string quartet she finds a note in her pigeon-hole from Edward Hunt asking if she is all right. She does not reply. To acknowledge her departure will lend it more significance than necessary, but that is not the reason she is silent. The reason is that she doesn't understand what happened at the concert so can't explain why she left.

No more notes from Professor Hunt arrive. The end of term grows closer, the implacable cycles of the city of books are quickened by the promise of summer and holidays; there are four weeks left; there are three; there are two. She works longer but has trouble concentrating. Her thoughts disperse mid-train, like aeroplane plumes in windy skies. Words are incomprehensible, become small trees, figures, insect tracks, flakes of bark, blades of grass, grains of sand. She begins to experience a vague at first and then pressing anxiety. She will be sitting in lectures or working in the library, coming back from the supermarket or walking along the cloudy streets and has to stop and turn her attention to it. But there is nothing to be done with the feeling. It cannot be palliated. She cannot push it away or get close to it.

The last tutorial with Professor Hunt arrives. She walks down to the college with the others on one of the last days in June. She won't be taught by him next year; none of them will, they will have finished Elizabethan and Jacobean English, and be moving on to the Restoration. Perhaps because of this there are no jokes today, no impersonations;

in fact, they are all rather quiet – even the boys, who took such delight in imitating him at the beginning of the year, and she knows now that each of them would say without hesitation that for all his idiosyncrasies Professor Hunt is the best tutor they ever had.

In the lodge she sees the porter. He says, 'I'll miss you next year, Miss Elizabeth. You'll have to come and visit me,' and she tells him she will, though she knows she will put off returning to the college indefinitely. They go through the tunnel, across the quad, into the building and along the corridor, past the rose garden swimming in sunshine, and knock at his door. She tries to embed it all in her mind but she cannot think for the hammering of her heart; in a strange way she cannot feel anything either, is simply existing, occupying this moment, then the next.

She can tell by his voice as soon as they enter that something is afoot. It is darker, quieter – stiller, if that is possible; if a voice can be dark, can be still. And there are other indicators that all is not well: he is not messing his hair, the boots are stationary, Hannah has forgotten her book but there is no obscenity, no copy wings its way noisily through the air to her; he simply goes to the shelf and hands a book down. What is more, it appears he is not going to read to them – something they have come to look forward to now because Professor Hunt is a great reader, one of the best; sometimes, listening to him, texts that have confounded her for weeks unravel themselves in a moment, become lucid, transparent, alive. But today he asks David to read instead, another sonnet, written a hundred years after Thomas Wyatt lived, by Andrew Marvell.

> *Had we but world enough, and time,*
> *This coyness, Lady, were no crime.*
> *We would sit down, and think which way*
> *To walk, and pass our long love's day . . .*

Marvell is not interested in the beloved except to mock; hidden in this sonnet is one of the most scourging attacks upon love she has ever encountered: the time the poet chides his mistress with wasting, it is made clear, will be the death of her; a heavy price to pay, if there was one, for failing to heed the call of the moment. But it is for these reasons that Elizabeth Stone enjoyed reading it. She rejoiced in the debunking of romantic love and its mores.

'A nasty little piece, for all its gilding,' he says. 'What do we make of it?'

'It's sarcastic,' says David. 'The Humber isn't a romantic destination.'

'"Lower rate" suggests not only "slower" but "lower", as in payment; things are commercialised, cheapened,' Kirsty says, pleased with herself.

'And the beloved is threatened with a marble vault; phallic worms try the "long-preserved virginity",' Hannah finishes.

'Good.' He is pleased with them: they are no longer the novices of nine months ago but scholars in their own right. He is pleased but the leg does not swing, the boots remain stationary, and she, too, is still on the rug; a numbness has descended upon her and now she is petrified, a small statue.

'The metaphysical poets are usually more interested in their conceits than the subject which gives rise to them,' he is saying, 'and it's no different with Marvell. This isn't a conventional love sonnet at all, though I think we know by now there's no such thing. Does anyone have anything to say about "quaint honour"?'

'"Quaint" was a euphemism for "cunt",' David says.

'Indeed. Hardly very romantic. Rather than uphold the value of his mistress's virginity the poet emphasises its "quaint honour", an oxymoron in which "honour" is negated by his use of "quaint" – a reference to female genitalia in medieval literature with which Marvell's audience would have been familiar. There are other euphemisms:

228

"youthful glue", "tear our pleasures", "rough strife", "iron gates" – "grates" in another edition . . .'

The discussion moves to Ovid and *carpe diem* love poetry. They return to the sonnet.

> *But at my back I always hear*
> *Time's wingèd chariot hurrying near;*
> *And yonder all before us lie*
> *Deserts of vast eternity.*

'The juxtaposition is between an empty future and a present dogged by the sense of time passing,' he says. 'And what do we make of the closing couplet – "*Thus, though we cannot make our sun/Stand still, yet we will make him run*"?'

The concluding couplet is the one part of the sonnet she puzzled over. She didn't understand it – for surely it is no feat to make a sun run that cannot be made to stand still; and if the sun did run, it would defeat the purpose of the complaint, which is ostensibly to gain time, not hurry it up. And she can make no more sense of it now, petrified as she is, her brain and her body free-floating.

She allows her attention to drift beyond the window. When she returns he is saying: '. . . "till the conversion of the Jews". What's Marvell referring to here? Elizabeth?'

Her heart tumbles back into her body; her mind begins to whirr. The conversion of the Jews? How does he manage to ask her questions she never knows the answers to? He is speaking to her for the first time in weeks – the first since the awful evening of the concert – and he is asking something she doesn't know. Suddenly she is tired of it, tired of the continual need to be right, to impress, put on a show. She wishes he had never discovered her, never picked her out, but left her to drift along with the rest in a sea of obscurity. And so, instead of making something up, instead of even excusing herself, she says flatly: 'I don't know.' She doesn't even look up.

'Oh.'

There is a short silence.

'Anyone else?'

Kirsty says, 'There was an upsurge of chiliasm about this time. Marvell is teasing millenarian hopes as incalculably remote,' and she hates her.

'Indeed.'

The word is a slap, she smarts with it, but instead of lowering her head she raises it and turns to look out of the window, as if she is bored.

She hears him say: 'The Jews were meant to convert at the Second Coming so the date falls within the catalogue of impossibilities. But after several hundred years they were no longer prohibited. Cromwell repeals. For the revolutionaries the millennium was imminent. Marvell isn't simply referring to a biblical non-time, he is referring to a very precise historical moment. Real time begins to be very menacing in this poem.'

Another few minutes and it's over. 'Essays in a pile on the table, please,' he says. The others crowd around the table but she goes to the door. He says: 'Elizabeth, have you got something for me?'

'No,' she says.

Everyone looks at her.

He frowns, then smiles. 'What,' he says, laughing, 'nothing at all?'

'No.'

The smile disappears. 'Not even an apology?'

'No.'

The third time has a finality she hadn't intended.

He seems to wake as if from a short sleep and says: 'Those people collecting their special-author papers stay behind, the rest of you, have a great summer.' Then he turns and begins sorting out a pile of Xeroxed hand-outs.

Damn. She had forgotten about special authors. She

remains along with Jessie and David and Marcus, lurking at the rear.

When it is her turn he says: 'Remind me which author you're doing.'

Now it is her turn to stare. 'Milton,' she says.

'Oh, yes.' He hands her the paper.

She looks at him. She would speak now if she could, would give up this pretence of not caring, but the whole world is conspiring against her – the levity of the day beyond the window, the next group waiting in the corridor, the sensation of being winded. In a different world, at a different time she could speak; but not here and not now – not with him so unwilling to help her.

She stands a moment longer as he collects the essays, slotting them together briskly against the wood, then picks up her bag and goes out.

The Seventh Night

Why did you do that? she said to herself. Why were you rude to him?

She said: I was afraid.

Why didn't you reply to his notes? she asked. Why did you run away from the concert?

I was afraid.

Of what?

That was a difficult one.

Of what I was feeling.

What was she feeling?

She closed her eyes. She said: I don't know.

Shortly before eleven Professor Stone's head hurt on the left side again and her left eye became blurred. She took more tablets standing at the sink with her eyes closed. It was cool in the bathroom and dark; she combed water into her hair and stood leaning on the washbasin for some minutes before going back to her desk.

She held her head gently and said: 'In a minute the tablets will work and you will feel better. You've made good progress, Elizabeth. The introduction is done and it isn't yet midnight. Now you must get down the first chapter.' But what she found herself thinking about was what she had remarked to Edward Hunt earlier that evening about the day being wasted, and she said: 'I wish I hadn't said it; I wish I had said anything but that.'

It was hotter now, the darkness a blanket; the world consisted only of small noises and everything was still. She finally began to type again at a quarter past but had got no further than a few words when she stopped. Was it true what he had said? That she had not come back for the Eliot papers? No. What had she come back for, if not that? Nevertheless, she let the question dangle in front of her for a minute and tried to look at it steadily. Then she remembered something else he had said earlier that evening, and now, come to think of it, the first time they had met: he had said she understood everything, a lot more than she let herself believe.

She held her head in her hands and pressed it. 'All right,' she said. 'All right. Just supposing the papers are not the reason I came back; well, if they aren't I don't know what is. It's true I thought of coming here before I discovered "The Music of Poetry"; I thought of it while I was ill – when I thought I was dying. I didn't mention it earlier but he knew. How did he know? How did he know what I had forgotten?'

Then she sat up straight and said: 'Think, Elizabeth, but not about that. This is the work you've waited your whole life to write, and this night you will write it.' But in spite of having the moment in her hands it was all she could do to stay in her seat. She heard a voice say: '*Thus, though we cannot make our sun/Stand still, yet we will make him run*' – and she still didn't understand that infuriating couplet. It was like Eliot's: 'Only through time time is conquered'.

She felt frightened and made herself think again of the long road, the destination very close now. How terrible never to make progress, to go on making the same mistakes all your life, never to move forward but only in circles. She had begun typing again fast: '*Repetition is a key musical device by which Eliot inducts his readers in assimilating the timeless moment*,' when a tinkling made her look up. It seemed to be coming from the lamp. She pressed the plug more firmly into the wall with her toe but it continued. She positioned the lamp further away but the glare of the screen was too bright. She sighed, adjusted her glasses and continued: '*Which is it: redemption or repetition? A lifetime burning in each moment or a lifetime of waste? The poet answers: "There is no end but addition".*'

Tinkle.

A muscle in her temple clenched and unclenched itself.

'*Returning makes progression possible while simultaneously alerting us to the fact that progress involves gathering the past into the present.*'

Tinkle.

She closed her eyes, then remembered what he had said: that the past was here, now, breathing down their necks. But that was ridiculous. How could the past be anything other than past? It could not remain perpetually arrested: that would be purgatory, limbo, a living hell. Reliving the past as one woke only in sleep to dream it again, never able to extricate oneself from its ever widening circles . . .

Tinkle.

She loosened the neck of her nightgown. He had said that she had lived a lie. How dare he? How could anyone say someone else had lived a lie? How would they know? 'I have not lived a lie,' she said. 'I have devoted myself to what I believe in. That is more than many can say and it has not been easy at times.'

Tinkle.

She scratched her head and began to type very fast: '*Eliot himself wrote: "Love is the unfamiliar name" that "calls", that "draws" us, so that we are moved to explore, to arrive at the beginning, at what we have always known.*'

She laughed. What a strange word. Lazy, lolling – almost ugly. *Love*. Words had a habit of becoming alien when you really thought about them. She frowned, then continued: '*This "previous state of existence", the notion that there run on parallel lines, as in a musical score, notes of being, particular frequencies, which resonate one with another*'

Tinkle.

'might explain why Eliot felt, by means of music'

Tinkle.

'genuine poetry could communicate before it was understood, tapping into a database of consciousness which'

Tinkle.

A wave of light passed over her and she heard the lamp smash against the far wall.

She sat still in the glow of the screen, then got up and turned on the overhead light. The fluorescence made the room feel like a bunker and illuminated the uneven walls, shabby carpet and mismatching furniture. The base of the lamp was in two pieces. She collected them and the broken bulb, and coiled the flex around the base. She put the lamp on the coffee-table and went back to the desk. What had come over her? She would have to pay for it tomorrow. She would say it had fallen from the table. She held her hands in her lap because they were shaking. There was blood beneath her fingernails. She didn't know how it had got there.

'What's the matter?' she said to herself. 'You can write this tomorrow. You don't have to do it now.' But the pain in her head and the stiffness of her arm and the stillness of the world beyond the window all told her that she had only this night.

She made coffee and drank it with her eyes closed, listening to something that sounded like crickets beyond the window. Summer nights had a sound all of their own; it was as if you could hear the earth ticking. In winter it slept so deeply it seemed dead. It was now midnight, 'midnight moment's forest' – that was Hughes, and the night was a little like a forest now, blind, pressing close; if it was a moment it felt like an endless one.

It suddenly occurred to her that she had travelled further this night than she had her whole life. The thought was a strange one and frightened her. She tried to think of something else. She thought: I am almost at the end now; but Eliot replied: '*Or say that the end precedes the beginning,/ And the end and the beginning were always there/ . . . /And all is always now.*' 'Now': there was another word that didn't bear too much thinking about, but words didn't when you got close to them. It is astonishing, she thought suddenly, how things – sounds, objects, colours – came to be, came to make sense to us solely through language. The world was so vast, so miraculous, so multifarious – and yet it remained up to words to mediate it. What was it like before language? What would experiencing such a world be like? She supposed no one knew, that experience residing before memory had developed. Then were words and time indissoluble? Could one exist without the context of the other? One word without the next?

She went back to the desk and peered anxiously at what she had written. She couldn't tell whether it was good or bad but had never written so quickly, so freely in her life. I must be careful, she thought. I am not myself tonight.

The pain in her head came again suddenly just after three and her left eye darkened. She held her hand over it, feeling the orb dart and quiver and knew that dawn was not far away now. She said to her eye: 'If you last just a little longer I will reward you.' She tried to think how she would do this. She said: 'I will let you rest for a week.' She had never addressed her body in this way before but tonight felt an uncharacteristic stab of compassion for it in all its chilblained, varicose-veined, Marks & Spencer-ed glory. It was odd to consider – if only in an abstract way – that it might have an intelligence of its own. Had it imagined sitting here in its fifty-second year? she wondered. Sitting for most of its life, in fact, before a page or a screen or a book, bent obediently to the task at hand; sitting and reading, reading and writing, writing a masterpiece. Well, it had taken thirty years – more; it was an awfully long time. A voice said: '*In place of the sensual banquet, the material gratifications of the conqueror.*' And what had she conquered? Herself, she supposed; and she had won. Was this what victory felt like?

For the first time she let herself consider what she would do if this meant what she thought it meant and discovered that she didn't know. 'But I will do something,' she said. 'There's always something to be done.' The thought did not have much reality, however, and she was gripped by a desire to run from the room – a desire so strong she could not help thinking that what she had written might be worthless because her current frame of mind could hardly be called 'detached'. She pressed on:

This is poetry's triumph over time [she typed]: *its memorability, the way it rings out over centuries, sounds the depth of this stuff called flesh and blood, makes it new so it can be understood all over again, so we can remember what we have forgotten, go away and come back.*

Then, before she could continue, her hands had dropped to her lap. And what about me? she thought. Why did I come back? He had said, 'Why now?' and she had not been able to answer.

She had always been wary of reading too much into things, of prioritising subtext, so it was with scepticism that now she allowed herself to consider again the last weeks of that term. And what if something did happen? she thought. It is long gone now. Though he had said the past was not gone; he had said it was there with them. He had said 'breathing down our necks'. She thought she would not see Edward Hunt again after that last tutorial but she had forgotten Milton. She had kept forgetting Milton; it became something of a habit, in fact. So she went back to return him on an afternoon of great light. Eliot wrote in

'Burnt Norton' of a pool, 'dry concrete, brown edged', 'filled with water out of sunlight'. Thinking of it now, that was just how Professor Stone would describe the light that afternoon, a substance that blinded even as it illuminated.

Her eyes were full when they returned to the screen; she blinked the tears away and began typing again:

Dante's insistence on the unspeakableness of the final vision compels his cumulative imagery, and therefore his substitutes for it; a dream, melting shapes in snow, the Sibyl's oracle scattered on the wind, a shadow in the sea; the failure of his utterance the means and the measure of his success. 'For it is ultimately the function of art, in . . . eliciting some perception of an order in reality, to bring us to a condition of serenity, stillness, and reconciliation; and then leave us, as Virgil left Dante, to proceed toward a region where that guide can avail us no farther.'

The failure of an utterance was the measure of its success; was her own successful or unsuccessful, then? Well, whatever it was, it was complete. She had here the first chapter and essence of her thesis. It just remained to apply the same technique to the other authors she had in mind and write a conclusion. She saved the document to a CD and closed the laptop lid. She would give it to Edward Hunt tomorrow – no, this morning. She would present him with the thing she had wanted to ever since he'd sent her the *Quartets*. She hoped he would be pleased.

It was now half past four and the light was coming, and Professor Stone knew the day would not be like the one before; not like any day before. She meant to get into bed but, laying her head on her arms for a moment, slipped into sleep.

She dreamed of the house by the sea, of the time the seals came to the bay, the sky leaden, the rocks statues and the sea impossibly vast. She and her mother watched the seals' silky heads bob above the water and the silver coils they left when they went under that spread like oil and went on spreading, as if their departure mattered more than their coming; as if they kept on departing long after they had disappeared. Then she was alone in the window-seat and the seals went on barking their strange prehistoric cries over the waters and she wanted her mother. When she woke she didn't remember the dream and her head was heavy, as if she had risen from death not from sleep, and she was filled with dread and with grief and it struck her with the force of a revelation that she did not want to be here, where she was, doing whatever it was that she was doing, writing words on a screen; and she wondered how long she had felt like that because she had always supposed that she had.

She tried to get up and go to bed but her head was too heavy and in a moment she was once again sleeping. This time she didn't dream of the house by the sea but of the kitchen where she had sat working at the large table and the stranger whose features eluded her. The kitchen was deserted now and she and the stranger sat in an inglenook fireplace she hadn't noticed before. Her bare feet were on the fireguard and her socks drying on the fender. The stranger's hair was damp and his cheeks flushed, as if he had been out in rough weather. He was reading aloud from a red book with gold letters on the spine and the cover and the woman with the shining hair and the knight in chainmail, and every word he read dropped like molten lead into the quiet around them and became solid matter. Presently he smiled and said, 'Got any idea yet?' but she shook her head, and though she wanted to find out what happened at the end of the book she could not bear to reach the end because she knew that then he would leave. Then she supposed that the stranger could also have been referring to himself, asking her if she knew who he was, but her answer would have been the same because she still could not make out his features.

This time she woke to whizzing followed by bangs, her hair sticky with sweat, coloured lights in the sky beyond the window. She tried to lift her head but it felt heavier than ever and she fell back into a waking dream in which she was a student again, pounding up the last flight of stairs in the great library to the Upper Room where books were waiting for her, books she had ordered – the most important books in the world – but when she reached the door, an attendant would not let her in: there was something wrong with her reader's card; it had expired, a digit was missing from the number, her photo had been obscured – she was unsure what was wrong exactly but she had to stand aside and watch others go in ahead of her, a long line of them. She could not see into the room beyond but from the doorway streamed a bright light.

Then she was walking along the road that led out of the city to the north, and the houses were giving way to hedges and the hedges to fields, and she was no longer young and she was crying, and woke with a jolt, her mouth working on air.

The professor wanted to move very much now, wanted to get up, as if her life depended upon it, but before she could raise her head the next dream was upon her, and this time she was skidding, scrabbling, pressed down and down further, pulsing in her ears and her heart bursting. She is standing on the landing of the house by the sea, the wind is high and the moon bright. Music is playing downstairs and the music is strange, out of time, half nursery rhyme, half opus, half tragic, half ironic, and she knows immediately that something is not right – knows she has to go down; that if ever she must go downstairs it is tonight; that if ever she must be brave it is now. She must go to her mother and wrestle her back from wherever she is, haul her in, hand over fist, make her hear and see her, but she is as still as a statue.

The more she tells herself she must move the more paralysed she becomes, and the longer she thinks about it the less able she is to think at all. 'Go back to bed,' says the sea beyond the window. 'This has happened before. Nothing has happened before; nothing is happening; over and over. It will go on happening. Everything is as it was.' But the music says otherwise. It is writing words above her, inscribing them in the air above her head. She tries to put both side by side, tries to see which is right. Then she lifts her head oddly, like a child drowning, and slides down the wall to the floor.

She doesn't know how long she crouches there but at some point she hears something else: she hears the front door open and shut softly as someone goes out. Now that it is too late – that she no longer has to move – the spell is lifted: she runs to the window and looks down. A tall figure is walking towards the cliff-path, the wind filling her coat like a sail. As they reach the top the figure is silhouetted against the sky and, for a moment, appears like a voyager on the cusp of some great adventure. Whoever it is does not appear to be doing anything: their hands are not in their pockets but at their sides and, despite the wind buffeting their coat and hair, they are as still as a stone. The darkness beyond the figure is immense, the sky low, but the figure gathers its coat around it, puts its head down and walks into it.

She is scattered, stretched across heavens, spun to the finest of threads. There is a roaring that terrifies her as she runs along the landing and down the first flight of stairs, down the second and third flight. The front door is closed, looks as if it has never been opened. For a moment she thinks it is all right: she will go into the room and her mother will be sitting in the armchair. But when she opens the door the room is empty, except for the music spilling from the blue box with the lid. She has made a mistake. She is too late.

She runs back to the front door and wrestles with the latch, slips, catches her arm and totters backwards. She is shouting, things are going black, she is falling down and getting up, wrestling again with the latch. She hears a window bang, the wind rise, feels the house spin. Then she and the house and the music are fading, her body is sinking into some substance thicker than air, she is watching it get further and further away, and she knows that everything will always take place after this moment; the moment that as soon as she wakes she will once more forget.

This time the professor woke unravelling at a furious rate of knots and cried out, waking or drowning, she wasn't sure which – though there were no mermaids or song, only fireworks going on over her head.

She managed to get up from the desk and got into bed. 'These are the things people regret when they are dying,' she said to herself. 'But not me. I have had my vision. I chose the dark room, I chose the deep water beyond all landmarks. It hasn't been easy, but it is over now. You can sleep, Elizabeth, you can sleep.'

She pulled the sheets over her and moved her leg back and forth because the pain had returned in her head. She began to cry and for once made no attempt to smother the sounds but listened to them as if they were made by some strange animal barking its discontent across wild and hostile waters.

A lifetime is not that long: that was what the professor of poetry thought as she slipped into sleep. The fact that a major part of it may have been wasted does not seem to be a cause for concern so much as wonder. That it is gone so quickly, spent so fast.

Water Out of Sunlight

There are poppies in the river meadows. The sky is blue silk. Elizabeth Stone is walking to Edward Hunt's room on an afternoon of great light with *Paradise Lost* and her last essay. Milton weighs heavily in her bag but the essay she cradles in her arms exudes electricity as if it wanted to scamper away from her. She is walking quickly but the afternoon does not seem to brook hurrying. Stillness is sealing and preserving each cobblestone and leaf, sunlight soaking the city in a kind of transcendence, submerging it in liquid amber. It is also warping it. Air bubbles like glass above gardens and bends like smoke in the middle of the road; the river swims, the spires riveted. She can hear the suggestive chink of tableware from gardens and the thwack of a cricket ball in the playing fields, distant at any time and place, but today doubly removed, existing as if in a dream. All is hypnotised, suspended; the sun has gathered the city up in its arms and rocked it, and its inhabitants are sleepwalking; cyclists labour, pigeons stumble; she feels herself sway on the kerb. The sunlight is so strong, it is as though many afternoons have been concentrated into one, the brightness of centuries into an hour. It is making her eyes water; it is the sunlight, but a passer-by would be forgiven for thinking that the thin girl lifting her glasses to wipe her eyes is crying.

She goes through the college, across the first quad and into the tunnel, and when she comes out, the light is falling in shards through her fingers, hammering red, white, gold, like notes on an anvil. Walls, grass and paths are revealed in snatches and she walks blindly, feeling the blows, her steps taking place somewhere far beneath her. The college is deserted. She doesn't think she has ever seen it so silent. Surely there should be a noise from the kitchens. A person on one of the paths; going into the well of a staircase or a dark panelled door? Perhaps there is an event – though she cannot remember there being one. It is the end of term, but there are still some lectures and tutorials, and some people had exams.

She goes up the steps by the horse-chestnut tree into the stone building and turns along the glass corridor. She cannot see the rose garden today. The light has hidden it behind a curtain of what appears to be dazzling water, and there is only this dry path along which to walk. In the darkness beyond, she knocks at his door, and as she does, the stillness of the afternoon deepens, the day takes on a knowingness she hadn't noticed before. Then a voice shouts: 'Come in!'

She goes in blinking. The room is full of shafts and blades, whirring motes and blurred lashes. It appears to be in chaos, and it looks as if the sunlight is responsible because the curtains have been tucked back and swathes of light are pouring into the room, appear to have rifled it, riddled objects from their darkness and scattered them haphazardly here and there; boxes, books, cassettes, records, photographs, mugs, ashtrays – nothing is where it ought to be. A kettle sits in an armchair, a model of the globe in the sink, Bach is propped indecorously in the wastepaper bin and the Fender surveys the room from the sofa. The garden of withered pot plants occupies the table; by a chair leg is a mug in which a small garden is growing.

'I'm up here.'

She turns to see him balancing at the top of a stepladder, his face flushed with irritation but also with labour – a first, she thinks: two whole shelves are cleared of books.

'What are you doing?' she says.

'Dusting.'

The word seems inadequate somehow.

'I'm sorry to disturb you. I brought my essay,' she says.

He comes down the stepladder, swaying precariously, and drops some books on the desk. 'Isn't it early?'

'Yes.'

She hopes he will take it from her but he flops into his chair and reaches for his cigarettes. She stands by the side of the sprouting mug, wondering if she can move towards the door again, but finally, afraid of offending him, she sits too.

The afternoon stretches away, pale with heat beyond the windows. Honeysuckle waves tendrils on the rug, roses cluster at the sill, but this is all she can see beyond of the outside world because the light is so bright.

He takes a first drag and exhales, saying: 'I take it you've recovered.'

'What?'

'From your "fit" at the concert.' Hefty twitching and pushing up of hair. 'And your little display of rudeness in the last tutorial.'

'Oh.' She looks down. 'I think so.'

Lots of swinging with the boot. 'Did it occur to you to let me know that you were all right after the concert?'

'Yes.'

The cigarette halts midway to his lips. 'It did occur to you?'

'Yes.'

'I see . . .'

'But I didn't know why I left. So I didn't know what to say to you.'

'Surely you could have let me know you were all right.'

'Yes. But I didn't know if I was. I don't know what happened. It's a mystery.'

'A mystery?'

'Yes.'

His mouth twitches as if he would smile, but he doesn't yet.

There is silence for a moment, then she says again: 'I brought my essay.' She holds it out, still not looking up, and this time he takes it.

His face changes as he feels the weight. 'How long is this thing?'

'About fifteen thousand.'

He sighs and shakes his head. He continues to shake it as he flicks through the pages, pursing his lips so that he doesn't smile instead. He frowns and says: 'How can you see to do this tiny stuff?'

She shrugs.

He turns a page round, better to inspect a chart. 'And what's this?' He looks vaguely outraged.

'That's a diagram.'

He puts down the essay and relights his cigarette; the leg has begun to swing again. He blows smoke away and says: 'I hope you haven't been missing lectures to do this.'

'Only a few unimportant ones.' In fact she hasn't come out of her room for ten days.

The beginnings of a smile are finally invading his face; there is a twitch at the corner of the eyes, a little shrug of the lips, strange currents that appear and then vanish again, like clouds moving across water. 'You realise this far exceeds anything you would be expected to produce at under-graduate level?'

She shrugs again.

'You realise that every essay you've produced for me has been way and beyond what everyone else handed in?'

'I don't know.'

'I suppose this is the last essay you'll write for me so you thought you'd make it one to remember.'

She continues to look at her knees. She wants to go now; she wants to get the moment of parting over with.

'You don't need to prove anything to me, you know that, don't you?'

'Yes.'

'None of this counts towards anything.'

'I know.'

'Do you write as much for the other tutors?'

'I don't know.'

A lie: she couldn't write as much for the others. The pain in her chest is lacing it tight. In an effort to distract herself she shifts her gaze to the rug. Sunlight is illuminating the fibres. The colours seem richer than before, the vistas deeper, the scenes more shifting.

He says: 'I find it depressing beyond measure that this might be the last essay you write for me.'

Unless she is dreaming there now appear to be small birds in the rug; what she took to be fleur-de-lis are birds of paradise. The birds are dancing, arching their necks. How could she have mistaken these brilliant creatures for abstractions, objects, mere pattern? Patterns didn't sing or dance. But the birds are singing – their beaks are open, they are calling to each other; they balance on the branches; their long tail feathers hang down.

She says: 'Can I ask something?' She is careful not to raise her eyes from the rug.

'Fire away.'

'When I am gone—' She corrects herself: 'After I leave – here . . .' She swallows. 'When I'm a graduate—'

'I understood the first time, Elizabeth.'

'If I should – if I should—' She clears her throat; she can't get enough air. 'If I should – if I should do something – and you get to hear about it—'

'Oh, I'll hear about it.' His voice is deep. 'I'll be watching you.'

The pain in her chest is suddenly so piercing that she knows if she isn't careful she will gasp or cry out, so she says nothing more and continues to watch the birds of paradise in the rug, though she cannot see them any more.

There is a heat in the room that makes thinking difficult, and when she speaks again she is no longer aware of her voice or the room or even of the professor, only the light all around them and the extraordinary pain in her chest. 'But if it should be something bad . . .' she says, her voice hoarse.

'It won't be. It'll be something good.'

Then she raises her eyes and looks at him and sees something she has caught only glimpses of before. Something falls away from his face; it appears to become darker. He seems about to rise, but instead he leans forwards in the chair and says: 'Elizabeth—' There is a knock at the door.

He closes his eyes and says: 'Fuck.' Then he opens them and says: 'Come in.'

A third-year peers around the door. His face is grey and shining – with anxiety, she thinks. She has seen it before with finalists. The boy doesn't look as if he has slept in a week. He says: 'Can I have a word, Edward? It's about my extended essay.'

He turns to her. He says: 'Wait for me on the stairs. Don't go away.'

Closing the door behind her, she hears him say: 'What's the problem, Simon?'

She stands in front of the door. She intended to leave at once, but instead finds herself leaning forward slowly, as if lowered by pulleys, and resting her head against it. She can feel his voice through the wood. She closes her eyes.

She doesn't know how long she stands there but when she straightens she feels the physical force of the door against her skull, the pull that hard objects exert when you have pressed against them for some time; the door must be made of granite if the sensation is anything to go by.

The pulling persists as she walks down the glass-walled corridor, as she passes the rose garden behind its curtain of water, as she opens the door to the quad and steps out.

Into the Rose Garden

She is no more than halfway up the street when a bump in her bag tells her she has forgotten *Paradise Lost*. Or, rather, she has remembered.

She cannot go back. It doesn't feel humanly possible. Her body protests; her legs refuse to move from the spot. But she must. Because to leave *Paradise Lost* in the professor's pigeon-hole is unthinkable. So she goes back down the cobbled street, through the gatehouse, the tunnel, the quad, and as she does, she feels she is wading into deep water.

She goes up the steps into the cool of the building and begins to walk down the corridor of glass, and then stops, because the curtain of light has now been rent, revealing something she has never seen before: the door, open. Beyond it the garden is shimmering; she can smell the freshly cut grass, smell the roses, feel the heat on her skin. It makes her frightened that the door is open though she cannot say why. She thinks about closing it, stands there a moment in the greatest perplexity, then hurries on.

She knocks at his door. There is no answer and she closes her eyes in relief. Now she will have to leave the book in his pigeon-hole and she will be excused for doing so. No – she's had a better idea: she will ask the porter to keep it behind the counter and give it to him in person. Why didn't she think of that before?

She is berating her own dim-wittedness, rushing back down the corridor, when she sees a figure in the garden and stops. It is so surprising to see anyone at all in the garden that for a minute she thinks she is seeing things, that the strange light is playing tricks with her, has created a mirage – or a ghost. The figure is standing with its back to her. She tries to make out who it can be but the light is so bright it is no more than a pillar of smoke. Whoever it is does not appear to be doing anything, not even looking around, and their hands are not in their pockets but at their sides, as if they have been petrified. Then, horribly, as in a dream, the figure turns. She stumbles backwards, her heart beating hard, but the figure has seen her, it is too late; there is nothing for it but to go into the garden.

The heat is staggering; that is the first thing she notices as she steps through the door – the sun is rebounding off the red brick and bouncing up from the paths. The second thing she notices is the scent of the roses, which is so strong it seems to curdle in the air. The third thing is the flowers themselves: enormous, ragged, feathered; velvet, silky; pleated, fleshy; ruffled, seething; coiled. She goes up to the professor – for it is he – and holds out the book. 'I forgot to give it to you,' she says, but he doesn't appear to have heard her. She says, a little more clearly: 'Thank you for lending me *Paradise Lost*. I'm sorry I forgot to give it to you earlier.' But still he doesn't move.

She was expecting him to be angry with her for not waiting on the stairs as he told her, but he doesn't seem to be – though she can't make out what he is feeling. He says: 'I thought I told you to wait.'

She looks down at her shoes. 'I thought it best not to.'

'Why?'

She shakes her head slightly, as if in pain.

He turns to look out over the garden. He says: 'I was just getting a breath of fresh air. The door was open. I think the gardener's around somewhere.'

Still not looking up she holds the book out.

This time he takes it, a little roughly, and says: 'Ah,

Milton, the great renouncer!' He flicks through the book and shuts it with a snap.

She is trying to think of something she can say so that she can leave, but before she can he says: 'What are your plans for the summer, Miss Stone?'

'Reading, I suppose.'

'Ah, yes. Third year. Serious stuff. What then?'

'What?'

'After you finish.'

She flicks back her fringe. 'I don't know.'

'Some other scholarship, some other body of higher learning – a glittering academic career.' There is something in his tone that is irascible, almost petulant; she would find it amusing if her chest wasn't hurting her so much.

'I don't know.'

He sways a little on his heels. 'And will you come back and visit your lowly tutor or will you outgrow him and move on to bigger, better things?'

She says quietly: 'I don't think anyone could outgrow you.'

'Oh, you will, you will!' He is adamant, seems to relish the thought.

She doesn't know where this is heading but she has already stayed longer than she intended. She feels that something is burgeoning inside her, and if she doesn't get away she might be ill.

She opens her mouth to excuse herself, when he turns and says, in a different voice: 'What do you want, Elizabeth?'

She looks at him. 'What?' she says.

'I said: what do you want?'

She blinks fast. 'I – I want—' For some reason it is hard to think. She stammers: 'I want to write . . .'

'Why?'

'What?'

'Why?'

'Because—' She swallows.

'Why?'

'Because I'm no good at anything else.' She glares at him, then turns away.

He says more quietly: 'I hope I haven't been instrumental in forming that belief.'

'No,' she says. 'I've always known it.'

Then he says, 'What happened to your mother, Elizabeth?' and she stares at him as if he has struck her, steps backwards, stumbles on the border of the path, and begins walking quickly towards the door.

He says: 'I know what happened. That's why you have so much self-hatred.'

She walks faster. She has almost reached the door when he says, 'Elizabeth—' in such a strange voice that she stops.

She hears him say: 'I know what happened, and you're still back there. You're so taken up with it you can't see what's here now. Look, Elizabeth. Look.'

She steps through the door but he is in front of her, blocking her way, catching hold of her hands. The instant he touches her, her spine becomes rigid and her head is thrown back. His eyes are black and glazed and he is burning her up with them, gazing at her so intensely that she feels evaporated, invisible. She fixes her own on a point a little higher than his waist; she is breathing fast and they are half closed.

He says, in a lower voice: 'You have to see, because this sort of thing doesn't happen often, sometimes not at all, and this is it, yeah, I'm sure of it.'

She pulls away sharply, involuntarily, in a sort of convulsion, but he doesn't let go. Blackness covers her eyes and her body is full of shaking blood. And it strikes Professor Stone now, lying in this room beneath the eaves, that at that moment something really was happening – but if someone had asked her then what it might be she would not have been able to tell them in even the most abstracted terms, except to say that her body seemed to be pulsing, that she must surely be beaming with light. That it was possible she was only half conscious because she could hear garbled voices and snatches of song and strange images as if replayed on an old cine-camera – the voices mismatching, the frames out of time, the film jumping and flickering. Except to say that she had been plunged into deep water, was travelling at the speed of light, buffeted by waves, coming up for air and going under. Except that they were both hurtling down a tunnel, that things shot backwards; except to say how absurd they looked, locked in some kind of eternal tussle; paper, scissors, rock; 'My thumb's stronger than yours' – till those thoughts shot away, too, at the speed of light.

But if you asked the professor now she would say: 'Hands. The palms warm and the fingertips cool. Hands, like other people's – and not like other people's at all.' She would say: 'The absurdity of these hands touching mine. Gripping them with surprising power. The mortality of knuckles, frailty of flesh, strange humour of half-moons; the miraculous living pressure of fingers.'

He drops her hands suddenly, as if realising they are no use to him. She stands frozen with eyes closed as he walks away.

The cobbled street is inclining. She doesn't remember it being this steep. She doesn't remember air being this dense either, but this afternoon walking through air is like walking through water. Halfway up the street she stops and is sick in the shade of a wall, and when she begins walking again she feels she is unravelling. She is not inside her body any more but back in the garden. She watches herself get further and further away from it as she continues along the street, and knows that everything will always be after this moment, set in a different place altogether, a place of permanent belatedness. The air in the quad and the street, the air passing through passages and archways is bright, suffused with pigment, with light and with stone and the smell of summer gardens immemorial. Brightness presses all around her and with it certainty, everything crystalline, transparent, exposed like a negative, and she sees the city, for the first and last time; entire; a map of the alleys and gateways, gardens and streets, the windows and spires, everything imprinted like copperplate on her retina; the slash of the river, the dark needle of a spire, the squares of honeyed stone, the ghostly towers, the blue-tinted dome; the streets and avenues, shapes and shadows, passing like ghosts, slipping over and under and through one another; quickly, slowly, haltingly; becoming consecrated, the way the view through a gate can become embedded, eternal in the mind's eye.

BOOK IV

'Quick now, here, now, always——'

*

'Little Gidding'
Four Quartets, 1942

The Eighth Day: Morning

Professor Stone woke later than usual that morning, the pain in her head already pronounced. She reached for the tablets but her left arm was limp. She tried to extend her fingers but her hand had contracted to a claw. The sight was blurred in her left eye. Healing pain, scar tissue: who was she kidding? There could be no doubt, really, that the cancer had returned.

She sat up. It was then that she knew the depths of her tiredness. Her head was swimming, her body drunk. She broke the tablets open with her right hand and took two sitting on the side of the bed. She stayed there for a long time, not thinking of anything, then got up and went to the window.

The sky was leaden, the poplars statues, the river meadows vaster than she had ever seen them. She was reminded this time so strongly of the view from that other window that the memory came with a jolt. She stood there a moment longer, then the aching in her chest made her turn away.

She washed in the basin with her right hand, squeezing the flannel against the side of it, running the comb through her hair. She buttoned her shirt by pressing the buttons against her chest but couldn't pull her tights on straight and settled for crookedness. She wedged her feet into her shoes without unlacing them, holding a pencil at the back, then packed, locked and left.

The pain in her head began to clear a little as she walked through the cloisters. She had tucked her left hand into her mackintosh pocket. Inside Hall, the light falling from the high windows was a physical pressure on her eyes; the smell of sausage and mushrooms and scrambled eggs made her queasy. The hubbub of the kitchen, the clatter of cutlery and swell of conversation assaulted her, though there weren't many students breakfasting this morning and those that were bore the look of the condemned; it could not be long now before the exams were over.

She discovered she could grip a little now with her left hand, though didn't trust herself with a tray and took a plate only. She sat at the edge of one of the benches and began to roll her boiled egg. Despite the cloudiness of the day the light was piercing and her neck damp with perspiration. She couldn't swallow the egg. She tried an apple but it was no better. Just as well, she thought, the sooner I get to the library the better; but she felt naked, exposed, on this last morning in the city, and as uncomfortable as it was sitting here on this bench she didn't want to be parted from it.

She felt strange, as if she was on the verge of some lone expedition, but with no one to wave her off or wish her luck, and she didn't know where she was bound, only a dark horizon, past which she would sail off over the lip of the world, into the infinite and irreclaimable beyond. She suddenly knew how her ancestors must have felt when they set off in their longships; there was something about the light falling from the high windows that made her think of those men of old. The Anglo-Saxons had a word for dread: '*morgenseoc*'; it meant 'fear in the morning'. She used to feel it as a child, watching her mother, wondering what sort of day it would be, but this morning the sickness augured something final, as if the day held terrors she could not yet identify; the wood had come to Dunsinane, the Oracle spoken; lots had been cast.

She tried to rouse herself from such thoughts but

succeeded only in slipping deeper, and the aching in her chest, which had been niggling all morning, had now reached such a pitch that she closed her eyes and held on to the edge of the table. What is it? she asked. This pain that rears up and strikes me dumb? It was usual for her to examine herself in this way. What was the matter? she asked herself. What did she want? The most obvious answer – that of life itself – did not occur to her. She thought: I want the thesis to be a success; I want that more than life, and although she had never articulated this thought to herself before it did not frighten her.

When she tested the answer against the aching, however, she realised it was not the right answer; it was not what she wanted now; what she wanted at this very moment, in this ancient panelled room filled with the sounds of plates and voices and passing feet, whose benches were lined with the ranks of the future and walls with dreams of the past, was something quite different. The answer presented itself as a Polish waitress stooped to collect her plate, accidentally bumping her and touching her arm in gentle apology, smiling so sweetly that liquid warmth travelled the length of the professor's body: what she wanted, more than anything, was to be touched. Could it be that simple? This thing she wanted most in the world? She was alarmed to discover that it could. 'Only connect,' she thought, and laughed at herself; E. M. Forster; Modernist mumbo-jumbo. She got up and went out beneath the gargoyles' gurning faces, crossed the quad. The sky was lowering. At the lodge she handed in her key. As she passed through the gate and bells rang out, 'First a warning, musical; then the hour, irrevocable.'

The street was deserted. Pink strings of fluorescent foam, glitter, neon horseshoes and shamrocks scattered the cobbles. An empty champagne bottle stood on the wall by the chapel railings, exuding a whiff of stale revelry, a limp balloon dangling vaguely obscenely from its neck. As she gazed at these remains of celebration, it occurred to her that she would finish this day what she had begun here years ago. 'You've done it, Elizabeth,' she said. 'It's taken a long time but now it's over. It is complete.' She said these things as she stood on the kerb waiting to cross the main street, as if she was both a runner in a race and a bystander cheering herself on because she felt beyond strange this cloudy morning, as if she was walking through a dream, though the touch and taste and sound of things were more real than they had ever been; she said these things because a fragmentation in her stomach, a weight-lessness in her limbs and the aching in her chest threatened some universal disassemblement; and because for some reason – in spite of everything – perhaps precisely because she had waited so long, she felt strongly that her job was not done, but that at the moment of emergence she would find her great work yet to come, must go forth not to honour but to trouble, and as in a dream re-enact over and over.

She passed the church, the Round Room beneath its blue dome. The square was withdrawn today and would not yield itself to her inspection. Every so often she clenched her left hand in the pocket of her mackintosh and was relieved to find that sensation was returning to it, though her left eye was still cloudy. She went through the passageway in the great library wall and crossed the courtyard. She hadn't visited the old place yet, so engrossed had she been in the archives, but nothing had changed. The walls were still brown, still pitted; the windows of many panes still depicted the scenes of history. There was the founder with the world passing upside down in his crown. As she went through the glass doors of the foyer it occurred to her for the first time that she was taking leave not of the city but of herself, because she had begun here, really begun. After you had left a place you loved, did you become part of it?

she wondered. Did your palms leave a trace on the wall where you leaned? Did your shadows linger in doorways or windows, haunt the bell-tower, sail with clouds over walls laced with ivy? Did some fraction of you become part of the taste of rain on wrought-iron railings or the ring of heels on old stones or the deep summer river, over-hung with alders, plunged into, forked over, embraced and exploding in pieces of water and light? Did the magic horse-chestnut trees sway with your breath or sigh when the sap moved inside them, arms reaching to boughs, fingers to twigs, toes wriggle down to root-tips scented with soil? Could streets remember your name and the sound of your steps, the place where you fell the night you pounded along in the rain, the alleyway where you leaned to get back your breath? If they could then she would leave herself here, among the ruins and façades and the long empty views stretching for miles, that hadn't changed for centuries and wouldn't for centuries to come; here, there, or elsewhere; in her beginning.

She showed her card to the attendant and the gate (Perspex, no longer wood) swung open. 'Bags in the cloak-room, madam,' a voice said, and an attendant showed her into a small, white, high-ceilinged room to the left of the lift shaft filled with lockers; this was new, too. She stowed her mackintosh and bag, took the laptop and began to climb the creaking steps of the tower.

The same! she wanted to shout at the banister, stone steps, half-circles worn by feet; the smell of dust and of paper, of skin and of time. It was all the more precious in view of the other changes, and so strange to be here again that for a moment the place felt holy to her. She craned to look up; she supposed there was something empyreal about the ascent to the Upper Room. She suddenly had an intimation this might be what Heaven was like – if there was a heaven; believers would swipe in, the gate would open and they would ascend spiral stairs to a lighted room where they would spend eternity among other enlightened souls reading books by the light of red and gold lamps, a Keatsian ecstasy of silence and slow time, endless hours marked by handless clocks that chimed no hour except the eternal Now. And down there would be Hell, she thought, peering into the lift shaft; there was something undoubtedly Tartarean about the basement; there, unoriginal souls would spend eternity ordering a book stack sorted by day and disordered by night.

She paused on the landing beneath the Upper Room and looked once more out of the deep-set window. Her breathing was audible, her arms hung by her sides. 'I will miss you,' she said. Then she mounted the last flight and opened the door.

White bookcases, large windows, parquet floor, moon-faced clock; the border of illustrious 'auctoritees' no more faded or cracked than she remembered (she supposed thirty-two years were a drop in a bucket compared to centuries); all was the same except for new chairs and desks, not yellowing pine, splintered and scuffed, but polished maple with green mats and leather seats. She closed her eyes and inhaled, then began to walk down the aisle.

The room was empty except for a handful of people, only two of whom looked like students. The sky beyond the windows was dark enough for the librarians to have turned on the lights but so far no one had done so and because of it, or perhaps because of the room's emptiness – or perhaps simply because nothing is ever as impressive as we remember – the room seemed homelier than it had been, more like a sitting room or a study than a public place, and the nameless auctoritees that bordered the walls nothing but tired old men, and it occurred to her that if the room did house gods, many gods and many voices, she could at last not be ashamed of adding her own.

It was a strange triumph, though, because greeting her like this, so naked and bereft of its regular devotees, her opponent had been brought low. It was as if she had been granted a glimpse of a long-venerated figure in an unguarded moment and after the moment of euphoria came one of deflation. As she passed one of the windows that looked on to the courtyard she glanced again at the room opposite. It was still, to all appearances, dark and uninhabited; if she had been hoping for some sort of illumination she was to be disappointed – the eyelid remained closed.

She found a desk close to the computers at the end of the room and opened her laptop. The quotation she wanted to check was kept in a book on the open shelves and she fetched it and found the page. There it was, Brémond saying 'in profane states of nature . . . we can decipher the great lines . . . discern the image and rough sketch of the mystical states of the soul for while listening, the "effort to understand relaxes".' '[E]ffort to understand relaxes' were Grand-maison's words after all; she had copied it correctly. She inhaled, was about to close the book, when her eyes were drawn to a footnote she did not remember seeing before.

No more need be said here about this particular facet of Milton's genius except to say that a much overlooked field of critical enquiry is now getting the scholarly attention it deserves. Promising work, with profound implications for our understanding of sound as a vehicle of poetic expression, is now being done. See Burr, Jonathan: The Sound of Sense: An Enquiry into the Margins of Knowledge . . .

Her stomach lurched and she felt the distinct need to urinate. 'Promising work', 'profound implications', 'sound as a vehicle'. Was it possible that she had missed another study so similar to her own? Was it possible that in all her years of counselling students about the necessity of exhaustive background research, of always – always – checking footnotes, she herself had fallen foul of those very same mistakes? No, it was not. She had read every book, every article, every review on the epistemology of sound under the sun; if the book Roth referred to really was so relevant to her own concerns she would have come across it when she trawled the search engines. Except, said a voice, and a small hand clutched at her heart, except if this particular footnote doesn't refer to a published work at all but a thesis like your own, awaiting publication.

She closed her eyes, then opened them, and turned to the bibliography. Her hands were shaking so badly she couldn't separate the pages but at last she found B. There it was: 'Burr, Jonathan: 'The Sound of Sense: An Enquiry into the Margins of Knowledge', Doctoral Thesis, 20–'. A white light swallowed her whole and for a moment she was nowhere. She sat in the smooth maple chair with its green leather cushion and felt the world as she knew it fall away from her. Then she forced herself to think again, to think clearly. Who was to say that this Burr had the same angle as herself? Who knew what he meant by 'the sound of sense'? Did he mean what she, the author of the new theoretical model 'A Poetics of Sound', meant – or something completely different? And even if his argument did run along similar lines, was it as radical, as far-reaching as her own?

She looked at her watch: too late to order the thesis that morning. At the enquiry desk she asked if there was any way she could see it that day. 'You don't need to order it,' the woman told her. 'You can look at it yourself. We're keeping theses in the basement now.' She thanked the woman, sat in front of the computer, found another shelf mark, filled in another pink slip. Her headache had vanished, her left hand moved easily – even her eye had cleared. Shock, she thought. It never fails to work wonders. Her knees were not holding out quite so well; as she went down the stairs she had to go slowly, hang on to the banister.

At the bottom, instead of turning into the foyer, she turned right, down one more flight, modern this time, concrete and hard-edged, where the air was palpable and the walls cold. She found the shelf mark, turned a handle like a ship's wheel and inched into the gap. A few minutes later she was sitting beneath a fluorescent bulb at a tiny Formica-topped table staring at a grey box bound with elastic bands. When she removed it she saw that the thesis inside was blue and bound in black tape. She stared at this, too, before she opened it to the introduction.

Too little has been made of the role of sound in our appreciation of literature in general and of poetry in particular. Would-be pioneers in the field have run aground before they got started by failing to realise that sound is a non-linguistic field and should be studied as such. In 'The Music of Poetry' (1942), T. S. Eliot, who propounded the theory of the auditory imagination and was a foremost proponent of the importance of the 'music' of poetry, talked of 'frontiers of consciousness beyond which words fail though meanings still exist'. This study traces a poetic tradition, a surreptitious but trenchant counter-current stretching from the Anglo-Saxon Scop to the twentieth century, a tradition in which meaning is reappropriated by the sensual from the cognitive . . .

She stared. And then, because there was nothing else for it, read on.

. . . the aural properties of verse operate on a different level from conscious thought. The way the human brain responds to sound and rhythm is anticipatory – even in infants, as if it has always at some level known it. It is akin to religious gnosis, the experience of déjà vu, of premonition, love at first sight, which Michelangelo describes as: 'La dove io t'amai prima', recognition from a previous state of existence . . .

. . . The implications of this seemingly trivial assertion are far-reaching. A floodgate of new readings of currently 'closed' works opens up. A poetics of space has changed the face of literary criticism; a poetics of sound should do no less.

She pushed the thesis from her with the air of one who has just learned something they do not need to know and sat staring at nothing.

A breeze was stirring the aspens in the private gardens beneath the Upper Room. The sky was darker. 'Did you find what you were looking for?' the librarian asked. She assured her that she had.

The eyes of the gods followed her as she returned to her seat. She had been wrong. Nothing had changed, after all, she was not triumphant, and the gods had known all along; mild-voiced elders, they bequeathed only a receipt for deceit. 'Timing,' she said, as she left the Upper Room. As she descended the stairs she had the impression that something inside her had burst; an organ of some importance had been broached. It had been seeping slowly at first, hardly noticeable, but with each step it flowed more freely, and by the time she reached the last flight she was awash on a current, a slick of debris, words, papers, scraps, shards, years, dispersing itself over darkening waters, beneath a sky that also darkened, until there was nothing left but the sound of the waters lapping and an increasing absence of light.

The statue, the square, the daylight were as she had left them, except now the air smelt of sulphur and the clouds, already low, formed a canopy brewing with intent. Beside a wastepaper bin she took the CD from her bag, but after a moment returned it; there would be no harm in showing him, there was no harm in that. She went through the covered passage into the square and the walking people, spinning bicycle wheels, the glimpse of passing traffic astonished her. It was a vision of the world familiar but illuminated for the first time in its complete and absolute indifference.

She sat on a bench opposite the dome. Movements, sounds, sights seemed to be going on miles above her. Her limbs were heavy as if filling with sand. She was aware of a thrumming, the type she imagined one heard under ether, in the bowels of a ship or a dream. She asked herself what she would do now and she didn't know. She thought: This time there will not be a miracle. But she felt no fear, only the promise of something like sleep.

Her hands lay in her lap and she considered them, the veins and the sunspots, the creases and ridges. She said: 'I am sorry, hands, because you served me well and I have not been good to you.' Her eyes travelled to her legs sticking out in front of her, the thin shins and dun-coloured tights. She said: 'And I am sorry, legs, because all your life you sat at a desk and you shifted on the seat of hard chairs.' She considered the sleeves of her blue mackintosh. She said: 'And I am sorry, arms, because you never wore bracelets and never hugged and never saw much of the sun.' Her head hurt very much then, and she closed her eyes and said: 'And I am sorry, head, because you worked for so long and I never rewarded you, only made you work harder.' Then her eyes were hot and the pain in her chest was very great and it occurred to her for the first time that it came from her heart. She said: 'And I am sorry, heart, because you beat fast for fear many more times than for joy, and never for love.' Then she opened her eyes and said: 'What happened?' And answered: 'I made a mistake.' She thought: What can I say? And the answer was: Nothing. Perhaps there had always been nothing.

She was feeling strange, insubstantial. If all the things that made someone up, she thought, that were strung like beads on a thread, flew apart and went skipping away over the floor, did the person come apart too? What was a human being? What made it up? Was it perishable or made of different stuff? Were we new in each moment, and hence – in a way – nothing? Or every moment – and hence 'All'? If, as Eliot said, 'All is always now'? If 'All' was always now, then did her grand idea – the idea that would have concluded her career as it should have concluded; that was brilliant, that was brave, that was entirely her own – exist in some absolute way even before she conceived it, in a realm of eternal realities? Did it matter that someone else had thought of it before her? Or perhaps at the same time? Did it matter that his work would be published and acclaimed while hers languished on a dusty shelf? Did it matter that it was written at all, or only thought of? Where did the existence of things begin? Where did it leave off? Did it matter that she had spent her life imagining she was doing something fine when, in fact, she was not? Had not? That she imagined she had lived each moment to the fullest when she had actually not lived more than a handful?

She was peering into a gulf terrifying in its infinitude – but she looked again and the day was beautiful; a child ran behind another holding on to his jacket; a Chinese family were having their photo taken against the gates of a college with twin spires; a gull, blown sideways by a sudden gust, cried and took flight. She had made a mistake. But the children were still playing, the family still laughing, the gull still in flight – getting higher now and higher.

The pain in her head was very bad and she bent forwards. A library porter, who was smoking close to the wall, watched her; for a moment it looked as if he was about to come over, but he did not, and after another he ground the butt beneath his shoe and went back into the courtyard. Thunder clattered. The first spots of rain wetted the cobbles. She stood up.

Professor Stone walked out into the square and the rain wet her and the wind filled her coat like a sail. Near the middle she veered towards the railings of the dome; it looked as if she might stop, but she did not; she walked on across the square and down the narrow street at the side of the church. As she reached the main street, bells rang out, and she suddenly remembered the taste of the city on the very first day she had arrived in her seventeenth year, the peculiar light that slanted across it; the heady nameless longing at one with those heavy skies laden with cold. She felt such tenderness now for her youthful despair. She thought: I will not see this city again, and I have loved it so.

The Eighth Day: Afternoon

'Off already, Miss Elizabeth?' the porter said.

'Yes, Albert. I finished sooner than I thought.'

'Professor Hunt'll be sorry to see you go. So will I. I thought we had you for at least another week.'

'Things wrapped themselves up sooner than I expected.' She smiled at him.

'Are you all right, Miss Elizabeth? You look a bit peaky, if you don't mind me saying, a bit on the pale side.'

'Thank you, Albert, I'm quite all right,' she said.

'When are you going to come and see us again?'

'Perhaps not for a while.'

'What a shame. It's not often we get the likes of you coming back.'

She laughed a little. 'What do you mean, the likes of me?'

'Well, someone of your stature, you know. You're one of the big names now aren't you, with your accolades and honours and what-have-you?' His eyes were obscured as his face was wreathed in smiles.

She said: 'You're an institution yourself, Albert. The college couldn't do without you.'

He inhaled. 'Well, the way I look at it, Miss Elizabeth, is this: there's horses for courses. Even if I could do what you do – and I couldn't, not in a million years – I don't think I'd want to and that's the truth. All that thinking!' He laughed at the very idea, then went on: 'No, we each do our bit. We're all given something; there may be a big difference in what that is but we haven't frittered it away. You get me?'

Droplets of sweat had appeared on the professor's forehead. 'I do, Albert,' she said. She smiled at the flagstones. 'I do.'

'Don't get me wrong. I haven't got any big achievements, just me family. But they're the world to me. And I got this job here at college. And you,' he brought his hand down heavily on her shoulder, 'you got your books.'

'Yes,' she said. 'You're right. We each – as you say – have what we've been given. You have your family. And I – I have my books.'

He frowned and peered closer at her. 'If you don't mind me saying, Miss Elizabeth, you don't look right at all. D'you want to sit down? D'you want a drink of water?'

'No, thank you.' She stood a little straighter. 'But I must be getting on – I have to see Professor Hunt and then I have a train to catch.'

'Of course. Would you like me to call you a taxi when you come back through?'

'Yes, that might be an idea, thank you, Albert.'

'Right you are.'

'Oh, Albert – the professor is in college, isn't he?'

The porter went to the other side of the counter. 'He'll be here till about six,' he called, then came through and opened the door for her.

She went down the steps holding on to the handrail. He watched her pass beneath the arch. As she turned into the quad he called: 'Miss Elizabeth, would you like an umbrella?'

'No, thank you, Albert.'

He watched her a moment more. 'Are you sure you're all right?'

'Yes, Albert, quite sure.'

Still he watched her, her hair flattened on her head, one end of her mackintosh belt trailing, till the corner of the tunnel obscured her.

*

273

She knocked at the door. Her eyes were closed and she was breathing slowly. When it opened he stepped back. She said: 'I'm going home.'

He said nothing for a moment, then: 'I thought you were staying another week.'

'I was, but there's no point staying longer. You were right about the Hyland Bequest. It wasn't that helpful.' She looked down and said: 'I'm sorry, I know you didn't want to see me again but I'm getting the train in an hour and wanted to say goodbye in person. I don't know if I'll see you again.'

He turned back into the room and said, in a voice thick with exasperation: 'Come in, Elizabeth, come in.'

She hesitated but he held the door wide.

She didn't take off the mac and he didn't offer to take it but she perched on the edge of the sofa and it was so wonderful to sit down and to be warm and to be still, if only for a moment, that she felt tears welling and closed her eyes in case he saw. She wanted to lie down and sleep more than anything in the world, and she could soon, she told herself, as soon as she got home. That was all she had to do now. Then he said sharply, 'You look pale,' and she opened them and said: 'It's just a headache. I've taken something. It'll ease up in a bit.'

'Coffee?' he said, still looking at her angrily.

'No, thank you.'

'I was just going to make some.'

'Oh, all right.'

When he turned to get milk out of the fridge she closed her eyes again. She felt as though she was swaying slightly but didn't know if it was visible. She sat back.

He filled the kettle at the little sink, looking over his shoulder at her. He said, 'You know, you do look very pale,' as if she should be ashamed of the fact.

She smiled faintly. 'I always look pale.'

He could say nothing to that.

The fizzing of the elements sprang into life and she listened to them in the dark room and to the rain outside, falling on the leaves and the paths and the rooftops. He cleared his throat and said, in a slightly more amicable voice: 'So, the *magnum opus* is complete. How does it feel?'

'Good, good . . .'

'Only "good"?'

She shrugged and smiled, and then because she was suddenly afraid she would cry again, she frowned and rummaged around in her bag for the CD. 'Here it is,' she said, without looking at him, and placed it on the table. 'I wrote the introduction last night.'

He took it and slipped it into the side of his computer.

'No,' she said in alarm. 'Not now. I meant you to read it when I was gone . . .'

But he was opening the file, the screen was loading, the title page appeared. She heard him scroll down, then scroll down again. Then he was still and she knew he was reading.

Outside, the rain suddenly fell faster as if a great tarpaulin had been shaken. It was so dark in the room now it felt like evening. A gust came in through the window smelling of rain and sulphur and freshly wet soil, of things new-broached and long hoarded, and she rested her head on the back of the sofa and turned to the window, where she saw herself and Edward Hunt and the white of the screen and the words move as he scrolled down. The kettle switched itself off but he didn't move.

Finally he said: 'It's beautiful.'

She looked at him. She hadn't been prepared for that – 'good' maybe; 'brilliant' perhaps she had hoped for. Not 'beautiful'.

His face was shining. 'It reminds me of your interview essays. It's got that wonderful immediacy, the spontaneity I loved.' Then he said: 'Elizabeth, are you sure you're all right?'

She nodded, though the pain was very bad. She said: 'I often get these things.'

'You should have a doctor prescribe something.'

He remembered the coffee – which she regretted – and began to pour hot water into mugs. 'Anyway,' he said, 'the introduction looks superb. I look forward to reading the whole thing.' He handed her a mug, launched himself into the armchair and lit up.

She stared into the steaming depths. Then, because she wasn't sure how much time she had, she said: 'Edward, I'm sorry things turned out as they did the other evening. I see I may have been "detached", as you said, perhaps even inconsiderate in the past. It was never my intention to be.'

His boot was swinging. He blinked quickly a few times and said: 'I'm looking forward to reading this. I really think you've got something.'

So he didn't want to talk about it. Well, that was all right.

She smiled and said: 'You never really know, though, do you? Till something's finished. And by then it's often too late.'

'Yes,' he said. 'Sometimes that's true. But not in your case, I think.'

Then she gave a small laugh, more of a gasp, really, and turned to the window. She appeared to be scanning the scene beyond the pane for something she had lost but there was nothing to be seen, only rain. She shook her head, an odd little jerk as if an insect had flown into her hair, and he watched her. She said: 'It seems—' She laughed and looked down at her hands. She said: 'It seems—' She gave the strange half-gasp again. She looked back towards the garden and said: 'It seems that—'

Then he said, 'What is it, Elizabeth?' in a voice so gentle it terrified her, and she pressed on as quickly as she could lest she crumble, and glared at him – and, though she hadn't meant to tell him, said: 'It seems that someone has written my thesis for me.'

There was a pause. Then he said slowly: 'What do you mean?'

She turned back to the window, breathing fast, her eyes very wide, her brows raised. 'Just that. Someone has written a thesis virtually identical to my own.'

'Indeed?'

'I discovered it this morning. In a footnote I'd overlooked, in a book I read months ago. The young man has just completed his master's. It's a very promising piece of work; I really was most impressed.' She laughed again. 'Perhaps it's just as well. I'm so busy with other projects I hardly know why I embarked on this at all. I mean – T. S. Eliot! What was I thinking?'

He said quietly: 'Are you sure it's the same? Have you looked at it?'

'Yes. He takes the auditory imagination as his starting point. He traces the same line, the same catalogue of authors I intended to, he makes prosody a field of enquiry itself – cites Michelangelo's definition of love at first sight.' She looked at him. 'Incredible, isn't it?'

'Yes,' he said.

They said nothing more for a minute and the rain fell so heavily beyond the window that tiny droplets splashing from the broad leaves of the ivy around the sill wetted her hand and the room was filled with the sound of rain and her breathing.

He said: 'I'm so sorry, Elizabeth. I know what this meant to you.'

'Yes!' she said. She laughed again. 'Not as much as some things, obviously. Some things are far worse.' She continued to peer desperately out of the window at the risk of appearing unduly interested in the shrubbery, which in fact she could see less of by the minute; now only the dim shape of the horse-chestnut tree and in truth not even that.

He inhaled deeply, then sighed. 'You'll write something else, Elizabeth.'

'No.' She shook her head fast.

'You've got many creative years ahead of you.'

'No.'

'Elizabeth, this is a blow, I grant you, but you've got more to come. I never doubted you would write something extraordinary. I never doubted it from the first moment I met you. Nothing has ever made me doubt it, and this hasn't either.'

'Then you're wrong.' A wave, rising inside her, threatened to break. She said: 'I won't write anything else. Not another word.'

He frowned. 'Elizabeth, you're a respected academic. I don't quite see—' and then his voice changed and he said: 'There's something else, isn't there? This isn't about the book.'

A white light flashed across her brain and for a moment the world went black. He got up, saying: 'What just happened?'

She was sitting back against the sofa, and when she answered her voice was hushed, as if it had been blown out. 'A headache, I told you.'

He went to the sink. He turned on the tap in a burst, filled a glass and came back with two paracetamol. He stood over her while she swallowed them and then went back to his seat. He banged a packet of cigarettes and took one in his mouth. He said: 'Are you going to tell me what's going on?'

'There's nothing going on.'

'I can read you, remember?' He tossed the packet on to the table. 'You're in a state; you've been in a state since you got here. What's the matter? Why are you unhappy?'

'What?'

278

'Well, are you happy?'

She took her hand away from her face and looked at him. She said: 'Are you?'

He stared at her for a moment, then inhaled deeply and turned to the window. 'Happiness is a big word,' he said. 'I occupy myself. I get by. But happy? No.'

They were silent and she shut her eyes, wishing she had already left. He was saying: 'This city, this college – I couldn't imagine being anywhere else now, but there are still days which are very empty.'

She was about to tell him she must go, should already have gone, had missed the train she had been going to catch and if she went on like this would miss the second, when she heard him say: 'In fact, there are days when I think of nothing but you.'

She heard the words clearly but they were so outside the realm of ordinary conversation that for a minute she hovered on the brink of comprehension, interpretations hurtling through her head in headlong pursuit, but before she could arrive at any satisfactory conclusion he was continuing, tapping his cigarette: 'And here you are – here you have been for over a week; it's a little overwhelming.'

She covered her eyes with her hand. She said: 'I have to—'

'Do you think of me?'

'What?' she said faintly.

'You heard me.'

She stared at him, then her body slackened and she stared at nothing. 'Yes,' she said. 'Sometimes. Often. I think of you.'

He said, 'Why did you come back, Elizabeth?' and his voice was raw and enraged, as it had been before.

But she was still staring at nothing, thinking: How strange life is. Because if he had said this then, my life would have been different. But he is saying it now. And I have to go away; I didn't have to then but I went anyway. Now I do have to and I don't want to. Then she thought: I don't want to live any more because living is too difficult. Out loud she said, 'I came back for the Eliot papers,' and she got to her feet. 'I really must go.'

She slung the hold-all across her shoulder and as she did so she tottered and put a hand out to steady herself.

He stood too, his look of blackest fire, and said: 'It doesn't look to me like you're fit to go anywhere.'

'Well,' she said, 'I am.' And she began to traverse the infinite distance between the sofa and the door.

He seemed both outraged and incredulous. He watched her, and when she had reached the door, he said: 'D'you know I never saw how selfish you were? But you are – terribly! Everything has to be done your way. You're too proud to admit the possibility of any other – you know it all. But you don't, Elizabeth. You've got it all wrong. You won't let anyone help you, you've got to do everything on your own. Well, perhaps you deserve to.'

'Quite possibly,' she said. There was a fine film of sweat on her head. She was having trouble turning the handle.

'D'you have feelings at all?' he said. 'Are you alive in there?'

She cursed the door knob, closed her eyes and said: 'I don't know about feelings, Edward, but I do know there's a train leaving in thirty minutes and I intend to be on it.'

He seemed to be stunned, then said: 'At least let me call you a taxi.'

She said: 'Thank you, but it won't be necessary.'

'Then take a bloody umbrella!'

'No, thank you.'

He strode to the coat-stand, grabbed a large yellow umbrella and thrust it towards her. She grasped her bag and the umbrella, the door opened; she was about to go through it when she stopped. I won't see him again, she thought, and she made herself look at him. Hair that sixty years couldn't tame. Shapeless jumper. Jeans with dents at the knees. Scuffed boots. The darkest eyes. Woman's hands. The most familiar and most unknowable face. Remember, she said to herself, remember all of this. Aloud she said, with great warmth: 'It's been so good to see you again, Edward. Please take good care of yourself.'

He stood looking incensed and helpless in equal measure and as she shut the door she heard him say: 'God damn you, Elizabeth.'

She passed through the lodge without seeing Albert and went up the street crying, without recourse to tissues or handkerchief or the other accoutrements adults resort to; she seemed to remember crying in this same street once before, though under more propitious circumstances. Unless she was much mistaken it had been raining then too. Her legs and arms didn't seem to belong to her, her head hurt, she stumbled a little, her heart was achingly slow.

Rumblings were breaking across the city, strange rattlings: the drops were getting heavier. She made it as far as the church in the square and went inside. She sat in one of the pews at the back and laid her head on her arms. The yellow umbrella slid to the floor. She would miss the train; she could get another. There was nothing to think now and nothing to fear. Was this detachment? she wondered. It felt a little bit like it.

Her attention was caught by a series of bleeps, followed by a long note that seemed to hover and throb, that dipped and rose before plateauing. Shifting her head on her arms she saw a man at the front of the church by the organ. He was turning a knob on an electronic device, and as he did, a red light swung slowly in circles. The faster the circle swung, the higher the note rose. She watched it rotate slower, then faster, heard the note crest then dive again, resolving itself finally into a red circle and a pure note that resonated in the coldness of the vestry.

The sound was unearthly and its wavering matched her sense of the moment's unreality. The circling reminded her of something she had seen long ago. When the light turned it appeared to warp, as if there was heat beneath it – heat it could barely endure – as if it wished to rise from the medium in which it moved and was in thrall. The light puttered, then petered, then came to a standstill. The man adjusted the organ and the bleeps began again. The professor closed her eyes.

A hand on her shoulder made her look up. He was standing in front of her, his hair plastered to his forehead, his eyes very black. He said: 'You've been crying.'

'No,' she said, 'not really.'

He sat down beside her and ran his hands over his hair. 'I knew something wasn't right. It hit me after you'd left. You're ill, aren't you? Please tell me.'

She closed her eyes and wondered again how he knew all about her and always had done.

'What is it?' he said.

And because this time there seemed to be no way of denying it, she said: 'Cancer.'

Instantly she wished that she hadn't, because she saw now that, however good he was at reading her, he hadn't expected this; he was looking at her with a sort of brokenness, the sorrow etched so plainly to see that she suddenly had a vision of him as a child, inconsolable; and she was a child again, too, looking on at what she had done.

He said: 'The headaches, the haircut, the lost weight.'

She was very tired. She nodded.

He was blinking, his mouth hung open a little. He said: 'Are you being treated?'

'I was. It's come back. Since I've been here, actually. I'm pretty sure of it . . .' She looked towards the front of the church where the tuner had reached middle C. The light began to circle again.

He passed his hands over his face and hair. He seemed to be thinking what to say. 'Why didn't you tell me?'

She kept her eyes fixed on the circle.

'Elizabeth . . .'

It is hopeless, she thought, so she looked at him, and saw the dawning in his eyes and the knowledge take him over, and when it had flooded his face she wiped her own and raised her eyes to the ceiling and saw something astonishing; saw quite clearly the painting she had wanted to see when she was a girl and had forgotten about until this moment; and saw that the trick to saying something unsayable was not to try, because the artist had painted the heavens remarkably simply, in purples and emeralds and blues; the spheres hummed, the great planets hung in all their unexampled glory; there were depths, illumination – but it was still, very much, just paint.

She heard him say, 'You love me?' and she looked at him. 'Since when?'

She shrugged. 'Always.'

He leaned forward and covered his face with his hands and she turned back to the painting.

When he looked at her again his eyes were glazed and his face seemed as if it had been wrung out and she saw again with astonishment that he loved her. She said: 'I thought I recognised you when we met. I thought I had seen you before.' Then the pain in her head came again and she bent over. He gripped her shoulders and said: 'Where is it?' She didn't move for a moment, then touched the left side of her head very lightly, and he put his hand there, and the sweetness of it was painful.

He said: 'Let me call a doctor.'

'No.'

'Elizabeth—'

She said: 'What good will it do? I have to get home. I have to see the consultant. But I can't do anything right now. I just want to be still . . . please.'

She shifted again and tried to rest her head on her arms and he said: 'Then let's not stay here. Let's at least make you comfortable.'

It was quiet in the church now. The organ tuner had disappeared. He rose, supporting her with one arm, taking the bag and the absurdly yellow umbrella and they went through the doors on to the street. Rain buffeted them, wind shook its fist, the sky was so low she thought they were walking into it. He did up her mackintosh reprovingly and she loved him terribly for it.

The street was full of tourists, buses steaming by, a guide was saying: 'Here you can see the building which houses a printing press that according to local legend is haunted, and over there, the oldest library in the world.'

He crossed them over. They dodged people and rubbish bins, umbrellas and bikes, but hadn't gone far when she said, 'I'm sorry, I have to sit down,' and he looked round, pushed open a door and a bell tinkled.

The place was dark and heaving and filled with the roaring of coffee machines. It was decorated in a rustic style with long tables, whitewashed walls and a large inglenook fireplace. He guided her to the end of a table by the window beside a family with young children and a dog, saying: 'Excuse me, this lady isn't well.' He pushed her mackintosh off her shoulders and crouched in front of her. He asked if she wanted a drink, seemed to be in two minds about leaving her, then stood fidgeting in the queue, turning back to check on her.

The world was a new place. Yet it was still behaving much as she remembered. So was she. They must both be adept at pretending. This is how it is when the impossible happens, she thought. It is impossible, and it keeps on happening. It was impossible to believe that Edward Hunt was going to come back to the table at any minute and look at her again in that new way, with that peculiar combination of ferocity and tenderness. It was impossible to believe he might touch her and she discover again that he loved her. Yet it would happen – here he was, this stranger, his face dark, smelling of rain, stumbling slightly, setting down two mugs, spilling one, saying, 'Fuck', going to get napkins. She couldn't help smiling.

He saw her face and the fear in his own vanished. The sudden joy was so blatant it was painful to see, and she thought again this was how he must have looked as a child, and studied her hot chocolate instead. He tore the top off a sachet of sugar and stirred it while looking at her. He mopped the spillage with a napkin and looked at her some more. He looked at her as she drank and as she turned to the window, embarrassed, and he looked at her when she turned back to the room and met his eyes somewhere between the two.

She sits in the coffee shop and a million things go on around her. Machines whirr, buses hiss, cyclists sail by covered with small plastic tents. There are children quarrelling over milkshakes, a baby who is bawling and attempting to abseil his father's chest. A dog is scratching, his leg thumping the floor. It begins to rain in earnest again and the bell tinkles as more people come in, shaking off umbrellas and sniffing; a group of post-finalists are among them, flushed with freedom, pulling sodden gowns away from their bodies and shaking off mortarboards, which for once have been put to some practical use. He says: 'Tell me when it began.'

So she tells him about the tiredness, about *The Dissident Corpus: John Milton and the Poetics of Difference*, about how it wasn't working and nothing she did made any difference. She told him about Wordsworth and *The Prelude* and toppling off the stage in the lecture theatre, then the weakness of her arm, the transitory blindness, the exhaustion, the rages, weeping in a tutorial. She told him about Doctor Wright, the scans, the therapy; the realisation that her book wasn't working; losing her hair, the empty chair, the conviction she was going to die, thinking about him and this city. Then she comes to the dream about the kitchen table and the bustling room and the stranger, and she looks around and she looks at the table and she looks at Edward Hunt and her eyes begin to fill.

He says: 'What is it?'

But she can't explain because she doesn't know, is not sure what is happening – or should that be what has happened? She shakes her head, looking around once again, and after wiping her eyes she goes on with her story, with amazement now; about the results that were clear, seeing Eliot leaning on his umbrella, the proof of 'Burnt Norton' and the idea for 'A Poetics of Sound', about writing to him and trying to seem professional, and the first two terrible days when she thought they wouldn't meet. And then she tells him about the long years before that when she did not think of very much else, which is something she hasn't told anyone – not even herself – before.

He brings his chair close and pulls her head on to his shoulder. He holds her like a child or a baby animal and she can hear his breath and feel his face in her hair and how much he is enjoying it, breathing deeply and savouring the moment. There is something humorous about the ferocity of his embrace, his oblivion to its recipient. She can feel the thinness of his body and the warmth of his skull and smell the rain in his hair. People are looking but for once she doesn't care and lets herself rest on him and it seems completely natural, as if she has always done this or was always going to, and is perhaps even a little tired of it.

For a while she is nowhere and everything is still. She cannot hear the children or the dog or the coffee machine or the crowd, can feel nothing except this unearthly heat where he touches her – this charge; so that when he pulls away her hair rises up and she is on fire and can hardly bear it.

Presently he asks her if she feels any better and she says: 'Yes.'

In another minute he says, 'Up to walking?' and she nods again, though to interrupt such deep pleasure is painful.

They go through the door, and the wind and rain hit them, but they put up the yellow umbrella and hang on to each other and it is as if they are walking into the sea.

The Eighth Day: Evening

'Where are we going?' she said, and he replied: 'Home.' She didn't know what he meant but she was content to walk beside him; indeed the novelty of being so close to him made her stumble. They were walking along one of the city's narrow side streets and beyond the stone walls either side they could hear the college gardens, emerald and dripping, and everywhere, everywhere the sound of the rain. As they turned into an alley he kissed her. The lips were softer than she had imagined, a little more hesitant, a little more moist. She could feel the vague shapes of teeth and gums behind them, the square bones of the jaw and the breath from the nostrils. Her knees bent a little as he released her and she stood for a moment with her eyes closed.

He kissed her again before they continued and once more at the corner of the street. They kissed beneath an archway and outside a sweetshop and on the corner by the Horse and Groom. Then they were turning into a cobbled street, stopping in front of a small white house with black timbers and bending to go through a low door.

He helped her out of her mackintosh and turned on a gas fire, his fingers fumbling with the switch. His face was red with wind and rain. He said: 'I want to call a doctor but I have to do what you say. D'you want to sleep, d'you want to eat, d'you need me to get anything from the chemist?'

She shook her head. She said: 'I've got some Nurofen in there somewhere.' He knelt and unzipped the bag and she watched in disbelief as this man hauled out her nightgown and toothbrush, her laptop and books; she would have looked herself but didn't like to interrupt. At last, when there wasn't much left to haul, she said apologetically: 'I think they must be in the side.'

He rummaged violently then handed a packet of tablets to her and went into the kitchen. He came back with a large glass of water and watched as she drank, then said: 'I'm going to get you some dry clothes and then we'll think about what to do next.'

She heard him go up the narrow stairs in the corner and sat back on the sofa, gazing at the low ceiling, the straining shelves, the pot plants, the CDs and enormous table. Then she put her head back and closed her eyes, which were filling, and tried hard to still her trembling chin.

He came back carrying a towel and dressing-gown, jogging bottoms, jumper and socks. He said: 'It's all I've got but at least you'll be warm. I'm going to put some soup on.' He went into the tiny kitchen and she heard cupboard doors shutting, a can being opened, the clicking of a hob. Her fingers were clumsy. She removed her tights and dried her hair and legs with the towel. She put on the jogging bottoms and socks and the jumper over her shirt. She put it on back to front to begin with and had to take it off again. Then she sat with her arms at her sides and tried to breathe slowly.

'How do you feel?' He sat down beside her.

She sat up and opened her eyes. 'Not that bad,' she said, and it was true, though she wasn't sure if the pain in her head was kept at bay by terror, exhilaration, or the Nurofen really were doing what was claimed on the box.

'Really?'

'Yes.'

He looked at her for a long moment, then said softly: 'D'you want something to eat? The soup's ready.'

She shrugged. She brought her hands up, let them fall back and they hit her thighs. She laughed. Then she sat still, breathing. She did all these things but she did not look at him. And then, for once in her life, Elizabeth Stone decided she would be brave, so she did look, and she smiled, albeit in terror.

It was the smiling that did it: if she hadn't smiled the evening might have passed differently. But she did smile and he smiled back – and then the smile went away and he was looking at her in the way that made her feel she didn't possess skin but only internal organs, and when he had looked at her a while like this he took her hand in his.

She shut her eyes and sat very still. Then she opened her eyes and sat back and her chest was rising and falling. She laid her arm along the top of the sofa and brought it back to her lap. Then she lifted her head oddly, like a child drowning, and her heart beat so hard that she felt sick. He said: 'How is the pain?'

She frowned, then blinked. 'Gone,' she said. 'For the moment.'

He cupped her head in his hand. 'Are you tired?'

She thought about this. 'Tired' was not the word, not any more; 'unreal' perhaps, 'bewildered' – and also, remarkably present, alert. 'Not tired,' she said. 'Just . . . here.'

His eyes travelled over her face and she felt his breath touch her. He sighed deeply. Then he said, 'Come with me,' and held out his hand. Her body followed.

At the top of the narrow stairs there was a landing, barely wide enough for two people to stand, and a small door. He lifted the latch and they went into a room filled with books. The smell made her happy; it would have made her happy if she hadn't been terrified. He led her to the bed and said: 'Sit down.'

Her breathing was audible. He unlaced her shoes, lifted

her feet out and put them side by side on the rug. He said, 'All right?' and she nodded, raising her eyebrows. She craned to look out of the window as if she had just glimpsed something there, but he said, 'Look at me,' and when she did she saw that his face was flooding with something it could only just contain.

He took off his own shoes and she shut her eyes and began to undo her shirt. She thought she might faint. She felt she was praying or fingering a rosary though she had never done either in her life and it probably showed because she wasn't getting on very well with the buttons. Then she felt his hands over hers and her own dropped to her lap.

He undid the front of her shirt, he undid each cuff, then slipped it down off her shoulders. He kissed her again, more deeply, cupping her head, then began unbuttoning his own.

Her eyes were glazed and wide, the pupils so dark they appeared to be depthless. He said, 'Lie back,' so she did. She folded her arms over her bra and concentrated on taking slow breaths. She stared at a paper lampshade. She thought: I have the same one at home. He took off her jogging bottoms and her feet fell plop, plop, against the bed.

He pulled off his jumper. She heard his hair crackle as it went over his head. She heard him unzip his jeans and she heard him stumble a little as he stepped out of them. She tried not to hear. She removed her bra and replaced her arms over her chest. She was aware that her breasts hung either side of her body. She was aware that no one had seen her breasts before. She was aware that her pants used to be white but were now a more ambiguous colour, and aware no one had seen that part of her either. Then it occurred to her that in a moment she would see his body, too, and she shut her eyes and didn't know how she would open them.

Was this what all mortals aspire to? Was this the great action, the event she had striven to be well 'equipp'd' for? She had prepared herself for something entirely different – she was woefully unprepared; the bridegroom would not find her waiting; her talents had been squandered; her wick was untrimmed, her flame quite put out. A muscle spasmed violently in her calf. She considered crossing her legs but thought it would look ridiculous. She realised she was still wearing her socks.

He lay down beside her. He was whiter, thinner, younger than she had imagined. There was a tan line at his neck. She tried to smile but her mouth wobbled terribly and she thought it best to return her eyes to the lampshade. He touched her and sighed with pleasure and her heart beat raggedly. He drew the blankets around her and kissed her face, he kissed her hands, he kissed her hair, and when he felt the rough scar beneath it he kissed this, too, so gently she wanted to cry out. He said: 'I have wanted to do this for the longest time.'

Fragments of darkness swam at the edges of her vision. Her arms remained pinned to her chest, whether because her breasts caused her more consternation than her pubis or because she was unable to move them she wasn't sure. He said: 'Elizabeth.'

She could no longer smile, or look at him, but after a moment she did succeed in unclasping her arms from her chest and lowered them either side of her, as if she was settling in a coffin. He took her wrist and unbuckled her watch and put it on the bedside table and lay down and she felt his warmth and his hardness and his heart.

He said, 'Remind me again why we didn't do this before,' and she said, 'I don't know.' He took her hands once more and kissed them. Then he sighed deeply and said: 'If only I could make you see how much I love you.'

She closed her eyes. She opened them. She tried to speak but her throat made a strange sound and she closed them again. She took a breath. She took another. She said: 'I have something to tell you.'

'All right,' he said. He was leaning on his arm looking at her. He didn't seem to be able to look enough.

She said: 'I.'

She said: 'I—'

She said: 'I—!'

She said: 'I am a virgin.' And when she had said it darkness swallowed her up.

He was silent a moment, then said softly: 'Are you?'

She nodded but didn't open her eyes. She could hear the sound of her breath and it was rasping. She was horrified but could do nothing to stop it. With enormous effort she looked at him.

It was even more terrifying than she had anticipated. His eyes were black and unbearably bright and held such terrible affection in them. Her own slid back to the lampshade. She said: 'I thought you ought to know.'

'All right,' he said. 'Thank you.'

She said sharply: 'Are you making fun of me?'

'No.'

The muscle in her calf was having a seizure. She said: 'I've disappointed you twice today. I didn't deliver the thesis I promised either.'

He laid his hand on hers and said: 'I'm sorry about "A Poetics of Sound" for your sake but now I can confess that I only ever really cared about the author. And she hasn't disappointed me at all. Besides, I guessed as much.'

She almost looked at him but remembered just in time not to. 'How?' she said, and her voice was no more than a whisper.

He said: 'Call it intuition.'

*

293

Then he put his hand on her heart, or the place she thought her heart might be, and Elizabeth Stone thought she finally understood all those poems about hearts and about love because if this was love she was dying of it and if this was a heart it was breaking, and if this was happiness she was only just bearing it – and then she thought, But I am bearing it, and she was. He moved his hand and she felt a fuse ignite and began to know that here was a miracle: that she had lived on paper and words and thin air and not known it. He began to stroke her body into life or into death and she woke in flames, at the crown of her head and the root of her tongue and the tip of her breasts and the ends of her fingers and the soles of her feet – and she thought she might revise her conclusion that thin skins were a problem because there was no problem here, only that she could not get her breath, only that it might stop.

Then he began to kiss her, quietly, searchingly, willing her to go with him where he would go; so she went, to the dark countries beyond the world's rim, to the place only the bravest go because they are unknown, the place not meant for her and meant for her alone, and the pain in her chest that had been her lifelong companion moved into her shoulders, and then it moved into her throat, and then it moved into her jaw, and crept into her eyes and slipped down the sides of her cheeks and ran into her hair like oil, and he said: 'How I have loved you.'

The books looked on. They would have to find ways of describing this mouth, this weight, this darkness, this pain; they would have to find metaphors for this feeling that made her heart beat fast and then slow, sounds to mimic skin touching skin, rhythms to approximate the waves ascending her neck, breasts and knees. She suspected she was dreaming but not as she knew it; she was dreaming awake and all the textures and colours and shapes of this world that laid themselves against her eyes, and the sounds of the city beyond the window she was dreaming into being – because hadn't she dreamed of this house many times and these roofs and this city and this man – and did that mean these things were real or imagined, in the future, the past or the everlasting present?

All was unknown yet remembered with the strange specificity of dreams, and now as he pushed her hair from her forehead she recognised this, too, with all the euphoria of Odysseus glimpsing the cliffs of Ithaca, yet all was undoubtedly real; indeed, there was a moment when he looked at her that it was unbearably so.

After that the kisses became a little quieter, and after that they became a little slower, and not long after that they made no sound at all but flew out of the open window and fluttered over the roofs and turrets and all of the gardens behind chained gates, and lost themselves in great palaces of light, the ones she had imagined angels to live in when she was a child but had never seen with quite such clarity as at this moment when the clouds parted above the newly washed city and she saw that the world was a strange and surprising place, could become so at any moment and probably always had been.

A bell sounded, clarion in the quiet of the room, and he got up and opened the window and a cool breeze came in. She turned to him and the darkness came again but the bells went on ringing. Unheard music was sweeter, but there was real music now – though she could not be absolutely sure, so easily did it enlace itself with the gathering grey. She said, 'Can you hear that?' and he said, 'Yes, it's the choir in the Music Room.'

The bells stopped but the singing continued, as dusk, dove-grey and quiet, drifted into the room, and with it, from a tear near the horizon, a little silver light. The dusk draped the room in sleep but the light, as it died, caught the letters on the spines of the books and glinted there as if it would speak.

Between the two figures, however, there were no more words, though there was music, rhythms of their own making, more insistent if less enduring than that of poems and arias. Again, said the music; again. Now, and now, and now. A succession of timeless moments.

Acknowledgements

Thank you to Robert Dinsdale, this novel's first reader, for valuable editorial work at every stage of the manuscript. Thank you to Carole Welch, my editor, for eradicating careless mistakes and making the novel much more reader-friendly, and to Hazel Orme, my copyeditor. Thank you to Faber and Faber for permission to quote T. S. Eliot, and Oxford University Press for permission to quote an extract from the Frank Kermode article 'Milton's Hero'. Virginia Woolf quotations come from *Mrs Dalloway*, those by Ted Hughes from his poem 'The Thought Fox', and by Geoffrey Chaucer from Book V of *Troilus and Criseyde*.